FELIX

Elite 8 Studios Book 6

Emmy Sanders

Beta Reading by Christie, Jen & Maxie of Smut Readers Society, and Lauren

Editing by M.A. Hinkle

Proofreading by Ky and Willow

Cover Design by Natasha Snow Designs

ISBN: 9781967130054

Content Warning: This book contains attempted assault of a side character.

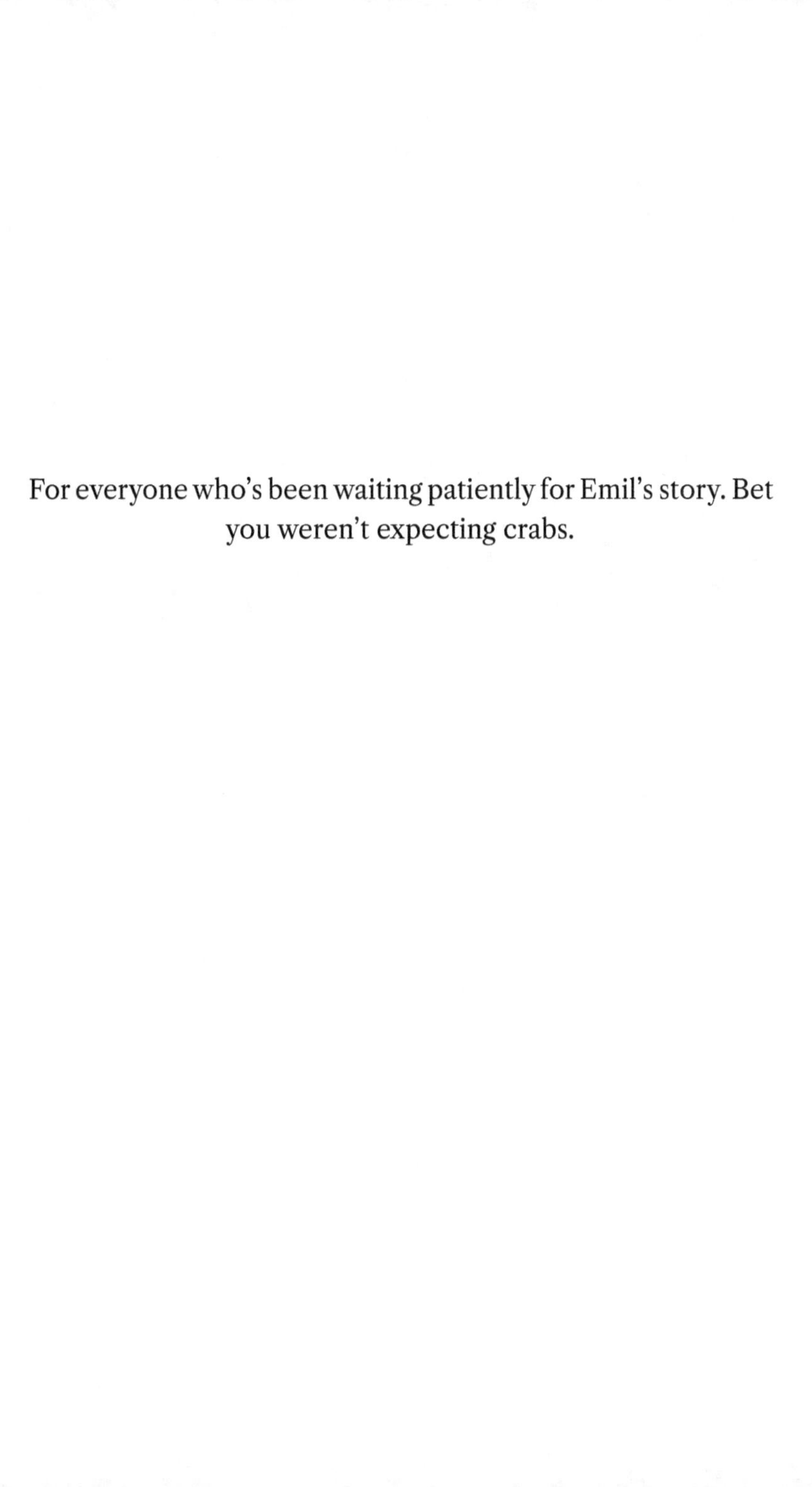

For everyone who's been waiting patiently for Emil's story. Bet you weren't expecting crabs.

Contents

Prologue
EMIL

Three Months Ago

Change sucks. I know I'm not the only one who feels this way. Most creatures in the animal kingdom operate on schedule. Routine. Humans are no different.

This human especially.

"Goddamn it," I mutter, stubbing my toe for the *third* time as I navigate my new kitchen. Who the hell thought putting an island in such a small space was a good idea? "Hate this. Hate moving. Hate unpacking. You've got it easy, Arthur."

My hermit crab doesn't respond.

"No, really. You didn't have to give up any of your cushy rocks, whereas my entire world got upended. And now I have a giant boulder where I don't want one."

I glare at the island as I stick some mixing bowls inside a cabinet next to the fridge.

"And before you say it, I know we didn't have a choice. We *had* to move," I grumble. "Asbestos is no joke. Doesn't mean I have to be *happy* about it."

Arthur still doesn't respond.

"And look at that. I'm having a one-sided conversation with a hermit crab. *Again*."

I sigh, wondering how it came to this. Actually, scratch that. I know exactly who's to blame for the fact that I now converse with a crustacean on the regular.

"This is all Alex's fault," I moan. I never would have brought Sir Arthurpod home if it weren't for my coworker, who took one look at the hermit crab and declared him my perfect companion.

I don't know what that says about Alex's opinion of me.

I don't know what it says about *me* that he was maybe right.

"Probably that I'm a lonely soon-to-be grad student who craves even the smallest sliver of attention and companionship despite my fear of abandonment and, subsequently, true intimacy?"

I let out another sigh. *Psych major for the win.*

Folding the last of my moving boxes, I head out into the living room, stopping to set the cardboard on the pile to be recycled. Arthur is burrowed into the coarse sand at one end of his terrarium, only the top of his spiral shell exposed. Probably wasn't even listening to me. I check his water, adding a bit to top it off, and then head for my new bedroom. I try not to cringe as I step inside the unfamiliar space. Unlike Arthur, I couldn't carry my home with me on my back. The walls in here are white and undecorated, there's a single window on one side of the room that looks onto the neighboring building across the alley, and the bookshelves are unorganized and half bare.

This time, I do cringe, unable to leave my textbooks piled on the floor as they are. I stack them on the shelves, ordered alphabetically by subject matter and then author, and only once they're resting in their proper place do I let myself fall into bed.

It's late, it's been a *long* day of moving, my coworkers who helped me are gone, and I should get some rest. *Or…*

My eyes catch on my open nightstand drawer, and I roll that way, peering inside. Snatching the lube, I roll back and make quick work of unbuttoning and pushing down my pants.

Perks of living alone, aside from my hermit crab, of course: *no need for closed doors.*

My head hits the pillow as I wrap a wet hand around my dick. It doesn't take long before I'm fully hard. Rucking up my shirt, I squeeze and roll my nipple while I brace my legs wide, giving myself leverage to fuck up into my fist. Unlike at the studio, I don't bother making a production out of it, but a groan still escapes my throat as heat pools low in my stomach with each pass of my cock through the tight ring of my hand. I lick my thumb before rolling it over my nipple again, the wet warmth sending a zing down my spine. In no time at all, I'm coming apart, ropes of cum painting my bare abdomen and chest.

Spent—and sticky—I pull in a breath. And then another. My body rolls in an aftershock.

"Well," I mutter, glasses sitting askew on my nose. "Suppose that's one way to christen the place."

The letter comes the next day.

"What are you?" I ask, staring at the innocuous white envelope taped to the outside of my apartment door as if it will magically explain itself. Probably a flyer from a local business.

I snag it off the surface and continue inside, my arms laden down with grocery bags from my early-morning shopping run. With my curiosity getting the better of me, I leave the food on the counter and open the envelope.

I pull in a sharp breath as I read the handwritten scrawl on the carefully folded paper. *Not* a solicitation. Not a professional one, at least.

Hey, neighbor.

Fun fact. If you go into your bedroom and look outside, you'll notice there's a window one floor up on the building next to yours. The blinds are black. Second fun fact—someone looking through said window has a perfect sightline to your bed.

First of all, bravo. Quite the finish.

Second, I promise I didn't mean to catch the show. But, well, there you were.

So here's me, letting you know you may want to close your curtains next time. Or not. Honestly, I would not be upset to catch that again.

Welcome to the neighborhood.

-C

"Holy shit," I whisper, my pulse sprinting so fast I'm left dizzy. My neighbor saw me *jerking off.*

I should be embarrassed—mortified, even—that I put on an unintended peep show. But I'm not. At least, not in the way I know I'm supposed to be. All that almost-shame is curling tight in my gut, heating my veins and making my fingers tingle in anticipation.

Did they like what they saw?

Do they really want to see it again?

This is where, logically, that shame should come. Because I don't regret it. I'm *thrilled* to have been caught. And I'm so damn horny all I can think about is that "or not" in regards to closing my curtains.

There's a reason I work in porn. And it has nothing whatsoever to do with the money.

Forcing a calming breath through my body, I put away my groceries before walking into my bedroom. My adrenaline is still high, pulse pounding, but my steps are even as I approach the window. Sure enough, there are a few windows on the building next to mine that I didn't notice yesterday. Probably because they're so far to the side I can't see them except from a certain angle. But in the case of one particular window—the one a floor above mine—that angle happens to line up perfectly with my bed, exactly as C indicated.

A wave of heat rushes through me.

Can they see me right now? The blinds might be cracked open; it's hard to tell. Are they watching? Waiting for a reaction? Waiting for me to snap my curtains shut?

I don't know what possesses me to do it, but I grab a sheet of printer paper and a marker, and I scribble my number in thick print. Then, I slap the paper against the windowpane.

My heart beats heavily as I wait. Chances are they aren't even there. I'm being ridiculous. And yet, less than a minute later, my phone pings. I drop the paper and grab the device from my pocket. A text waits.

Unknown: Hey, Specs.

"Holy shit," I whisper again.

I adjust my glasses and change the contact to "C," and then I type out a response. Maybe it's because of C's own bluntness in their letter or that nearly irresistible offer of "or not," but instead of being polite or appropriately apologetic about what they saw, I decide to throw caution to the wind for once in my goddamn life.

What's the harm? I don't know this person. And they don't know me; not really.

There's safety in anonymity, even if it's only an illusion.

Me: I'd say I'm sorry, but I'm not.

C sends me a grinning emoji that immediately sets me at ease.

C: Never asked for an apology. Does that mean you're going to leave those curtains open?

There goes my pulse again.

Me: You really want me to?

C: Is that a serious question? That was hot as fuck. I'll watch you anytime, Specs.

My thumb hovers over my screen before I type back.

Me: How old are you?

C: Perfectly legal.

They send a wink, and I blow out a breath.

Me: I'll leave them open.

C: Lucky me. When's the next show?

Holy shit. Am I really going to do this?

Me: Tonight?

They send a frown.

C: Working. I'm free now, though. What's your refractory period like?

I huff a laugh. I'm a twenty-three-year-old with a high libido and a penchant for being watched. My refractory period is damn near zero if there's an audience involved.

Me: I'm good to go. Wanna watch me fuck myself with a dildo?

C sends a skull and crossbones emoji, and I grin at the implication that they're dead from that response.

C: Specs, I can honestly say I'd love nothing more. Show me what you've got.

Fuck.

Inhibitions nonexistent in the face of my single greatest weakness, I set my phone on the bed, check to make sure I'm standing in a spot where my neighbor can see me—even though I can't see through their blinds in return—and drop my pants to the floor. My pulse hammers as I drape myself over my bed, reaching into my nightstand for lube and the biggest dildo I have.

I'm well aware that, in a sea of humans, I'm a fairly average fish. I'm average height for a guy, not overly thin but not bulky either, I have plain brown hair and eyes, a decent smile, and I wear glasses. Frankly, I blend into the crowd.

But when there are eyes on me, none of that matters. There's not a high I've discovered that's better than *this*. I know nothing about C. I don't know their gender. Whether they're my age or sixty. I don't even know if they find me attractive or only see me as a free source of porn. *Ironic, really, considering my job.*

But none of it is important. All that matters is that they *see* me. That they're watching.

A shiver rolls down my spine as I kick off my socks and underwear, uncaring where they land. I get on my hands and knees before bending low, putting myself on display.

My phone pings.

C: Look at you, Specs. You like this, don't you? You like showing off.

You have no idea.

I don't respond, instead bringing lubed fingers to my ass as every fiber of my being vibrates in excitement and heady *want*.

Funny, just yesterday I was lamenting this change in location and the upheaval of my comfortable routine. But less than twelve hours later, I'm wondering if maybe this move was the best thing to happen to me. It's no secret my life is predictable. Some would even say boring, apart from my job in porn. I go to classes, I study, I eat, and I sleep.

And I'm happy with that. I like my life; I do.

But sometimes, even when I'm stubbornly rebelling against it, I know change can be a good thing. And this change? Maybe even great.

After all, what more could an exhibitionist want than a willing voyeur right outside their bedroom window?

Chapter 1

EMIL

Present Day

"Hey, boo."

"Hi, Alex," I mutter, too preoccupied by my phone to raise my head and give my coworker a proper greeting. Specifically, preoccupied by the text on my phone.

C: Did you know when you wake up, you stretch your arms above your head and knead the air like a cat?

Me: I do not.

C: You do! Every time. It's cute.

A smile quirks my lips, and I shake my head, typing out a response.

Me: Did you know it's creepy to watch people sleep?

C: Pft. You love it, Specs. Don't pretend otherwise.

They've got me there.

"Who ya texting?" Alex asks, startling me as he plops onto the bench beside me in our locker room at Elite 8 Studios. He swipes his floppy blonde hair off his forehead, giving me a grin. The guy goes by Tink on set, considering he looks like the Peter Pan fairy.

"Oh, uh..."

I scramble for a suitable response.

My secret pen pal of three months who watches me masturbate through the windows of our respective apartment buildings and who texts me randomly throughout the day to chat about everything and nothing in particular?

Yeah, no. Not telling my coworker that.

"My sister," I lie, slipping my phone away.

Alex narrows his eyes. "Mm. Which sister?"

"Younger?" I answer unsurely.

"Uh-huh," he says, crossing his leg over his knee and bouncing it. "And doesn't Rebecca have a no phones policy at her school that would be in effect this time of day?"

I open and close my mouth. *Christ*, try to cover up a simple quasi-friendship-with-voyeuristic-benefits sorta situation and the guy turns into Sherlock freaking Holmes.

"There's something you're not telling me, Kent," Alex says slowly.

I straighten my black-rimmed glasses, huffing a laugh at the nickname. *Never mind Sherlock. Lois Lane is on my tail.* "You caught me, Lois. Saw the signal light up, so I'll be on my way to save the world and stuff."

"That's Batman, not Superman," he points out, squinting at me. "Everything all right?"

"Of course," I tell him, standing and grabbing my bookbag.

He hums, looking like he doesn't believe me. "For what it's worth, it was nice. The smile you had when I walked in."

I don't know what to say to that—how to explain the source of said smile—so I keep my mouth shut. Luckily, Alex goes on.

"Watch out in the halls, boo. Jerome has a few guys by the private rooms waiting on auditions."

"Yeah. Thanks, Alex."

He nods, and I slip out the door, releasing a breath. Bag over my shoulder, I head down the hall.

I've worked at Elite 8 Studios—a producer of gay porn—for a little over two years, so this building and the people in it are familiar to me. A comfort, even, despite the well-intentioned snooping from certain coworkers. I might keep some things close to my chest, but the guys here, Alex included, have my back. And I appreciate that.

As Alex noted, the hall leading to the private suites is dotted with a few unfamiliar men hoping to land a job via the studio's most recent casting call. Nathaniel, the assistant producer and second-in-command to our boss Jerome, is standing near them, a clipboard in hand as he calls for a Mitchel.

I hurry past, keeping my head down and passing the large Elite 8 Studios sign lit up in bright yellow neon. *That's Vegas for ya*. Outside, the day is bright, and I hitch my bag more securely over my shoulder as I walk toward my car. Seeing as I filmed a scene late this morning with Trevor, named Bruiser on set, I have a few days before I'll be back.

We all have nicknames, or *porn aliases*, here at the studio. There's Tink. Bruiser. Dixon, aka Dix, who's worked here far longer than I have. He's dating Niko, also known as Adonis. And Teddy, of course, the resident teddy bear who drunk-married Niko's friend Kipp. We lost some of the other regulars, who quit for one reason or another, hence the call for new talent. But there are a handful of guys who film part-time, too. And me? Well...

I go by Felix.

That piece of me gets left behind as I slide into my car and shift focus. I have a different sort of work to do this afternoon, one where my companions only know me as Emil. The lab where I'm a research aide is inside one of the psych buildings on campus. I'm a first-year master's student, which means I'm well acquainted with these buildings, but my unpaid job as an aide is new.

"Hey, Emil," Lucy says as I enter the space. Like me, she's working on this graduate study. We met just last week.

"Hi, Lucy. How's it going?"

"Good. I talked to Nicole." *The project lead.* "She asked us to go through these forms and add the approved candidates to the electronic database. We're supposed to transfer all the info over and assign each a number."

"Sounds easy enough."

Lucy nods, and I pull up a chair next to her in front of the computer. I look through the forms as Lucy opens the program where we need to input the candidates.

"Are they all from the same nursing home?" I ask, flipping through the papers.

"Um, not sure. It should say, though?"

"Yeah, it does. Sorry, I have a tendency to speak my thoughts aloud," I admit. "It's a chronic problem."

Lucy shoots me a smile. "No worries."

"What's this?" I ask, pointing to a line on the form that says *study eligibility*. "This one indicates 'N-D.'"

"Oh, uh... Non-dementia. For the control group, maybe?"

"Nicole said it's a blind study, though. So the participants should all have some degree of dementia, including those in the control group." As soon as the words leave my mouth, it comes to me. "Oh, a baseline? The non-dementia participants would provide a comparative baseline for the cognitive training."

"Wouldn't the control group do that?" Lucy counters.

"For immediate effectiveness of the training, yeah. But not for long-term impact, right? We're trying to determine whether these cognitive games help with memory retention, so comparing the results to a group without dementia would provide an indicator into what's considered a 'normal' degree of memory loss after the fact."

"I hadn't thought of that," Lucy says, huffing a small laugh. "You know, I feel bad for saying I love this stuff when our study is focused on dementia, but I really do love this stuff. It's fascinating."

"I know what you mean," I reply, nudging my glasses into place. "It's like a puzzle, except we don't know the picture. We have all the pieces, but we have no clue how they're going to come together or into what shape. And, at the end of the day, it might not even make a recognizable whole. But that doesn't matter. Our job isn't to force the pieces to be something they're not. We just stand back and interpret whatever we've created."

Lucy shakes her head. "Shit, I think you might be a bigger nerd than me when it comes to this stuff."

I chuckle. "Guilty as charged."

"Come on," Lucy says, a smile on her face. "Let's get these candidates in the system."

It takes about an hour to work through the thirty-two forms Nicole left for us. It's not the entirety of the study group, but it's a good start. Once done, Lucy and I head our separate ways. I don't have classes today, but I do have plenty of coursework to get done, so I drive straight home to dig in. I just make a quick stop at the convenience store down the street first, seeing as I'm low on energy drinks—a bad habit I can't quite bring myself to quit.

As I'm stepping out of the store, admittedly distracted by thoughts of the paper I have to write, I bump into someone.

"Sorry," I mumble, regaining my balance, only to nearly fall on my ass when I see the guy I stumbled into.

He's tall. Like, *really* tall for how lean he is. He looks like a damn model or maybe even a K-pop star, with fine features, dark eyes winged with equally dark liner, and black hair falling messily above his shoulders in an artful, layered style. He's about my age, if I had to guess, and for the briefest of moments, he stares at me in shock. Then his expression smooths out, and he *smiles*.

"I, uh...sorry," I say again, jolting when my phone rings. I shoot the guy an apologetic wince before turning away and fishing the device out of my pocket. When I reach the corner, I glance back, expecting him to be gone. He's still watching me. I walk out of sight, putting the phone to my ear. "Um, hello?"

"Hey, bro."

"Bec?" I ask, checking the time on my phone. I guess school is out. "Something wrong?"

"No," Rebecca says quickly. "I just... Ugh, don't tell Mom and Dad, but I miss you guys. I wanted to hear a familiar voice."

My shoulders come down, and I let myself into my building, heading toward my apartment door. "I'm happy to be in your ear whenever you need it, Bec. Are you settling in okay?"

"Yeah," she says. "It's just different."

I bet. Rebecca started at a boarding school this term. Our parents were worried about her moving out at only sixteen, but my younger sister is a bit of a violin virtuoso. She was adamant she wanted to attend a high school dedicated to fine arts, and our parents—after much discussion—relented and let her go.

I'm not surprised Rebecca doesn't want to admit to them that she's having difficulty with the transition. She's stubborn like that.

All us kids are, in our own way.

"I'm sure you'll be used to things in no time," I say, trying to reassure her. "But call whenever you want, okay? Just not during school hours."

She snorts. "I'm well aware of the rules. Would you tell me a story?"

"Seriously?" I ask, bending down to check on Arthur now that I'm inside my place. "I thought you said you were *too mature* for stories these days."

"Just this once. Please? But don't tell Jules or I'll blab about that poster of his you ripped."

My mouth falls open. "Blackmail, Bec? Really? That was over ten years ago."

"And he's never forgotten. Neither have I," she sing-songs.

"All right, cool your conniving little jets," I grumble, setting my bag of energy drinks on the coffee table and sitting down. My paper can wait a while longer. "I'll tell you a story."

"Yay," she cheers, sounding so much younger than the angst-ridden teenager she is these days.

Smile on my face, I start out, pitching my voice theatrically. "Once upon a time, there was this mean ogre named Julian who terrorized the town."

"Oh, God," Rebecca says, chuckling. "This is gonna be good."

As I spin an impromptu tale for my younger sister, I feel as if I've fallen back in time. I used to do this for both Rebecca and Henry, the baby of the bunch, when I lived back home.

Most days, I don't miss the mayhem of my childhood. As one of five children, it was always loud, messy, and chaotic around our house. I was the quiet, middle child who blended into the wallpaper. And I liked it that way. Mostly.

But I'll admit there are times, like now, when I feel a fond pang of nostalgia for those days now long gone.

But that's life. And, if anything, I'm self-aware enough to recognize the way I live now is in direct opposition to that lifestyle for a reason. It was hard falling by the wayside all the time. Feeling unheard. Unseen.

I never want my siblings to feel that way, which is why I do my best to be there should any of them need it. Like now, with Rebecca.

When we end our call—Julian the ogre having succumbed to a gruesome death neither of us would wish on our real brother—I set my phone beside me on the couch. It's late enough that I should probably start some dinner. And then I really do need to make progress on that paper. But I can't quite help snatching up my phone again and opening my text thread to C.

Our recent exchanges are full of a mishmash of things. Talk about what I'm studying. Psychology. TV shows we're both watching. BBC's *Life*, mostly. The damn weather, even. And then there's C's commentary on my...*performances*, those particular texts making me blush now that I'm not in the heat of the moment.

This stranger outside my window knows more about me than most people in my life these days. And yet, apart from their love of David Attenborough-narrated nature documentaries, I know almost nothing about them. For all I do know, they could be an eighty-year-old grandma. I sure hope not. It would be truly mortifying to find out I've been semi-flirting with an octogenarian, let alone flashing my asshole their way. *Yikes*.

Yet I can't shake the feeling that my mystery voyeur is younger than that. And male, even though I don't have any evidence to prove it. It's a gut feeling. An educated guess based on what I *have* learned.

Of course, I could simply *ask* and see what they say. But, by unspoken agreement, neither of us has broached the topic of C's identity. Maybe I don't want to know. Maybe it would ruin this game we play and the stupid smile I seem to have over a person I've never met.

Maybe I'd feel compelled to close my curtains, and I don't want to do that.

Even so, I can't help but wonder...

"Who are you?"

Chapter 2
CHRISTIAN

"Hey, Christian. Could you cover my table?"

"Which one?" I ask Noel, adjusting the skimpy-ass booty shorts that are trying to ride up my ass.

"Ten?"

I look over at the table of rowdy men my friend-slash-coworker is talking about and groan. "Noel..."

"I know, I know. But please?" he says, hands held together beneath his chin. "You're so much better with them than I am."

I capitulate easily, knowing it's not Noel's fault he got stuck with the group. Some customers are going to be trouble; you just know it. And Noel, well... He's not the best at fending off trouble.

"I got it," I assure him, giving his shoulder a pat as I pass. Pasting on a big smile, I approach the men in business wear.

As a club that boasts *the finest boys on The Strip*, you don't come to Knee Highs for the music. You come to ogle half-naked men dancing in cages or those serving overpriced drinks. Tonight? I'm the latter.

"Hey, boys," I greet, cocking a hip as I reach the table. "What can I get for ya?"

The guy closest to me eyes me up and down. "Well, shit. How about one of you?"

The rest snicker, and it's all I can do not to roll my eyes. "Sorry. Not on the menu. How about a hurricane? The bartender makes it strong."

The guy isn't deterred. "Aw, c'mon now, sweet thing. Give us a twirl?"

"If you want to see the back of me," I reply shortly, grin in place, "that can be arranged. But then you'll be left without a server. Order or not. Your choice."

He huffs but asks for a bourbon. I go around the table, nodding at each drink order, not bothering to write them down. I have a weirdly good memory for these sorts of things. Mission accomplished, I turn to go.

I wish I could say the slap to my ass is a surprise. It's not.

Spinning, I grab Asshole Number One's wrist, applying enough pressure that he leans forward to reduce the strain.

"You touch without permission again, and you'll meet the bottom of my boot," I tell him, flashing my pointy heel his way before dropping his arm.

He rubs his wrist, laughing it off. "Oh, this one has claws."

"And teeth," I say, snapping them together before turning and walking away. *Fucking alphahole.*

"Shit, you okay?" Noel asks as soon as I reach the bar.

"Fine," I tell him, waving off his concern as I start inputting orders. Unfortunately, that sort of behavior isn't uncommon here. Even worse is that our boss turns a blind eye to the way his employees are treated inside this club. *Another alphahole*, if I do say so myself.

Max, my favorite bartender, catches my eye and lifts a brow. He's a good guy, and I know he'd gladly step in if needed, but I shake my head. I can handle it.

Finished at the touchpad, I give Noel's arm a squeeze and get back to work. Most of my tables tonight are polite. They're here for the show and to enjoy drinks with their friends, and they don't give me any trouble. Table ten, though...

"Another beer, pretty?" That was Asshole Number Three.

"*Pretty moody* is more like it," Number One says.

I flash a toothy smile. "A beer. You got it. Anything else?"

A couple other guys place orders, attention shifting between the dance cages and Asshole Number One, who just *looks* like he's biding his time for another crack at me. I try to edge away before he has the chance, but his hand whips out, grabbing my arm.

I blow out a slow breath. Violence was not on the agenda today.

"Come on," he cajoles. "What would it take to get a real smile out of you?"

He tugs me closer, forcing me to take a step lest I lose my balance.

So much for peace.

I give the guy a real smile as I tip up his chin. And then I hitch my leg over his lap and plant the heel of my boot at his crotch. His eyes widen, and his Adam's apple bobs.

"I did warn you," I say sweetly.

"Christian!"

Ah, hell.

I drop my leg and take a step back as my boss comes storming over, a firm set to his jaw I've seen a time or two. *Or ten.*

"My office. Now," he says.

I don't wait to hear whatever apology and free drink offer he gives the table. I just walk away, shaking my head when I catch Noel's worried gaze and heading for the boss's office. He catches up before long, face a little red.

The door hasn't even clicked shut when he says, "What the hell were you thinking?"

"I was thinking I'd had enough of that guy manhandling me."

He works his jaw, looking unimpressed. "I've tried, Christian. But enough is enough. You're done here."

I scoff, unable to help it. "Because I defended myself?"

"Because you have a history of being antagonistic with the customers," he spits back, circling his desk and plopping into his seat. I bite my tongue, *hard*, as he glances at the screens along one side of the wall that broadcast the goings-on inside the club. "I've given you too many chances here, but you're bad for business. You're fired."

I almost open my mouth. Almost tell him it's not *my* fault some people are assholes who don't know how to keep their hands to themselves. Almost tell him there's this thing called respecting a person's bodily autonomy, no matter their occupation or what they choose to wear, and *hasn't he heard of it*? Almost tell him he's a total and utter prick.

But there's no point. Me running my mouth—*again*—isn't going to change his mind.

I give a nod before turning for the door.

"Leave your keycard with Max," he says.

"You got it."

I don't slam the door. Don't yell. I simply stop by the employee change room, grab my things—including the keycard that opens the back door—and walk through the club to the bar.

"Max," I call out.

He eyes me, expression falling when he sees me holding my things. "He give you the boot?"

"Mhm. Here," I say, handing over the card, certain my boss is watching me right now from inside his cushy office.

"Sorry, lovey."

I shake my head. "Don't. It's not your fault. He's a crap boss, Max. You know he is."

"Yeah, well... The world is shit. Everywhere you go."

"Maybe I refuse to accept that," I say, my gaze landing on Noel at the edge of the room. My chest squeezes tight. "Do me a favor and watch out for him?"

Max's eyes find Noel, his expression softening. "You know I will. Take care of yourself, Christian."

I knock the bar top. "Always do."

Noel catches up with me on my way to the door, looking downtrodden. "Christian, I'm so sorry. This is all my fault."

"It's not," I assure him. "You know he's been looking for a reason to fire me."

Noel winces, but he doesn't refute it. "What will you do?" he asks, looking over his shoulder. The club is busy tonight, tables full. A guy named Jonah is shaking his ass inside one of the cages, drumming up tips from the onlookers nearby.

"Honestly? I don't know," I admit. "I'll land somewhere, I'm sure."

"I, uh..." Noel steps closer, speaking so low I nearly miss him over the music. "I know of somewhere that's hiring. Remember my cousin Tanner?"

I rack my brain when it clicks. "The one that works at the porn studio? He does set design, right?"

Noel smiles a little sheepishly. "That's the one. He, uh, said they're looking for new...*talent.*"

My eyebrows pop up. "You mean porn stars."

He groans but pulls out his phone. "I know it's kind of out there, but look. The pay is *ridiculously* good, and they even have benefits and health insurance and stuff."

"Seriously?" I ask as Noel shifts his phone screen my way. I skim the ad, curiosity piqued.

"Open auditions end tomorrow," he tells me before looking over his shoulder again. Max gives him a hurried wave, and Noel curses, tucking his phone away. "Shit, gotta go. Let me know what you decide?"

"I will. And Noel? Be careful."

He nods, but I don't feel all that reassured as I watch my friend weave back through the crowded club. Heaving a sigh, I head out the door and into the vibrant bustle of the city. I didn't bother changing out of my tiny shorts, so I get a few looks and even a catcall, but I ignore it all, taking the bus home.

My apartment's heavy wooden door creaks when I push it open. I flick on the lights and drop my keys into the bowl under the switch. My mail sits atop the same table. An overdue bill. A statement from the nursing home.

I head past, stopping at the window inside my bedroom.

A smile curves my lips when I see my neighbor across the alleyway. He's on his bed, a book out in front of him and a pad of paper beside it. His brown hair is a mess, telling me he's been studying for a good while, and I have the most perfect view of his ass as he bounces his legs through the air behind him.

Unable to resist, I pull out my phone and fire off a text.

Me: Hey, Specs. Looking cozy.

He glances at his phone, and then his head whips my way. I huff a laugh, grinning, even though I know he can't make me out behind the blinds. Does he have any idea it was me he bumped into the other day outside the convenience store? I highly doubt it, considering he doesn't even know what I look like. He's never asked for details about who I am.

My heart sure had beat fast, though, a combination of surprise and awe at suddenly being face to face with the guy who outright invited me to watch him get off three months ago and who hasn't closed his curtains once since. His light brown eyes were even wider in person behind those thick-framed glasses of his, and he was *right there* for the first time, so close I could touch.

But then his phone rang, he turned away, and my chance to say something—*anything*—was lost.

A ping breaks through my thoughts.

Specs: Hey. You're home early.

I let out another sigh.

Me: Yeah. I got fired.

He jolts slightly.

Specs: Crap. I'm sorry.

Me: It is what it is. Can I ask you something?

Specs: Of course.

Heading to my dresser, I change out of my shorts and pull on something softer, more comfortable. Then I trade my tight shirt for a loose tee. When I get back to the window, I stop in front of my sewing table, letting my fingers drift over the familiar plastic of my Bernina sewing machine.

She was worth every exorbitant penny.

Taking a seat, I glance at Specs again. I don't know why it's always so easy to talk to him. Maybe because I consider him a friend, even if the circumstances that brought us together are admittedly a bit strange.

Me: Do you think we're in charge of our own destinies?

It's a question that's been on my mind a lot lately. Sometimes I wonder if my path in life has already been set. If I'm destined to end up like those who came before me: stuck in jobs I have no passion for, with few friends and even fewer joys in life. I don't want that. I want more. *Better*.

Specs reads my text, and from this distance, I can just make out the crease in his brow as he frowns. If I could—and if he'd let me—I'd smooth it away.

Specs: I don't believe in destiny.

Me: No?

Specs: No. There's so much that happens in life that's completely out of our control. Existence is chaos. We're just atoms bound together in evolutionarily advantageous bundles, and along the way, that led to neural networks and high-functioning brains. You can pick out patterns in people and guess at their actions, but you can't truly control anyone but yourself. The diversity on our planet alone? No, I don't think that has anything to do with divine intervention. I think it's evidence of the tenacity of life.

My heart beats fast, breath whooshing out of me as a smile curls my lips.

Me: Damn. You're sexy when you talk nerdy.

Specs ducks his head, trying to hide his smile, but the divot in his cheek gives him away. He nudges his glasses up before typing again.

Specs: To answer your original question... I don't believe in destiny, and no, I don't think we're in control of every facet of our lives. But I do think we're responsible for making the best out of the situations we find ourselves in.

I hum.

Me: How do we know if the choices we're making are the right ones?

Specs: I think you just have to trust your gut.

Me: You're very wise.

He shakes his head.

Specs: Not really.

I snort. Pretty sure the guy is a literal genius.

Me: Accept the compliment, Specs. You have a nice ass and a nice brain. Both great qualities.

He looks as if he's chuckling.

Specs: Thanks, I guess.

Me: Better. And you're welcome.

I spin my phone in my hand before opening up the website Noel showed me. *Elite 8 Studios*. There's not much I can access without a subscription, but I find the ad for the casting call and read it over again.

Adult entertainer. Exclusive filming rights. Open auditions. Generous compensation.

Could I fuck for pay? The idea isn't unappealing. If anything, I'm intrigued. Despite what my more handsy former patrons might have thought, I'm no prude. I enjoy sex quite a lot. I just also believe in respecting a person's boundaries, and I expect my partners to do the same.

But when it comes to fucking... There's empowerment in making another person come. In making them feel good, even if only for a little while. I've never done that in front of cameras, but it could be fun.

My gaze pings out the window again, and I huff a laugh. Pretty sure Specs would enjoy the hell out of that.

Switching over to Noel's contact info, I shoot him a text asking for his cousin's number. Surely it couldn't hurt to find out more about this Elite 8 Studios.

Specs said to trust my gut.

And my gut is telling me I'm ready for something new.

Chapter 3

EMIL

C: Well, well. Isn't this a nice way to wake up?

I swipe my phone open and groan, lust tightening my balls as I slowly stroke my morning wood. I turn my gaze out the window, still a little sleepy but much more awake now that I know C is watching. Shifting, I get my sleep pants down under my ass so they have a better view.

C: That's a pretty sight, Specs. Gonna get your nipples wet? I know how much you love that.

Fuck. Is it weird that my neighbor knows so much about my preferences? My last boyfriend knew less than this stranger outside my window.

Setting my phone beside me, I suck two fingers into my mouth and rub over my nipple. Electricity pings across my synapses as the bud pebbles. When I give it a twist, my hips reflexively punch off the bed.

C: Mm, there you go. Will you come for me, Specs? I wanna see it.

"Holy hell," I mutter, biting my lip as I jerk myself faster. My glasses slip to the side as I stare at C's text. At the encouragement, which isn't new. But asking me to come for them sure is.

C: Nipples. Don't forget.

A whimper falls from my lips, my body already tensing. I give my nipple a good tug, imagining it's the wet suction of a mouth instead, and the thought has me cresting over the hill in a flash. My eyes slip shut as I come across my fist, everything in me drawn tight in a burst of mini-explosions and crackling flames.

It's always more intense when C is watching.

Another ping comes from my phone, but it takes me a moment to catch my breath and open my eyes.

C: Gorgeous.

Shit.

Remarkably, I feel my cheeks flush hot at that. It's ridiculous, really, how a single word can affect me. I shouldn't let it. And yet I can't help but hoard the compliment and the warmth it brings. Maybe it doesn't matter who C is in the end. They make me feel good. That's enough.

I roll off the bed and clean myself up before returning to my phone.

Me: Thanks for watching.

C: Anytime.

They send a wink, and I smile. What a weird friendship we have.

C: Class today?

Me: Work.

I switch out my clothes as C types their response.

C: Guess what? I got a new job.

Me: That's great! Only took a few days.

C: Yep. I think I'm going to like it. No more late nights, either. Bonus.

Sitting on my bed, I glance at C's window, admittedly a little curious about their life. I don't know where C used to work. It's one of the things we never discussed. Although, technically speaking, they don't know where I work, either. I haven't told them about the studio. Only about my psych degree and, in vague details, the research I'm involved in.

I wonder what it is they spend their days doing. I wonder what makes them happy.

Me: Well I hope this job works out better for you.

C: Thanks, Specs. Me, too.

Getting up, I wave a goodbye and head toward my bathroom to shower. I don't have a scene at the studio today, but we have a team meeting, which everyone is expected to attend. Since I know a brunch buffet awaits, I skip breakfast, but I do stop to feed Arthur his daily meal of pellets before I go.

"Hey, buddy," I say, grabbing the specialized pellets I get for him from a local pet store. Arthur is a small hermit crab, so I crush them a bit before putting the pieces inside his shallow food bowl. He perks up, shell popping out of the sand as his beady little eyes take stock of the situation. I chuckle. "You're a weirdo, you know that?"

Arthur scuttles closer, his tiny orange legs carrying him across the terrarium.

I sigh. "Of course I would find you cute—the least cuddly pet on the planet. You're basically an armored spider."

He doesn't seem to have an opinion on that. Arthur simply waits until my hand is out of his tank, and then he scurries over to investigate the food. He sifts through the broken-up pellets for a moment before pausing. I swear he looks at me as if to say *this again?*

"You'll get something fresh tonight," I assure him. "Watermelon?"

Arthur gives me his back, and I roll my eyes.

"Diva."

Checking the time on my phone, I head for the door. The studio is about a twenty-minute drive from where I live. The building itself is entirely nondescript. If you didn't know what it was, you might assume it was a warehouse. I let myself in through the coded door, confused, at first, as to why it smells like a spice cupboard exploded in here. But then I catch sight of the festive fall display someone decorated the entryway in.

A few of my coworkers are mingling in the hall as I pass. I shoot them a little wave before heading into Studio 1, where our meeting will be held. Several of the performers are inside already, and Teddy holds up his hand in greeting. I head his way, eyeing the table of bagels and other breakfast foods as my stomach rumbles.

"Hey," the bigger man greets. Teddy is in his mid-thirties, a stockier guy with muscle. His brown hair, beard, and abundance of chest hair lends credence to his *teddy bear* persona. But from what I've heard—mainly from Teddy's husband Kipp, who doesn't seem to possess a filter—the man is a lot kinkier than his gentle smile and easygoing presence would suggest.

Not that I'm one to judge. I let my neighbor watch me masturbate.

"Hey, Teddy."

"How's it going?" he asks. "Settling in at the new place all right?"

I manage not to blush as my thoughts shift to C.

"Yeah," I tell him, clearing my throat. "It's finally starting to feel like home."

Doesn't hurt that the walls aren't bare anymore, and I've stopped stubbing my toe on the damn kitchen island.

A flash of blonde appears in my peripheral vision, followed immediately by a voice I know all too well. "How's my favorite crab daddy?"

"Alex," I groan, my insides squishing as my coworker hugs me tight.

"Having crabs is nothing to be ashamed of, Emil," the tiny troublemaker says, stepping back and looking around. "Where's Kipp?"

"Work," Teddy says, a soft smile on his face that seems reserved for his husband. Kipp doesn't work here at the studio, but he's been hanging around a lot lately, sometimes even watching Teddy while he films.

Husband goals.

Alex pouts. "Darn it. I miss my Kipper."

"Your?" Teddy asks, lips twitching in amusement.

"He was mine first, Teddy Bear," Alex claims.

"Actually," Niko cuts in, his long, curly hair tied up in a bun, "Kipp was *mine* first."

Alex waves him off. "Semantics. There's plenty of Kipp to go around."

"He would so love this conversation," Teddy mumbles.

"Everyone?" Nathaniel calls, standing inside the door in his typical argyle and khakis. "Seats, please. We're going to get started."

"You know," Alex says, winding his arm around my own and leading me over to the chairs, "I met this really cute guy the other day. He's new at Rowan's garage."

Rowan, one of Alex's boyfriends, is a mechanic. Their other boyfriend, Finn, does software development. When I first met the two, I thought it'd be the other way around. Rowan is the shy, quiet type, whereas Finn... Well, he's covered in tattoos, piercings, and has flaming red hair.

"Okay?" I ask slowly, wondering why Alex is telling me about the new guy at the garage. We take seats beside one another, ending up in a row behind Teddy, Niko, and Dixon. Dixon, for his part, is grumbling about his latte and some guy named Rip.

"Want me to set the two of you up?" Alex asks.

It takes me a moment to process his question. "Wait, what? No, I... What?"

Alex snorts. "You haven't dated much since you started working here, boo, and I thought, well, maybe you'd want to? Or not."

"I, uh..."

I'm not sure how to explain to Alex that dating, for me, feels like navigating a minefield. Granted, I'm sure everyone has their own unique challenges when it comes to finding a potential life partner.

But for me... There's a level of trust I need that I haven't been able to find on the handful of dates I've gone on in the past couple years. In fact, since starting at Elite 8 Studios, I haven't slept with anyone outside of the job. Not once. It's been easier that way.

Safer.

A first date isn't particularly scary, but I don't know that I want to bother with it right now. There's a lot on my plate between work, classes, and the research study. And *love*, well... It can wait.

I don't have time to give Alex an answer before the studio door swings open and Jerome walks in. Our boss is the production manager here at Elite 8 Studios. He doesn't own the company, but everyone knows he's the one in charge. And as his leather jacket and no-nonsense expression might suggest, he's a bit of a hardass.

Once you get to know him, though, you realize exactly how much he cares about the people inside these walls. His ferocity extends to protecting his employees, even if, at times, his yelling is a little rough on the ears.

"All right, everyone," Jerome booms, coming to a stop inside the door and motioning for the man next to him to step forward. "Time to meet your new costar. This is Christian Ducat, herein known as Vixen."

I choke on absolutely nothing.

Because *holy shit*. It's the guy I ran into by my place. The tall, dark-haired maybe-model with the smokey eyes. And today, he's wearing a *skirt*. A short, black, pleated skirt over high-top shoes. His shirt is white and cropped, showing off his slim stomach. And there's a dainty silver chain around his waist, held in place by the piercing at his navel.

"Oh my God," Alex whispers beside me, sounding frantic. "*A femboy*. Emil, it's a femboy!"

"You know we had open auditions last week," Jerome goes on. "Vixen here is one of two performers we've hired. The other won't be joining us for another few weeks. But, in the meantime, make sure to welcome your new cast member. Be polite. Show him around. Don't be asses."

There's a general chuckle that goes around at that, and Vixen's lips lift into a smile. His eyes sweep the room, taking everything in, but when they land on me, he freezes. Those eyes go round, and my pulse kicks up in response. I chance a glance behind me, wondering what has him looking so astonished, but I don't see anything. When I face forward again, that smile returns to Vixen's face, full-blown this time. And then, he winks.

What.

"Two quick notes," Jerome says, his voice cutting through the din.

"*Top, top, top,*" Alex chants under his breath, his fingers crossed in front of him. "For the love of all that is dirty, say he's—"

"Vixen is an exclusive top," Jerome confirms.

Alex grabs my arm, squeezing tight. "I knew it!" he hisses. "A *blouse.*" At my confused expression, he explains, "A feminine top, boo."

"Second thing," Jerome calls. "We're trying out something new. Starting in a couple weeks, we'll test pilot a series of live stream videos for a new elite tier of subscribers."

A murmur goes around at that, and Alex releases his death-grip on my arm.

"Vixen has agreed to be one of the participants," our boss says. "We'll do some promos in the coming weeks to prepare for the launch, so expect to see added scenes on your schedules for filming. That's it for now. Enjoy brunch. Introduce yourselves. Be good boys."

Teddy snorts, and Jerome turns to Vixen, saying something quietly. Alex launches out of his seat as conversation starts up again, the cast and crew talking about the changes coming our way.

But I'm stuck on that wink.

He wasn't looking at me, right? Surely not.

Alex is one of the first to reach our new costar, a good head shorter as he stops in front of him. He's all smiles, and Vixen grins in return, laughing lightly at whatever Alex is saying.

I meander over to the buffet table, not wanting to crowd the new guy right off the bat. And, if I'm being entirely honest with myself, a little intimidated. But there are plenty of introductions to go around. Mine can wait.

I busy myself with making a plate of food, grabbing a poppy seed bagel and some fruit. But as I'm setting down the knife for the cream cheese, I hear a gentle, "Hey."

My inhale is small, and I turn, coming face to face with none other than Vixen himself. He gives me a tiny smile that has my heart trying to leap into my throat, so I clear it, clumsily holding out my hand.

"Um, hi. I'm Emil."

Vixen's hand is warm against my own. Soft, apart from the calluses on his fingertips. "Emil," he says, rolling over my name slowly. He releases my palm. "I'm Christian."

"Right. Um, hi."

Shit. I said that already.

Vixen—*Christian*—simply smiles. "It's really good to meet you, Specs."

My brain skitters to a halt.

The world tilts just a little.

Everything goes deathly quiet.

And then Christian adds, "Officially, I mean."

Christian.

C.

Specs.

I pull in a breath, my heart kicking a big *thump* inside my chest as sound returns around us in a rush, the chatter of my coworkers like the buzzing of bees. I don't believe in coincidences that big. There's only one logical conclusion to be made here, but it's one I'm having a hard time wrapping my head around because the reality of it is so far from what I expected, it doesn't seem possible.

This gorgeous man looking at me with the dark eyes and the soft smile...

He's my *voyeur*.

Holy. Freaking. Hell.

Chapter 4

CHRISTIAN

Specs looks freaked out, his big eyes blinking at me in slow repetition.

No, not just Specs, I remind myself. *Emil.* My kinky neighbor finally has a name.

I can't blame him for being spooked when I was equally as shocked to walk into this studio and find him staring back at me. I suppose, in a ridiculously roundabout way, it makes perfect sense. Emil clearly gets off on being watched, so him working in porn fits. I just didn't expect it.

Nor did I think *this* is how we'd finally meet.

"You…" Emil manages after a moment, his question evident in the half-formed sentence.

"Me," I confirm gently.

He shakes his head a little, and my gut sinks. Is he…upset? Before I have a chance to ask, someone steps up next to us.

"Hey!" the newcomer says. "I'm Tanner."

"Oh," I say. "Noel's cousin."

He nods, offering his hand to shake. "Yep, that's me."

Emil edges away, a blush on his cheeks. For a moment, I consider chasing after him. But I don't want to put him on the spot any more than I already have, so I accept Tanner's handshake and let Emil have his privacy. Hopefully, he just needs a few minutes to process.

"Thanks so much for answering my questions the other day," I tell Tanner. "I really appreciate it."

"Of course," he says, seemingly happy to have given me a rundown and recommendation of the place.

Talking to Tanner did help solidify my decision to audition for Elite 8 Studios. But it was meeting Jerome and Nathaniel after the scout sent me to the studio that really sealed the deal.

I wasn't sure what to expect of a business that makes bank from sex work. But the place is clean, the people respectful, and when I laid out my conditions—in particular the fact that I don't want to bottom—neither Jerome nor Nathaniel batted an eye. They both nodded, Nathaniel made a note, and Jerome asked me if I had any other limits they should be aware of.

I was shocked, to say the least.

When they offered me the job, I didn't hesitate to accept it. I thought of Specs. Of trusting my gut.

And now, somehow, that decision led me right back to the man himself.

I find Emil in the crowd, his back to me as he talks with the boom operator who introduced himself as Marco.

"Have you done this before?" Tanner asks, pulling my attention.

"Porn?" I check.

He chuckles. "Well, yeah."

"No," I admit, huffing a laugh. "Brand new."

I don't think mentioning my brief stint in high school drama would be relevant. Sure, I was told there would be scripts to follow for certain scenes, but fucking in front of the cameras is a lot different than what I did a decade ago in my high school gym.

"Well, I hope you don't mind me saying it, but fans are going to love you," Tanner says.

"That they will," another voice cuts in, the only feminine one here. A woman with a perky ponytail and impeccable makeup holds out her hand. I'm careful to avoid her talons as we shake.

"Christian," I offer.

"Raylin," she answers in kind, letting me go. Her eyes sweep over me from head to toe, appraising. "Nice hair. And love the skirt. Do you wax?"

I cough. "I'm guessing I do now?"

"Sure do, sweets. I'll see you on Wednesday." With that, Raylin gives me a wink and walks off.

Tanner winces. "Don't envy you that."

"Yeah, well..." I shake my head, huffing a laugh. "I suppose it's a small price to pay."

Over the next half hour, I meet the remaining members of the cast and crew. There are a lot of faces and names, but I do my best to commit each and every one to memory.

When I see Emil near the edge of the room, finally on his own, I break away and head in his direction. He spots me coming right away and straightens, pushing his glasses up his nose. I've seen him do that a hundred times, if not more, and a smile pulls at the corners of my lips before I think better of it. Emil looks wary.

I stop in front of him with a small sigh. "I'm sorry."

His eyes widen. "What for?"

"For surprising you? I didn't know you worked here, Emil. Please believe that. And it wasn't my intention to catch you off guard, but I couldn't *not* tell who I am. I wouldn't have felt right keeping that to myself considering, well, we'll be working together."

He nods, brows furrowed.

"Did I wreck things?" I ask.

There go his eyes again, bouncing wide. It's a little surreal to be standing here in front of Specs, seeing all the nuances of his face I couldn't make out clearly from my window. It's a good face. Open and inviting. But I can't help but feel like I've disappointed him. Like maybe he didn't *want* to know the person who's been watching him from behind the blinds. Maybe that was part of the appeal.

But Emil shakes his head. "No. You didn't, uh...wreck anything. I'm not upset. I just, uh... I never thought... *Shit.*"

His cheeks start to redden, and I cock my head.

"I just..." He cuts off again, fidgeting with his glasses.

It sinks in. Slowly.

"Are you...*shy?*" I ask in awe.

He blushes harder.

"Oh my God. *Specs*," I nearly whisper, unable to stop my grin. "I've seen you butt-ass naked with four fingers up your ass, and you never once had your hands in front of your eyes like you do now. What are you doing?"

He groans, but there's a smile on his face that has me huffing a laugh.

"Are you seriously hiding from me?"

"I can't help it," he says, literally peeking through his fingers. "I'm so embarrassed."

My smile slips. "Emil, I'm sorry. I wasn't trying to make you uncomfortable. We don't have to talk about...that."

His hands drop, leaving his glasses crooked over his perplexed expression. "I... I'm not embarrassed by *that*. Or mad,

I promise. I just... I never expected you to be..." He waves a hand up and down in front of me before finishing with, "*You.*"

"And...is that a good discovery or a bad one?" I check.

His eyes slip down to my skirt before trailing back up to my face. "Please don't make me answer that."

Oh.

My insides ping, but Emil glances quickly away again, and, since the last thing I want to do is embarrass him further, I offer a change of topic. "Would you show me around the studio?"

"Me?" he asks.

"Yeah, you," I answer, chuckling. "Is there someone else I'm staring at?"

He pulls in a sharp breath, and, *ah, damn it.* There's that blush again. I hold back a groan. Specs might very well be the end of me.

"I can do that," he finally says.

"Lead the way."

I trail after Emil as he heads out of Studio 1, many of our coworkers still inside enjoying the brunch buffet. The hall is quiet, and Emil glances over at me as we walk.

"You probably went down that way," he says, pointing down the hall where I met with Jerome and Nathaniel. "Those are offices and private rooms that we use for some of our solo videos."

"Do you do a lot of solo stuff?"

He shakes his head. "Not me personally, but some of the guys do toy promos or jerk-off type videos."

He says it so casually, as if talking about sex is far easier for him than whatever it was making him blush a moment ago.

At the next hall, he says, "There's our gym. It's not huge, but it has some decent equipment from what I've heard. I don't use it."

I hum, and he leads us on.

"Cosmetology, storage room for props, and here's our break room," he says, motioning toward each. He stops at the break room, pushing the door open, and I peek inside. "It's always stocked with snacks and drinks. You're welcome to any of it."

"That's really considerate."

"Yeah, it's a nice bonus," he says, letting the door shut. "Last up is the locker room."

He opens that door, too, and I step inside. The room is well-lit, with a bank of lockers and some large mirrors along one wall. There are sinks and toilets, and around a corner, a row of curtained shower stalls. I walk back toward the lockers, looking at the names on each.

"Which is yours?" I ask, fingers running over the metal doors.

Emil steps over to the one that reads "Felix" and gives it a tap. "This is me."

My lips quirk. "Suits you. It's very..."

"Nerdy?" he says with a laugh.

"In the best way," I answer, meaning it.

He clears his throat. "Well, Vixen suits you."

"Does it?"

He nods, although his eyes flit away again, like he's self-conscious. It's so strange to see. I never would have pegged my neighbor as the shy type, not after what I've seen him do.

"The people here..." I say slowly. "They're good, aren't they?"

I got that impression during my interview and while meeting everyone today, but I trust Specs would tell if that's *not* the case. I'd hate to end up in another toxic work environment.

He nods, though. "Yeah, everyone is seriously great. Jerome wouldn't let anyone get away with shit. Nor would Alex. The guy might be a menace," he says with a huff, "but he's a *good* menace."

"Alex is Tink, right?"

He nods again.

"Can I ask how you got into porn?" Quickly, I add, "Unless that's personal."

"It is, a bit," he says, shifting on his feet. "But I have a feeling you can guess."

Yeah, I can. Emil is an exhibitionist. I wonder if the people here know that about him. If they know he likes to show off, even in the privacy of his own home where the only person who can see him is me.

Emil's cheeks color a little, as if his thoughts went the same direction as mine.

"And you?" he asks. "How'd you find us?"

I'd say fate, but I know Emil doesn't believe in that. I'm not sure what I believe—if there's any sort of rhyme or reason to the chaos of this world or if, as Emil said, it's all just a beautiful sort of happenstance.

"Chance, I guess?" I answer.

"Lucky us," he mumbles almost entirely under his breath.

"Lucky me, too."

Emil ducks his head, cheeks flushed, and it's so endearing, my chest squeezes tight. He makes for the exit, leaving me jogging to catch up.

"So, that's everything," he says, holding the door as I pass through. "If you have questions or whatever, just let me know."

"Emil," I say softly.

He stops, facing me in the hall outside of the locker room.

"I'm glad I got the chance to meet you," I tell him seriously. "But I understand if this changes things between us. I don't want to make you uncomfortable. *Ever*. I'll follow your lead."

He blinks. "Nothing has changed."

"No?" I ask, a little surprised.

"No. Except... I know your name now. And we'll probably be fucking at some point."

I huff a laugh, and Emil smiles, a small thing.

"But the other stuff?" he says, shaking his head. "Hasn't changed."

Relief hits, making me realize just how worried I'd been about that. I would have hated to lose Emil's friendship. Even more than the view outside my window.

"You can always close your curtains," I tell him, needing to do so for my own peace of mind.

The slant of his lips this time is all smirk. "I know."

Well, then. There's the brazen show-off I know so well.

I chuckle, and Emil waves me down the hall. We rejoin the stragglers in Studio 1, and I learn a little more about these men and one woman I'll be working with. Emil leaves before me for class, but his, "See you later, Christian," feels like a promise.

Before I go, Nathaniel hands me a schedule. Jerome has me slotted in with Raylin in a couple days for, *yep*, hair removal. On Friday, I film an intro to myself, letting the fans know who I am, probably flashing some skin. And then, next week, I'll work with my scene partner for the lives, getting comfortable before we film for real.

There's no name yet beside my own, and I can't help but wonder who I'll be paired with.

I know who I'm *hoping* for.

When I get home, it's early still. Only midafternoon. I sit down in front of Bernie, her plastic body free of dust or smudges. She's the cleanest thing in my apartment and always will be, not that the rest of the space is all that untidy. I thread some white, all-purpose thread through her needle before grabbing the bundle of fabric I'm turning into a skirt.

My mind and body settles into the familiar rhythm as I start to sew. I remember sitting in almost this exact spot when I was only twelve years old, back when the apartment belonged to my grandmother. My mom had just dropped me off for a visit, and, at the time, I was upset with her because she wouldn't buy me a skirt I wanted from the store. *"It's girls' clothes,"* she told me. *"Not for you."* When my mom left for her job at the diner, my grandma sat down with me on the floor in front of the couch and asked if I was a girl. There was no distaste in her tone, only honest curiosity. She genuinely wanted to know, and I could tell my grandma would have supported me no matter my answer.

I shook my head, though, because even then I knew I was a boy. I just liked skirts.

My grandma squeezed my shoulder and brought me over to her sewing machine, and, together, we made me a skirt. My mom never knew. Not about that one. I'd wear it every time I visited my grandma, and I'd take it off before my mom came to pick me up.

My grandmother was the only person in my life who asked me who I was growing up. Who listened instead of telling me no.

The day I moved in here, that sewing machine broke. I cried when it happened, and it took a good few months before I was able to bring myself to buy Bernie. I don't regret it, but I do miss the old metal machine I learned to sew on.

Thoughts of my past scatter when a light flicks on across the alleyway. Specs's light. He walks into his room, disappearing for a moment into the area where I can't see him. When he returns, he looks toward the window.

With only a moment's hesitation, I reach over and pull up the blinds. We stare at one another for a long beat, and I wait to see what he'll do. If he'll close his curtains.

He doesn't. He plops onto his bed, sets an energy drink beside him, and opens up a textbook.

With a small exhale, I go back to sewing my skirt. I wonder what Specs will think of the white.

Chapter 5

Emil

"You want me to do the lives with Vixen," I repeat.

"If you're amenable," Jerome says, his foot kicked over his knee as he sits behind his desk. "It's either you or Adonis, and I'm asking you first. Frankly, I don't trust Tink not to say something he shouldn't on a live stream. And Dix, Bruiser, and Teddy are all tops."

I nod, strangely flattered that Jerome seems to consider me part of the core group here at Elite 8 Studios. There are other guys Christian could do the videos with, but Jerome wants me or Niko.

"Um, yeah," I answer, heart kicking an extra beat at the idea of being paired with Christian. "I'll do it."

Jerome links his hands atop his flat belly. "Good. I'll have you two do a test run next week. No sex, but we'll make sure you're comfortable, figure out camera angles, that sort of thing. We're going to allow viewers the ability to comment in real time, so we'll have to be on top of that. I'll have an assistant monitoring the chat for anything that needs to be removed, but I'm leaving these videos unscripted, so the two of you can accept some direction from the viewers. Within limits, of course."

Holy shit.

"Yeah, um... Sounds fine," I manage to say.

Sounds like a goddamn wet dream.

Jerome gives me a short nod. "All right, then. You're scheduled for Tuesday. Get on out of here."

"Yep."

Standing, I take my leave. The halls are strangely quiet as I walk, apart from the sound of a machine in the gym clanking. So quiet I can hear my heartbeat in my ears.

Christian is going to fuck me. Or do *something* with me. Honestly, it doesn't even matter. He's going to touch me live in front of who knows how many people. They're going to see it in real time. Comment in *real* time.

Slinking inside one of the private rooms, I let out a breath. "Fuck," I mutter, leaning against the door and squeezing my eyes shut. My hand slips down my stomach without conscious thought, curling over my cock through the material of my jeans. I'm shaking, so horny I'm nearly lightheaded. It'd be so easy to slide my hand inside my pants and rub one out. It wouldn't even take long. Half a minute maybe; I'm that keyed up.

But I don't.

I uncurl my hand, drop it to my side, and breathe long and low as I let all that burning need turn to a simmer. My therapist would be so proud that I'm choosing to practice self-control.

Once my body is in check, I head back into the hall.

"Hey, boo."

"Holy fucking—" I grab my chest, pulse thundering. "*Jesus*, I didn't see you."

Alex snorts. "Clearly. *Soo*, what were you doing hiding out in one of the private rooms?"

"I wasn't hiding," I shoot back, even though it's a lie. I was.

Alex cocks his head. "I was kidding, but you're being awfully suspicious, Kent. World-saving stuff again?"

I huff a laugh, my pulse starting to come down. "Yep."

"All right, keep your secrets. For *now*."

That's not ominous.

"How are classes going?" he asks.

Alex graduated recently with a degree in art. He's one of the only people in my life—apart from Christian—who asks about my coursework. Of course, thinking about that makes me realize, all over again, that *Christian* is my C. I'm still not over the fact that the maybe-octogenarian peeking through my window turned out to be a smoking-hot guy in his twenties with a belly button piercing and legs as long as a giraffe's.

And *fuck*. Don't think about that. Not about his legs. Not about the belly chain. Not about his mesmerizing eyes or the pitch-black hair that's long enough to grab ahold of.

"Good," I say loudly. "Classes are good. I'm, uh, doing some research this semester. Did I tell you that?"

"No, you most certainly did not. What kind?" Alex asks, giving my arm a little tug. I walk with him to the break room.

"It's a clinical psych study on the effectiveness of cognitive training for memory retention in dementia patients."

Alex's eyebrows pop up. "I'll pretend like I understood half of that. Why dementia?"

"I didn't pick the topic," I explain as Alex grabs a snack. He holds up a granola bar, silently asking if I want one, but I shake my head.

"What topic would you pick?" he asks, sprawling onto a nearby couch like a cat.

"All of them?" I answer with a laugh.

The thud of the door banging into the wall has me jumping.

"I did *not*," Dixon says, coming into the room in a huff.

"Did, too," Niko counters, sauntering in after him. He shoots me and Alex a wink.

"What's this about?" Alex asks, perking up. He's never one for passing up potential drama.

"He said 'I love you' during our scene," Niko says, a shit-eating grin on his face.

Alex snorts, and Dixon pinches the bridge of his nose, looking exasperated.

"You know I fucking love you, Niki," Dixon grumbles. "But that's not what I said."

"Should we go check the footage?" Niko asks.

"You are the most insufferable man I have ever met in my goddamn life," Dixon retorts, grabbing a drink and twisting off the cap.

Niko grins. "Yet you suffer me just fine."

Dixon grinds his teeth together before stomping out of the room.

"Love you, too!" Niko yells, turning to us with a look of glee. "He is utterly incapable of admitting when he's wrong. Excuse me."

As Niko jogs out of the room after his boyfriend, saying something about how *being grumpy only makes you hotter, you know*, Alex chuckles. "I like watching their foreplay."

"Is that what that is?" I murmur.

"Mm. So what do you think about our new costar?"

I choke on my spit, and Alex's eyes narrow.

"Fine," I eke out.

"Uh-huh. He's very tall."

"Sure," I agree.

"And pretty."

I don't comment.

"*And*," Alex says pointedly, "I'm fairly certain he has a seven-and-a-half inch dick."

I cough. And cough again, my lungs seizing. "*W-what?*"

"I mean, not like that info will stay private for much longer," Alex says, which is true. Dick sizes are listed on our bios, for Christ's sake. "But he was in to film his intro, and I heard him talking about it."

It's not like it matters. Not really. A dick is a dick, and knowing how to play your partner is more important than the size of the instrument.

But.

"That's, um...good for him," I say.

And me. Very good for me.

Alex's lips twitch. "Not sure where he hides that thing under his skirt."

"Oh my God," I groan. "I, um. Have to go. Yep. See ya later, Alex."

"Bye, boo," he calls, cackling as I leave the room to a flood of mental images I try my best to dispel.

It's just a dick. Attached to a guy I happen to find very attractive. A guy who lives across the alley and watches me jerk off, and *holy fuck*.

This whole time, it's been *him*. For three months. The guy I've been chatting with and, yes, at times flirting with, is a reality far better than any fantasies I had conjured.

I didn't think that was possible.

And the fact that I get to *have* him, at least a little? At least within the bounds of these walls? It's a thrilling, terrifying prospect. Because, as much as I don't want to admit it to myself, now that I've met him, I could like him. I really could.

But Lord knows, when it comes to intimacy, I'm more than a little screwed up.

When I get home, I kick off my shoes and head into my bedroom. Christian's blinds are up, but he's not in front of the window. My fingers itch to text him, even though I have no idea if he's home.

I grab my phone before I can chicken out.

Me: Hey.

He appears in the window half a minute later, and I let loose a breath. He smiles, blowing a kiss from the tips of his fingers.

Christian: Hey, Specs.

Me: You free?

He knows what I'm asking. His smile widens, and he takes a seat, plopping his elbow on the windowsill, chin in his palm.

Christian: Watching.

Fuck. I have such a problem.

And yet acknowledging it doesn't stop me from tugging my shirt over my head. I walk to my nightstand and look inside, contemplating my options. There's a whoosh in my ears, the kind that drowns out rationality. I pull out a seven-and-a-half inch dildo and climb onto my bed.

My phone dings.

Christian: Are you going to fuck yourself for me?

Yes, that's the plan.

I kick off my pants and underwear, eyes flicking to the window. My gut bottoms out as I catch Christian's gaze. It's the *good* kind of swooping, like when you're riding a roller coaster and gravity has you spiraling toward Earth. It's danger, but a welcome one.

I contemplate for only a second before asking Christian something I never have before.

Me: Can I call you?

He smiles, nodding, but before I can hit his number, my phone rings. I answer, turning it on speakerphone and setting it on the bed.

"This okay?" I check.

"Yeah, Specs. I'll finally get to hear what you sound like."

Shit.

I lick my lips, grabbing the lube and wetting the dildo. I lean back with it in hand, spreading my knees, letting Christian see all of me.

This is the one place where I can't hide.

Notching the toy against my entrance, I exhale. The toy slips in, and Christian makes an aborted sound, as if *he's* the one being breached. "Damn, Specs."

"I'm going to be filming with you," I say, inching the toy in further. "Talked to Jerome today."

"Yeah? That'll be fun."

"Uh-huh," I breathe, halfway there now.

"And you're okay with that?" he asks.

"Yeah."

Excited. Scared. Horny as fuck just imagining it.

"The fans will be watching live," Christian says.

My breath stutters, the fake balls of the dildo coming to rest at my ass.

"It'll be like they're right there in the room with you," he adds, and I groan, my cock jerking. Christian huffs a laugh. "You really do like that, huh?"

"What...gave me away?" I ask, pulling the dildo nearly all the way out and fucking it back in. My mouth parts, breath leaving me at that smooth glide. At knowing Christian is watching. I can't help but wonder if he's imagining it's *him* sinking inside me instead.

"Not sure if you know this, Specs," he says almost fondly, "but you seem to have a little thing for being watched."

I choke on a laugh.

"You're gorgeous like this," he goes on. "Uninhibited. And don't forget to stroke your cock. He looks lonely."

I mutter a curse, hand flying to my dick.

"Mm, there you go. You're like this in your videos, too. I watched a couple this week."

Lightning crackles down my spine, and I dig my toes into the sheets, pace stuttering. "You did?"

"Mhm. I've never seen anyone as raw as you when it comes to sex. You're completely devoid of artifice on that screen. Same way as you are right now, here in front of me. It's stunning."

My breath puffs out of me as I work myself over. Not only stroking my cock, but pumping the dildo in and out of my ass, again and again until it feels as if I'll explode. Christian helps me along.

"I'm gonna enjoy being the one to make you come."

With a muffled groan, my body twists, my grip on the dildo slipping as my hand flies over my cock. I jerk, my muscles locking tight, ass strangling the toy as sparking energy fires through my veins. My cum coats the sheets in front of me as Christian makes a sound that rivals my own.

"Fucking hell, Specs."

I pant, catching my breath as I roll to my back. "Do... Do you jerk off when...you watch me?"

Christian hums, a quiet sound. "I haven't."

I crane my head to look up at his window. "Why not?" I ask, feeling almost...disappointed by that. "Does it not turn you on?"

"Oh, Specs," he says quickly, shaking his head. "You turn me on so much it's painful. Don't doubt that."

I grab the dildo, pulling it free and making a mental note to wash my sheets. "Then why?"

"It felt like one thing to watch and entirely another to participate," he says simply. "And, frankly, watching you is kind of like looking at art. I'm okay with enjoying the view."

I blow out a breath, sitting up. "You could if you want. I'd be okay with you participating."

It looks as if his lips quirk into a smile. "Noted."

"Um, Christian?"

"Yeah, Specs?"

"Thanks for watching."

This time, there's definitely a smile. "Anytime."

Chapter 6

CHRISTIAN

"Hi, Grandma."

"Christian," my grandmother says warmly, opening her arms wide. "Get over here."

I head over to her chair and give my grandma a hug. Like me, she has dark hair, although hers has more silver running through it than black these days. We look a lot alike, in fact. I never knew my dad, but it's clear I take after the Korean half of my family, a fact my blonde-haired, blue-eyed mother seemed to love and hate in equal measure.

"How's jail?" I ask, leaning back.

My grandma chuckles. She moved into an assisted living facility—as she insists I call it—after a nasty fall busted her hip. She doesn't get around all that well these days, and her decision to move, as she likes to remind me, was the best option.

Doesn't mean I have to like it. I miss seeing her at home, in the apartment where I now live. I'll always think of it as *hers*.

"It's far from a jail cell," she says, giving me a gentle prod. "Back up. Let me see you."

With a laugh, I step back and fluff my skirt. Opening my arms wide, I ask, "Well?"

"That's a gorgeous one, sweetheart. Chiffon?"

"Yep," I say, sweeping my skirt under me as I take a seat on the end of her bed.

"Bet those layers took a while."

They did. The skirt is long, reaching all the way to my ankles, and layered enough for the white fabric not to be see-through. It wasn't the easiest material to work with, but I'm really happy with the end result. I paired the skirt with a black crop top today and boots of the same color. I like the blend of soft and hard.

"It was tricky, but Bernie was a champ," I tell my grandma.

She smiles, always happy to hear about my sewing. "Give any more thought to selling your pieces?"

I fidget with my skirt. "I don't know who'd buy them, Grandma."

She hums. "Boys like you, I imagine."

I nod, but I wouldn't have a clue where to start when it comes to opening a business. The legalities alone make my head spin, not to mention figuring out how to sell online. It's so much to learn, and I'm not even a professional seamster. I don't have training. Sewing is just my hobby.

"I'll think about it," I tell her, grateful, at least, for her unwavering support.

My grandma smiles, and conversation turns to other topics. I stay with her for a good while, the two of us chatting and playing war with a deck of cards until it's her lunchtime. As she goes to eat with her friends, I head to work.

I'm filming with Emil today.

Well, pseudo-filming. It's more a trial run to make sure everything runs smoothly with the live feed. But it will be me and Emil. On a bed. Together.

My stomach does a strange little hop just thinking about it. I've seen the man on a bed—*naked*, no less—dozens of times. But this will be different.

Because I'll be there with him.

I use my code to get into the building and follow the sound of chatter to Studio 2. Alex and a man I don't recognize are inside, practically giggling as they huddle together in front of a laptop. Some of the crew is here, too, getting the set ready.

"Hey," I say, heading toward Alex, since I know him best. The man makes it near impossible to feel like a stranger.

His blonde head pops up, and he gives me a swift smile, followed by a once-over. "Damn, boo. *Love* the skirt."

"Thanks," I reply, giving it a pluck.

Alex pokes the man next to him in the cheek. "Christian, this is Kipp, Teddy's boytoy."

"Husband," Kipp corrects, shoving Alex's shoulder.

Alex snickers. "Same diff."

Kipp rolls his eyes before giving me a smile. "Hey. Nice to meet you."

"You, too," I answer. "Is Emil here yet?"

"In the locker room," Alex says.

I thank him and head that way, leaving Alex and Kipp to whatever they're in cahoots over. When I push the door to the locker room open, I find Emil seated inside on a bench. I'm not at all surprised to see a textbook on his lap, but the sight still makes me chuckle.

Emil looks up, huffing a self-conscious laugh before shutting his book.

"Studying?" I ask.

"Shocking, right?"

"Quite," I tease.

I walk slowly past the bank of lockers until I find the one labeled "Vixen." A smile pulls at my lips as I trace the letters with my fingertip. When I turn Emil's way, I catch his eyes darting down my body before he looks away.

Mm. Would it be wrong of me to ask what he was looking at just to see his blush again?

Probably.

"So, ready to go to bed with me?" I ask instead, taking a seat beside him.

Aaand there's that blush anyway. *Oops?*

"Yeah. Uh. Yep," he says.

I keep my grin to myself. "Have any tips for me?"

His eyes widen. "Tips?"

"For being in front of the cameras," I say, wondering where, precisely, his mind went. "Anything I should know so I don't mess up filming?"

"Oh." He huffs a laugh, nudging his glasses. "Yeah, um... You'll want to be aware of where the cameramen are. Keep yourself angled toward the wide shot, and if you're, like, going down on someone, tilt your head a bit so your face is in view."

Well, *damn.* There's a picture.

"And normally, I'd say don't look at the cameras," he adds. "But in this case, I think we're supposed to. But, um, also look at me a lot because people like to see that."

"That I can do," I say easily.

"Um, good," he mutters. "Yeah, so that's pretty much it. But don't worry too much about getting everything right. Jerome won't expect you to have it all figured out the first couple times, and he or Nathaniel will tell you if you need to make adjustments."

"You really like it here, huh?"

I can tell from his tone. Emil speaks about the people here with a sort of fond familiarity that's usually reserved for family, not coworkers.

"I do," he answers. "I know what a lot of people think about sex workers. But the people here...they're good. And I don't think sex is something to be ashamed about. I might have my hang-ups, but that's not one of them."

I'm tempted to ask what his hang-ups *are*, but I refrain. "I agree. Sex can be an amazing experience. I think, for some, powerful even."

He nods. "Yeah, um... Yeah."

"What?" I ask, having a feeling he was going to say something else.

"I just—I figured you were pretty open-minded about it considering, well, the first thing you ever told me was to leave my curtains open so you could watch me jerk off."

I huff a startled laugh, eyes caught on Emil's little smirk. "I didn't *tell* you to. I said I wouldn't mind it. There's a difference," I defend with absolutely zero heat. "I never thought you'd actually do it, you know."

"Well," he says, blushing again.

"Mhm. Well, indeed."

Emil picks at the seam of his jeans. "Um, are you ready? We should probably get out there."

"Yeah. Let's do it, Specs."

Emil puts his book in his locker before we head to Studio 2. The set looks complete now. There's a bed stationed against one wall, with a fluffy white comforter on top, and other details fill out the room—pictures and decor, all of it making the space look like a real bedroom. Above are lights suspended from the ceiling, and just outside the set sits a large camera on wheels.

"Wow," I mutter.

"Pretty neat, isn't it?" Emil says.

I nod.

I can't say I ever had dreams of being on the big screen, but I did enjoy my high school stint in acting. There's something magical about being on stage, or, in this case, on set. You get to put your all into it, and no one can tell you to stop being so bold or dramatic. No one tells you to wipe off your makeup or take off your skirt.

I think, for me, theater was a way to feel comfortable in my skin when my parent wouldn't allow for that. It's different for me now. I *am* comfortable in my skin. I express myself the way I want to every single day.

But as I stand in front of the lit-up set, I'm hit with familiar jitters I haven't felt in years. I won't be reading Shakespeare today, but *this* is something I know how to do. It's something I didn't realize I missed.

"You're smiling," Emil says, looking at me curiously.

"What can I say?" I reply. "I'm excited to get into bed with this cute guy I know."

He huffs a laugh, looking down at his shoes.

"All right," comes Jerome's big, booming voice. "Felix, Vixen, you're here. Good. Tink and...Kipp. Get outta here. You'll be watching from a private room. Keep your comments on the up-and-up, gentlemen."

Alex snorts, clearly not making any promises. But he and Kipp leave the room, the laptop with them.

"Let's get this started," Jerome calls.

I give Emil's arm a nudge. "Come on, Specs. We're up."

Emil walks with me over to the bed. I hop up first, patting the spot next to me, and he climbs on, a small smile on his face.

"Here's how this will go," Jerome says, addressing the entire crew. "Because we can't edit these lives, we're going with a single camera setup, like a typical home video. Otherwise, we risk another getting caught in the shot. Vixen, Felix, there's a tablet on the end table next to you. It's opened up to the live chat. As you'll see, Tink and Kipp are already having a good time."

I glance at the tablet. The text is enlarged enough for me to be able to read it without getting closer, and, at the moment, it's filled with eggplant emojis, a few suggestions to take off our clothes, and one rather explicit request involving Emil's ass and my tongue. I chuckle, realizing the camera must already be recording, at least to our limited viewers down the hall.

Jerome shakes his head, heaving a sigh. "Let's try taking a few of those comments down just to make sure we can."

The assistant at the edge of the room nods, his own tablet in hand. A second later, some of the eggplants disappear.

"Good, good," Jerome says. "All right. Felix, Vixen, go ahead and get started. Move around a bit, try out some positions, imitate sex. We'll make sure everything looks good from our end."

"Damn," I mutter, quirking a smile at Emil. "I guess we're skipping the foreplay and jumping right into it."

He chuckles, adjusting his glasses. "Here," he says, lying back and motioning me forward, reminding me that he's the pro in this situation. My pulse jumps as he opens his legs wide in invitation, and I hitch up my skirt, crawling forward and settling on top of him.

He blows out a breath, our faces so close I can feel it.

"Okay?" I say quietly.

He nods.

"So... What sort of things don't you like?" I ask, focusing on Emil as the crew moves around us. "Jerome said the studio sticks to relatively vanilla sex, but do you have any hard or soft limits? Anything I should stay away from?"

Emil swallows. "Um. No degradation," he says. "Don't call me a slut or anything like that."

I nod. "Okay."

"No DP, either," he goes on. "One dick or toy is plenty. And use your other arm," he adds as I stroke his hair back from his forehead. "You're blocking my face."

"Right," I say, lips twitching as I switch arms.

"And, uh, no spitting unless it's to wet my asshole," he says, making my pulse—*and cock*—kick up. He clears his throat, clearly having felt that, considering our crotches are nestled together. "Everything else is fair game."

I hum, my thoughts running wild. I know Emil enjoys playing with dildos. Maybe he'd let me do the same for our first video. I could stretch him open with something small, maybe have the viewers pick. And then go bigger. And bigger. And then, maybe, I could dick him down until he shoots all over his stomach and those pretty pink nipples of his.

"Don't forget to check the chat," Jerome calls, making me jolt.

"Right," I say, eyes pinging to the screen.

You guys are hot.

Bow-chicka bow wow.

eggplant emoji

water spray emoji

Take it off!

I snort. "What do you want to see go?" I ask, grinning at the camera.

Not the skirt!

Emil clears his throat. "Yeah, um... You should definitely wear the skirt for our video."

"Yeah? This one?"

There's a chorus of emphatic *yes* from around the room.

I chuckle.

"The, um, chain was nice, too," Emil says, not quite meeting my eye, even though his dick is pressed to mine and his legs are bracketing my hips in an intimate hold. "Not that I don't like the little jewel you're wearing. But, uh, yeah. The chain was pretty."

"Noted," I say softly, my pulse thrumming. "Emil... Could I kiss you? Before we do this for real, I mean."

His eyes flash to mine, and he licks his lips. "Um, yeah. Sure. But you can't call me Emil while we're film—"

Emil's words cut off as I bring my lips to his. His body melts, pliant below me, his fingers gracing my sides and lifting my shirt. His lips are smooth. Soft. The bottom is plump. It's only practice, but I find myself sinking into it wholeheartedly. Everything else vanishes until there's only Specs and me. His lips and mine meeting for the first time, our bodies tangled, hearts beating less than half a foot apart. It's sweet, and it's serene, and it's absolutely filthy... And I want more.

Fuck, do I want more.

With effort, I pull back, and Specs blinks up at me.

"Okay?" I ask.

"I, uh. Yeah. Good," he answers, fingers slipping beneath the hem of my shirt. They trail up over my ribs before reversing course, making me shiver. Emil seems to catch himself, hands stilling.

"You can touch me," I assure him. "Anytime. You have my permission."

He nods quickly, a blush rising on his cheeks. The sight of it makes me want to kiss him again. So I do, a tiny peck meant to set him at ease. But Emil catches my lips in return, a beautiful smile lighting his face, and my breath hitches. His air becomes mine as butterflies take off in my stomach, and I realize...

Oh, no.

Do I have a crush?

I dismiss the thought immediately. I've never wanted a relationship before, and I don't want one now. It's only affection I feel.

Right?

"All right," Jerome shouts. "New position. Change it up."

Right.

Lifting, I swing myself around, putting Emil and I in a sixty-nine. I heft my skirt so it's not over his face, and it settles against his chest, giving him what I'm sure is a perfect view of my thong.

"Oh my God," he mumbles, palms landing on my thighs.

"Okay?" I ask, looking back.

"Oh my God."

"Sooo," I say slowly. "This is the part where, if your cock is in my mouth, I should be aware of my angles, right?"

Emil coughs, hands flexing on my thighs. I hide my smirk against his leg.

Oh, yeah. This is going to be a lot of fun.

Chapter 7

EMIL

I'm no stranger to fucking. I've done a lot of it here at the studio. I've been railed over countless surfaces, had sex that's slow and sweet, had plenty of dicks in my mouth and ass and in between my thighs. I've had to wash cum out of my hair more times than I can count.

There's not much I haven't seen or done.

But as I watch Raylin give Christian a touchup in preparation for our very first live video together, I'm hit with nerves like I've never experienced before. I don't know if it's him or the upcoming scene, but my heart has been beating heavily since the moment I walked through these doors, and I'm already descending into that foggy place where everything shuts off and I lose any and all control over rationality and reason.

There are plenty of people who enjoy being watched. Who enjoy exhibitionism. But not all of them feel a near desperate urge to have others present when they come. Not all of them would do just about anything to make that happen.

When I started seeing my therapist, worried about where my impulses might lead me, she suggested I find a safe way to explore my kink instead of trying to shove it down. One that wouldn't land me with a public indecency record.

I found Elite 8 Studios.

Inside these walls, I *am* safe. The cameraman, the crew, everybody here has consented to watching me have sex. It's part of the job, and no one bats an eye. And it feels *good*. Every time I do a scene, I get high off the knowledge that people are watching. That, even later, people will continue to watch. Viewers will see my videos days, weeks, *years* later, and that fact gives me a thrill any time I stop to think about it.

But I have never, not once, felt like *this* on the cusp of filming. I don't know if it's the promise of live viewers this time around—knowing countless people will be watching me at the same moment I'm being fucked or who knows what else. I don't know if it's the idea that they'll have a say in what happens to me. I don't know if maybe it's Christian himself—this man who's been my personal voyeur for months, who I've gotten close to, who will finally be touching me for real.

I can't say if it's one reason or all of them, but I'm so far gone, I would drop to my knees right this instant if anyone asked it of me. I would do it for any member of this cast or crew, and I'd love every goddamn second. And I *have* done scenes like that before, where my costars took turns on me. Hot as hell.

But then? I was in control. I was doing my job.

Right now? My control feels nonexistent.

"Everybody ready?" Jerome calls. "We're five minutes to showtime."

Oh, God.

I give my boss a swift nod, my mouth running dry. My hands shake as I head to the refreshments table and grab a bottled water. The cool liquid helps a little.

"Hey. You okay?"

The softly spoken words come from Christian. I turn to find him watching me with what looks like concern. *Fuck*, he's hot. The white, fluffy skirt. The belly chain he wore today that's peeking out from below the hem of his cropped shirt. The subtle makeup and the dark hair that's falling around his face, only adding to his allure.

I've never wanted someone to touch me as badly as him.

"Emil?"

"Fine," I croak.

"Are you sure?" Christian asks. "If you're not okay to do a scene today, we can call it off."

I shake my head quickly and set down the half-empty water. I understand why he's asking, I do. But his worry is misplaced. "I, uh... I'm good. But, uh..." I blow out a breath, and Christian's concern only seems to grow. "I'm going to need you to take charge during this scene."

"Do you have stage fright?" he asks.

I nearly bark a laugh. "No. Christian, I'm so turned on right now, I'm having trouble seeing straight."

His eyes flare wide, and he looks me up and down, pausing at my crotch. My cock is rock-hard, tenting my jeans.

"I want this," I make sure he knows. "I'm good, I promise. I just..."

"You need me to be the one making the decisions," he says, stepping close. Close enough that I can feel his body heat. Close enough to smell the faint whiff of something minty and fresh coming off his person. "You want me to take charge so you can enjoy the fact that everyone is going to be watching you and wishing they were me."

I let loose a breath.

"One minute," Jerome yells. "Felix. Vixen. On set. *Now*."

"Come on, Specs," Christian says, grabbing ahold of my hand. "I've got you."

And that, I believe.

Christian leads me over to the bed as the crew makes final adjustments. We sit beside one another, everything in me spun tight. I barely register what's going on around us. My heart is hammering. Anticipation is making my limbs tingle. Jerome yells for places.

I've done this a hundred times or more. But this is different. Better. *Intoxicating.*

I think I've found my new addiction.

Jerome holds up his hand, and everyone quiets. He counts us in with his fingers.

Five.

Four.

Three.

Two.

One.

The light flashes red. We're live.

"Hey, everyone," Christian says from beside me, his voice pitched into something flirtier than how he normally speaks. "I'm Vixen. And this is Felix. And *you* are the lucky subscribers who get to watch us live. How are we doing today?"

The tablet next to us scrolls with text, and I'm thankful Christian is handling this like a professional because I can't even get my eyes to work enough to read the messages.

Christian laughs, all light and throaty. "Well, thanks, Big-Boy23. I like my face, too. Now I have a simple rule before Felix and I get started. Is everyone listening?"

Christian's hand links with mine, and I blow out a breath, squeezing his fingers tight.

"If you're a dick, I'm gonna ignore you," Christian says plainly. "But if you're polite, I might just take your suggestions. So are we going to be good today?" There's a brief pause before he says, "Good. I'm glad we have an understanding. Now... Who wants to see me edge Felix so hard he passes out when he comes?"

Oh God.

Christian laughs. "I know, he's damn cute, isn't he? Come on, Fe. Let's lose the shirt."

Thank fuck Christian helps me because I'm not entirely sure I have full motor function right now. I glance toward the camera, eyes skipping to where Jerome is standing in the wings. He's watching the feed from the tablet in his hands, and he looks up, giving me a nod. No one is holding up cue cards to redirect us, so I go with the flow, letting Christian tug off my shirt. He pushes me playfully onto my back and crawls over me, his eyes as dark as night.

"Here's what I'm thinking," he says, leaning down to kiss my collarbone. The next one lands on my chest, so very close to my nipple. "I'm going to let our viewers decide what I fuck you with."

My head swims.

Christian kisses above my belly button before going on, his voice projecting enough for the boom to pick him up easily. "But I get to decide for how long. Lift your hips, Fe."

I lift, and Christian tugs down my jeans. My cock is tenting my briefs, and I'm suddenly grateful Jerome told us to keep this video under an hour because I'm already desperate to come. Desperate for, *fuck*, anything.

"Ch—Vixen. *Please.*"

Christian flashes me a smile as he slinks up my legs, looking like a cat on the prowl. He slips his fingers beneath the band of my briefs, lips suspended above my cock. After an endless moment that almost has me begging—*again*—he lifts the material, but only enough for the end of my dick to slip free. He tilts his head just so, his smirk telling me he remembered what I told him about angles, and then he kisses the top of my dick.

I curse under my breath, hips hitching.

"BellyDancerBoi wants to see your cock, Fe," Christian says, knowing what it does to me to hear that. *God*, he knows exactly how much that turns me on. "Think I should let him?"

I nod furiously, and Christian chuckles, finally, *blessedly*, slipping my briefs down my hips. As soon as they're cleared, I spread my legs wide, past the point of caring how damn wanton I look.

"Should I let them pick a toy now?" he asks.

"Yes," I gasp. *Fuck*. "Please."

"Mm. You beg so prettily," he practically purrs, palms slipping up my thighs. "They like that. So do I."

Christian's touch feathers away an inch from my cock, and I huff a breath.

"Turn over, Fe."

I've never flipped so fast in my life.

Christian chuckles again, talking to the viewers. I miss most of it, my pulse heavy in my ears as Christian's fingers drift slowly up and down over the backs of my thighs, occasionally brushing my ass cheeks. He shifts me slightly, giving my hips a small push, and I go where he tells me to, knowing he's positioning me for the camera. The next second, something cool and wet slips over my asshole.

I moan, pushing back, and a small toy slips inside my ass.

"Fuck," Christian says. "You're ready, aren't you, Fe?"

"Yes," I pant out.

There's pressure again, and another object slides in. Anal beads, I realize. He's fucking me with an anal bead wand.

"He does have a gorgeous ass," Christian says, pulling the second bead out before pushing it in again. It stretches my rim before settling inside, and he teases me with it for a minute. Eventually, a third bead joins, bigger than the first two. "They want to see you take all six, Fe. What do you think? Can you handle it?"

I nod against the sheets, not knowing how large the final bead is, but trusting Christian. He knows what my limits are, so he wouldn't have chosen a toy bigger than I can handle.

"Want it," I manage. "Fuck me, *please.*"

He teases me again, pressing, pressing, and then another bead slips in, stretching me wider. The tip of the toy is *so* close to my prostate now. I can feel it, brushing against me, as Christian fucks the fourth bead in and out.

"Another," I groan.

"Look at you, Fe," Christian says, *slowly* edging the fifth bead in. He pauses with it at the widest point, his hand skimming my ass. "They're all watching you, you know. Every single one of them, waiting for your ass to swallow the toy."

My pulse thunders, and I push back against his hand, needing it. "*Please*, Vixen."

Christian hums, the sound happy and light. He pops the fifth bead in, and I let out a breath. I know I should turn my head, not have my face planted in the sheets. And I should be talking more, interacting with the viewers like Christian is.

But all I can focus on is the sixth bead he now has pressed against the rim of my ass.

"You want this, Fe?"

"Yes. *Yes.* Please."

Christian pushes the bead inside of me, pausing and reversing course before it can settle fully. He does it again and *again* before finally letting the sixth bead slip all the way in, my body holding it tight. His thumb brushes along my rim. "Gorgeous," he breathes, the word making me tremble. "NotYourBoyfriend says you have the sweetest ass he's ever seen. Should I fuck you with this now, show him how much you can take?"

I pull in a shaky breath. Expel it. *"Please."*

His palm slides over my ass, a gentle sign of approval. And then he starts tugging out the toy. Each bead stretches my rim before popping free, and only once the first bead remains in my ass does he reverse course. I grip the sheets tight as they slide back in, filling me wider, each notch of the toy a welcome jolt that sends heat spiraling through my body. When he gets to the fifth bead, he angles the toy down, and *there*. I groan, the first bead playing over my prostate as Christian fucks the fifth bead in and out. He pushes it further, giving me the sixth, and although it's no longer hitting me just so, the width is greater, and *that* is just as good.

"How's that, Fe?"

I groan something unintelligible, and Christian chuckles. He doesn't stop playing with me. He alternates five beads, prostate, six, over and over again. My legs start to shake, and my balls are so tight against my body I worry I might not be able to hold off from coming for much longer. But Christian tugs the toy out before I can cross that edge, leaving me bereft. I curse, my cock painfully hard and ass far too empty.

"Not yet," he says in a sly tone. "Turn over. It's time for toy number two."

I practically fall onto my back as I spin. I right my glasses, looking toward the tablet. The chat is filled with comments, more coming in every second. It's dizzying in the best possible way, and I ache to grab my cock, to find some relief. But I don't.

Christian continues to talk to the viewers, smiling at the camera every once in a while as he grabs a couple items off the foot of the bed. He's shirtless now, although I'm not sure when that happened. My eyes dip down the planes of his torso, settling on the chain around his stomach, my own contracting at the sight. His skirt is bunched around his knees like a cloud, and I have the distinct thought that if he's an angel, he's the filthiest one I've ever seen.

Christian holds up a dildo, turning toward me with a grin. "We have a winner. Grab your knees, Fe. Open up."

Holy hell.

"I'm not sure I'm going to survive this," I mutter, although I do exactly as he requests.

Christian smirks, settling near one of my bent legs so as not to block my ass from view. He notches the dildo against me, his other hand brushing mine beneath my knee.

"You'll survive," he says, slipping the bulbous crown inside my body. I blow out a breath. "And just think, once this part is through, and you're nice and stretched and ready to blow"—he edges the dildo in further—"I'll fuck you while everyone is watching. And they'll get to see exactly how gorgeous you are when you come."

"*Fuck*," I groan, my head arching back as Christian pushes the toy the rest of the way in. "Do it. Come on."

His hand wraps around my cock, and I jolt. "Oh, Fe..." He kisses my knee, hand stroking once. "You forgot the magic word."

I huff. "Please, you dick. Fucking fuck me."

Christian barks out a laugh, and I have only a moment to marvel at the sound before he's pulling out the fake cock and shoving it back in. I groan, holding my legs, keeping myself wide open as he fucks me over and over. I'm distantly aware of the fact that we're still in the studio. That there are people all around us monitoring the shoot and making sure everything goes off without a hitch. I know I should be checking in, peripherally aware of whether or not Jerome is giving us cues, considering he can't speak up during the lives.

But all I can focus on is the feel of that fake dick in my ass. At the energy in my body building and building as my orgasm draws closer. At chasing the motion of Christian's thrusts so the toy hits right where I need it to. I'm close. *So* close. And I want to come. I want everyone to see it, like Christian said. I don't care what that makes me—needy, debauched, a mess of epic proportions. I get off on it, plain and simple. And *fuck.*

I. Want. To. Get. *Off.*

Christian pulls out the dildo.

"No," I groan, reaching for my cock.

Christian grabs my wrist, rolling over my body and pinning my hand to the bed. Slowly, he does the same with the other. His eyes are vibrant, his skirt settling between us as he *grinds* his cock against my own. I squeeze my eyes shut, chest heaving.

"Felix."

I open my eyes.

"Can I fuck you now?" Christian asks, his tone serious. It's only then I notice how flushed he is. His cheeks. His chest. Probably his dick, too, although I can't see it.

"If you don't," I say slowly, "I will be extremely upset."

His lips curl into a wicked grin. "All right, Fe. Let's show your fans how well you can take my cock."

Oh fuck.

Yeah. Call me an addict.

And Christian?
He might just be my new drug.

Chapter 8
CHRISTIAN

Emil looks intoxicated. There's no other word for it. He looks drunk on whatever it is that gets him so hot any time an audience is involved.

It's captivating. And to be the one pulling the strings?

I did *not* anticipate how much it would affect me. I knew I'd enjoy it, sure. Sex with a cute guy? Especially one I already have a connection with, like Emil? It wasn't going to be bad.

But this... This is beyond, and I haven't even fucked him yet.

Emil stays put as I ease back, his hands reflexively tightening into fists before relaxing against the bed, a small sign of surrender. I make a point of checking in with our viewers. It's hard to keep track of all the comments pouring in, but I swing my gaze over the screen quickly, replying to a couple compliments about Emil because I think he should hear them. When I glance at Jerome, he gives me a thumbs up.

Must be doing something right.

Jerome already told me the skirt would need to go if I fuck Emil—it's too bulky to stay out of the shot—so I slip it off, letting the fabric fall near the foot of the bed.

Emil exhales, his gaze skipping from my belly chain to my dick. "Fuck. You really are big."

I'm not as enormous as some of the guys here, but my dick is certainly longer than average. It's usually a pleasant surprise for my partners. By the look in Emil's eye, I'd say he feels the same.

I give myself a slow stroke as I climb over Emil's body. He swallows thickly as our dicks rub together. "You can take me, though, isn't that right? You'll love *every second* of it and ask for more."

Emil's eyes slip shut, a ragged breath leaving his mouth. "Please, Vixen. Fuck me before I get someone else to do it."

The screen lights up at that, messages streaming through. "They like that," I say, chuckling as I lean down to nip his ear. "They all want to fuck you, Fe. You're irresistible."

"Then *why*," he says with a panting breath, "are you still out there when your cock should be buried inside of *me*, right where it goddamn belongs?"

Fucking hell.

I grab a condom from beside the tablet and roll it on swiftly. Emil makes a frustrated sound when I slip off his body.

"What are you…"

Sitting on the edge of the bed, I pat my thigh. "Come get it, Fe."

He's up and across the mattress in an instant. He throws his leg over my lap and grabs the base of my cock, and, before I've truly prepared myself for it, he sinks down. One moment, light brown eyes are meeting mine. And the next, there's heat and pressure surrounding my dick, and Emil's ass is coming to rest on my thighs.

We groan in unison, my hands clutching Emil's waist as he wriggles into place, adjusting around the girth of me. With my legs spread as they are and Emil's back to the camera, I have no doubt the hundreds or maybe thousands of viewers watching have a perfect view of Emil's ass as he lifts himself nearly all the way up and falls down again. My hand flies behind me for support as Emil repeats the motion, setting a pace that lets me know he's not fucking around. His hips roll over top of me, lifting and sinking, and I'm not sure he even cares about anything else around us. His goal is singular, his eyes closed and head tipped back, his mouth parted around words like *yes* and *fuck* and *more*.

He's gorgeous and completely uninhibited, and it's all I can do to hold on for the ride. It takes me a good long minute to remember we have an actual job to do. That this isn't just...*us*.

Sinking my fingers into Emil's hair, I tug his head to the side so neither of our faces are blocked. He doesn't miss a beat, riding me like his life depends on it.

"Look at you, Fe, milking my cock," I rasp. "Goddamn hungry for it, aren't you?"

"Yes," he pants, his blunt nails raking down the backs of my shoulders.

My body rolls in a shiver, hand tightening in Emil's hair. "Are you gonna come on my cock, Fe? Gonna squeeze me tight and shoot all over yourself so everyone can see how beautifully you fall apart?"

His response this time is a garbled moan, and then, his lips are on mine.

Fuck. *Fuck*.

He kisses like the chaotic proof of life he talked about. Like everything, in this one moment, is beautiful evidence of all that's out of our control. It's wild, and it's passionate, and I don't know where this shy psych major gets it from, but I'm in awe. I'm completely under his spell.

When his pace starts to stutter and his breath catches, I realize he's about to come. Jerome drilled one thing into my head above all else. The money shot. You have to get the money shot. And in a live video, there's no chance for redos.

Spinning the both of us, I press Emil's back to the bed. Our lips separate, and I grab his leg, hoisting it over my shoulder and hoping like hell it gives the camera a good angle of his ass. With one knee on the bed, my other foot on the floor, I fuck into him as hard as I dare. His cock bobs, and he gasps out breath after breath.

"Come on, Fe," I say, bending down to lick his nipple. I suck it into my mouth, flicking it with my tongue. "I'm not gonna stop you from coming this time."

Emil reaches for his cock, but he's already coming. I lean back as the most gorgeous moan spills from his lips. Cum hits his stomach, his chest, his chin.

Fuck.

As soon as his body stops spasming around me, I pull out, tear off the condom, and stroke myself furiously. Emil drops his leg and sits up, a hazy look on his face as he hovers with his lips right in front of my cock. His hands land on my waist, fingers drifting over the chain.

"Come on, Vixen," he says, voice hoarse. "I think I more than earned your cum."

I lose it. Just like that.

I paint his tongue, his cheek, the glasses sitting crooked on his face, and Emil takes it all, his eyes shining with nothing but satisfaction. He looks like an utter mess, thoroughly fucked and marked, and I drop down and bring my lips to his, the both of us falling back against the bed. I can taste myself on his tongue, but that means he can taste me, too, and *fuck* if that isn't a gratifying thought.

I kiss him hard, my cock spent. His, too. I kiss him, and then I lick the cum from his cheek as he laughs. My heart skips when I see the smile on his face.

"Well," I say, swiping my hair back as I sit up. I shoot a grin our viewers' way. "My very first time in front of the cameras. Think that went all right?"

Comments pour in, and I offer a hand to Emil. He accepts it, letting me pull him up, and without overthinking it, I swing around and settle behind him, my chin tucked over his shoulder and arms around his waist. The assistant next to Jerome is writing on a cue card, so, while he's doing that, I check the chat.

"Look, Fe. They want to see more of your asshole."

Emil snorts, an indelicate sound that has me grinning. "And your dick," he comments.

"Oh, JimmyLovesC wants me to fuck you in a skirt next time. Think that could be arranged?"

Emil smiles, looking down at his lap. I kiss his cheek.

The card the assistant holds up says to mention the next live video in a week. I take that to mean it went well and give the camera a smile.

"Well, you're in luck," I tell our audience. "Fe and I will be back next week, same time, same place. Meet us here? Bring your suggestions and your own lube. And, if you ask nicely enough, maybe Fe will show you how much he likes sucking cock."

Emil's uptick of breath tells me he would, in fact, like that very much.

"Say bye, Fe."

He huffs a breath. "Bye, everyone."

"Bye," I add, waving at the camera. The light turns off, and I swear the crew breathes a collective sigh of relief.

"Thank fuck," Jerome yells, accepting a water from one of the assistants. Another comes toward the bed, setting two robes beside us.

"Um," Emil says softly, shoulders a little stiff now in my embrace.

I let go, cool air washing over my skin as Emil stands up. He slips his robe over his shoulders.

"That went as well as we could've hoped for a first run," Jerome says, addressing the room at large. "We're going to set up a mobile camera for the next shoot. I want those close-ups, damn it. The slight delay should give us adequate time to switch feeds. Bill? Where's Bill?"

As Jerome confers with the cameramen, I give Emil's arm a nudge. He looks over at me, eyes drifting away like he's suddenly feeling shy again.

"Was that okay?" I check.

He lets out a small laugh, pulling off his glasses and cleaning them with the edge of his robe. "Yeah, it was good."

"I didn't overstep at all?"

"No, Christian. You know exactly how to play me."

Emil replaces his glasses and, seeing my frown, rushes onward.

"I don't mean manipulate. I mean..." He rolls his eyes, but I get the feeling it's more at himself. "You've been watching me pleasure myself for over three months," he says quietly, his back to the rest of our coworkers, who are moving about. "You...know what I like. And you used that knowledge. Very well, I might add."

"So you had a good time?" I ask, well aware I'm fishing. I just... I need to hear it. I need to know we're okay.

"I'm pretty sure that was obvious," Emil mumbles, so full of sass it makes me grin. "It was great, okay? I was really into it, and you took charge like I asked, and..." He groans slightly. "Why are you still sitting there naked? There's cum on your shoulder and that chain is around your stomach, and *Christ*. Could you just...be a little less hot, please?"

Bubbles pop inside my chest as I stand. Emil's head tips back to track me, and he swallows, his eyes never leaving mine.

"I had a good time, too, Specs," I tell him honestly. "That was, quite possibly, one of the hottest encounters of my life."

His throat bobs again. "Really?"

"Really," I say, grabbing the ends of the belt hanging loose from his robe and tying it shut. "You're wildly sexual, you know that? You might come across as this quiet thing, but I've seen the real you."

He pulls in a breath.

"For others, this might be a show," I say softly. "But for you, it's more than that. And I think it's brave, letting people see it, even if they don't realize what they're witnessing."

Emil's mouth falls open, his eyes wide.

"Vixen. Felix," Jerome calls.

Emil's head whips away as our boss comes over. I grab my robe off the bed, swinging it around my body.

"That was well done, both of you," Jerome says. "I'm going to set up a time this week to go over the video and discuss adjustments moving forward, but we didn't have any major fuck-ups, so I'm pleased. Vixen, that was impressive. You're going to fit in well here. And Felix...I noticed you were less chatty than usual. Anything wrong?"

"No," Emil says quickly, flushing. "I just, uh, asked Christian to take the lead."

Jerome hums. "All right. Well, it worked out. Go get cleaned up, eat some lunch, check your schedules for that meeting," he practically yells, already walking away.

I huff a laugh. "Showers?"

Emil nods, and we head out of Studio 2. Silence descends as we walk the short distance to the locker room. I shoot Emil the occasional glance as we go, but he keeps his gaze resolutely on the floor. When we reach the locker room, he heads for the showers without a word. The water turns on a second before there's a whoosh of a curtain.

I stop at my locker, removing my belly chain and slipping a simple curved bar into the piercing at my navel. Once the extra jewelry is in my bag, I head toward the shower stalls. I pick the one next to Emil's, hoping that's not a taboo thing to do.

"You all right?" I ask.

"Huh?"

"It's just... Did I say something to upset you? You seem a little..." I don't say withdrawn, but it's the truth. "Quiet."

I wait, my shower heating. It's perfectly hot by the time Emil answers.

"You didn't upset me," he says. "I just, uh... I'm not really used to people noticing me. And you...do."

"How couldn't I?" I counter.

I think he huffs a laugh, but it's quiet underneath the noise of the showers. "Most people aren't like you, Christian. And I don't mean because you're this ridiculously gorgeous guy who wears skirts and is, like, this perfectly sexy combo of masculine and feminine. I just..."

This time, it's me huffing a laugh as Emil pauses.

"I just mean you pay attention," he says. "Most people don't. Not really."

There's a pinch in my gut at the implication that the people in Emil's life haven't paid attention to him. It's a sad, sobering thought, and I wish I could walk into his stall and wrap him up in my arms. But I don't know if that would be welcome. I don't know if he'd want that from me.

"Well, I think you're captivating, Emil," I say, making sure he can hear me over the running water. "And I'm really glad I saw you jerking off all those months ago. I'm glad it led to this."

After a moment, he asks, "What do you mean?"

"I mean coming here and already knowing you? It's nice. More than nice. I'm glad I get to work with...my friend? Are we? Friends?"

"Yeah, Christian," he says, sounding as if he's smiling. "We're friends. Weird ones, maybe, but hell... I sleep with all my friends, so that's par for the course."

I bark a laugh. "Friends who play together stay together?"

"Jesus," he groans. "You sound just like Alex."

"I'll take that as a compliment," I say, my lips quirking.

"You might not want to," he practically mumbles. "That guy is something else. And he makes you get pets you never even knew you wanted."

"He...what?" I ask in surprise. "Are you telling me you have a pet? Specs! I've never seen it."

Emil groans again, his water shutting off. "*Itsacrab.*"

"What?"

"It's a crab," he moans. "I have a crab."

He sounds so utterly perturbed by that fact that I laugh. Loudly.

"Let's not talk about it," he says, his voice coming from further away. "We can just...never speak of this again."

"All right," I reply. "We don't have to talk about your crabs."

"One. *One* crab," he calls. "Jesus. My life."

I laugh, and Emil continues to mumble, but he doesn't sound all that put-out. Quickly, I finish rinsing myself and shut off the water, the bubbling in my stomach urging me to catch up with the man outside my stall. Maybe it's not the gut feeling Emil was talking about, but it's a good feeling nonetheless.

I think I should follow it.

Chapter 9
EMIL

"Um, hello?" I say, blinking at Christian, who's standing at my door.

My door. Here. At my apartment.

"Hi!" he says brightly. "Can I come in?"

I step aside, and Christian sweeps into the room, looking around quickly before holding out a small paper bag.

"Here. I stopped by a pet store, and they said if you had a crab, it was probably a hermit crab. And that...he? she?...would like dried shrimp."

Shocked, I peek inside the bag. "You got dried shrimp for my crab?"

Christian grins, and I finally have the wherewithal to take him in. He's wearing maroon-colored joggers today and a sleeveless white shirt. His hair is tied half-up in a bun, and *fuck*. Apparently, *hot* is Christian's default.

"Um, thanks," I manage. "He does like shrimp."

"Perfect. Can I meet the little fella?"

"Oh Lord," I mutter. "Please, *please* don't let this influence your opinion of me."

Christian gives me a strange look. "Why would it?"

I sigh, long and low, before walking over to Arthur's terrarium. With a flourish of my hand, I say, "Christian, meet Sir Arthurpod, His Royal Cuteness, Burrower of Sand and Creator of Dreams."

Christian's grin is slow. "Sir Arthurpod. Because he's an arthropod?"

"Yes," I mumble.

"And what was that next part? His royal..."

"Cuteness," I fill in.

Fuck my life.

"And, uh..."

"Burrower of Sand and Creator of Dreams," I finish quickly. "Don't even ask. The last one was Alex."

With an expression I'm hoping is amusement and not concern for my sanity, Christian leans down and looks inside the tank. Arthur is barely visible, blending in with the sand and rocks around him. "Hi, Sir Arthurpod. Nice to meet you." Turning to me, he asks, "Does he like to be held?"

"No," I say with a snort. "He's prickly and guarded. Just like me."

Christian's eyebrow wings up.

"Here," I say, grabbing the package of dried shrimp. "He'll come out if we feed him."

Sure enough, once I drop a bit of the shrimp into his food bowl, Arthur starts to move. Christian hums and then lets out a surprised laugh as Arthur scurries across the sand.

"Holy shit," he says. "How freaking cute."

"You think that's cute?" I ask. Arthur is investigating the shrimp now, his legs moving rapidly as he picks off almost imperceptibly tiny pieces to bring to his mouth.

"I mean, yeah," Christian says, squatting down in front of the glass. "Look at him. He's tiny and orange and adorable, but his eyes mean business. He'd probably kick my ass given the chance. Will he always be so small?"

"Uh, no," I answer, honestly surprised that anyone but me finds Arthur adorable. "He's young, so he'll get a bit bigger still."

"How long do hermit crabs live?"

"Upwards of fifteen to twenty years in captivity if they're cared for properly," I tell him.

His eyes meet mine, wide. "Jesus. You could have him when you're forty. What else does he eat?"

I sit on the floor next to Christian, watching him as he watches Arthur. "Lots of things. Meat, fruits, veggies. Shrimp is a favorite of his. And he really likes coconut and melon. Hates broccoli."

Christian huffs a laugh.

"He needs calcium, too, for his exoskeleton," I say.

His eyes meet mine, soft as he blinks at me. "Does he prefer to be alone?"

I get the feeling he's asking about more than Arthur, but I answer for my crab. "They're social, actually. I've been meaning to get Arthur a buddy, but I wanted to get settled with him first, and...I guess I'm a little worried, when I *do* get another, they won't get along."

Christian hums. "Won't know unless you try."

Guess so. But trying is the scary part.

"Want to watch some TV?" Christian asks, popping up.

"Uh, what?" I say, thrown.

"TV," he repeats, shooting me a grin as he walks over to my couch. He sprawls out on top of the cushions, laying his head in his hand and making himself at home. "We're on the fifth episode of *Life*. Have you watched it yet?"

It takes me a second to answer him. "You...you want to watch it together?"

"Yeah, Specs," he says, his smile making my pulse accelerate. He pats the cushion in front of him. "If you want to."

Slowly, I get to my feet and walk his way. "You're nearly too tall for my couch," I mumble.

"I'll manage," he says, scooting back so there's room for me in front of him.

Heart pounding, I sit down, hoping Christian doesn't notice how awkward I feel. "You, uh, really like David Attenborough, huh?" I say, grabbing the remote.

"The man could narrate my shopping list, and I'd eat it up," he says, making me laugh.

I start episode five of the nature documentary and set the remote down, having no clue what to do with my arms. I end up resting them on my knees.

I have never in my life been so hyperaware of my own body. My limbs feel too big. My breaths loud. Why am I so nervous? This man has seen me shove a tentacle up my ass.

"Specs," Christian says softly, startling me as his hand winds around my waist. I tense, and he freezes. "Sorry, I—"

"No!" I blurt before he can let go. "No, it's fine. I, uh..." What did he say to me that one time? "You have my permission to touch."

I nearly cringe, but Christian just chuckles, his fingers planting more firmly against my stomach. "Come here," he says.

When I don't move, not sure what he means, Christian gives me a little tug. My back meets his stomach, and then he tugs again, guiding me to lie down in front of him. I let him mold me like clay until we're all but connected from chest to crotch. When he gives my top leg a shove and fits his own over mine, locking us together like puzzle pieces, I let loose a breath.

Christian's hand returns to my stomach, fingers resting over my shirt. "Okay?" he asks.

"Yeah," I say on an exhale, my voice quiet.

"Okay," he repeats.

Slowly but surely, my tension starts to unwind.

Yeah, this is okay. Kinda nice, actually. Weird but good.

Before long, my head is in the crook of my elbow and my breathing has evened out. Christian is a warm presence behind me, and for a while, I forget about studying. I forget about reading and the papers I have to write. I watch one of my favorite shows with someone who's quickly becoming one of my favorite people.

And I let myself simply...*relax*.

"Emil. *Emil.* Hello?"

Rebecca's waving hand has me jolting back to awareness.

"Shit, sorry. What'd you say?" I ask, adjusting my glasses.

She looks at me curiously. "You were just completely zoned out. What were you thinking about?"

"Uh..."

The memory of my neighbor's hand and how, when I jerked off this morning and caught him watching from his window, I imagined it was his fist wrapped around my cock instead?

"You really don't want to know," I mutter.

"Don't wanna know what?" Henry asks, returning from the restroom and plopping into the booth next to me. Our younger brother looks between me and Rebecca.

"Whatever had Emil's face going all…" Rebecca rests her chin in her hands and bats her eyelashes.

"That was not my face," I retort.

"Was, too," Rebecca says. "I bet you were thinking about *boys*."

I groan, and Henry goes, "Ew."

"What?" our sister says, looking at Henry. "I'm sure your face goes all schmoopy when you think about boys or girls *you* like."

Henry shakes his head, taking a sip of his soda. "Nope. Don't care about all that. Sex makes people stupid."

Rebecca shoots me a look, eyebrows raised.

"Henry," I say slowly. "I'm sure Mom and Dad have already talked about this, but if you're sexually active—"

"Like I said, *ew*," Henry cuts in. "Not interested. Pass the ketchup?"

Rebecca passes the bottle, eyes meeting mine again. Henry is fourteen, and I know he already started going through *changes* a couple years back. He's well into the early teenage years of rampantly running hormones where sex might be on the mind. It was on mine when I was his age.

But maybe, for Henry, that's not the case. I wonder if our parents have thought to talk to him about the spectrum of asexuality.

I mull it over as my siblings bicker about Thanksgiving this year and whether Dad should cook ham or turkey.

When we leave the diner, it's early afternoon. I drive my sister back to her boarding school where Henry and I picked her up from a few hours ago. Rebecca doesn't live far from home. It's only a two hour drive, and she could have opted for a weekday-only boarding option. But, overachiever that my sister is, she decided on full-time so she could enroll in extracurriculars on the weekends.

I'm just glad she didn't choose a school further away. It would have made an impromptu visit like this much harder.

When I park the car, Rebecca leans over to give me a hug. "Thanks, Emil."

"What for?" I ask, patting her arm.

She leans back into her seat with an exasperated look on her face. "For coming, you doof."

Oh. Well, I don't tell Rebecca I was a little worried about her after our phone call. She looks good, though. Happy. Even if she *is* missing home at times.

"No problem," I tell her. "We'll see you at Thanksgiving?"

"Wouldn't miss it," she says, turning to look into the back-seat. "See ya, little bro."

Henry waves a hand, gaze never straying from his handheld game.

Rebecca rolls her eyes. "Later."

"Take care, Bec."

I watch Rebecca head into her dormitory before easing the car out of the parking spot. Henry keeps playing his game.

I often wonder why my parents waited so long between having me and Rebecca. Julian is the oldest of us at thirty-one. Eloise is next at twenty-seven. That puts four years between the two of them, as well as between me and Eloise. But there's a seven-year gap from me to Rebecca. And only two between her and Henry.

My mom told me they were happy with three kids. That they didn't want to try for more. Until they did.

I couldn't help but wonder, especially when I was young, if that was because of *me*. If, maybe, I turned out not to be what they wanted from a third child.

Realistically, I know that's not the case, only my insecurities talking. My parents love me. They've never asked me to be anything I'm not. But rationality and *feeling* don't always go hand in hand.

"Hey, Henry?"

My brother doesn't look up from his game. "Huh?"

"Do you think, one day, you might want to date?"

I see him shrug a shoulder in the rearview mirror. "Dunno."

"Are there any genders you're interested in?"

He shrugs again. "They're all okay. I just think kissing and bumping parts is a waste of time. All Tyler talks about anymore is girls and boobs, and it's so stupid. He used to be fun."

I hum, suppressing my laugh. "You'd rather just play video games, huh?"

"Yeah."

I nod, wondering if Henry might be ace. Or maybe he'll start wanting those things in a few years. He's young still.

"Just so you know..." I tell him. "If you ever have questions about kissing or dating or any of that, you can ask me, okay? However *you* feel about it is okay, and I promise there are other people who think the way you do, too. You don't ever have to do anything you don't want to just because other kids are doing it."

"I know," he says, rolling his eyes. But then he adds, quietly, "Thanks, Emil."

"Yeah," I say, feeling... I don't know. Proud, maybe, of my baby brother for being his own person.

Henry and I lapse into silence, and I turn the radio on while he keeps himself busy with his game. The two-hour drive back to Las Vegas passes relatively quickly, and as soon as I pull into our parents' driveway, Henry bursts from the car and runs inside. I follow at a more subdued pace, chuckling as the front door slams into the wall and bounces nearly all the way closed again.

I shut it once I'm inside and peek into the living room. "Mom?"

"In here," she says, followed by, "Henry, use a glass!"

I follow the noise into the kitchen. Mom is pulling a glass out of the cupboard as Henry bounces on his feet. She takes the orange juice carton from his hand, shooting me a smile as she pours him a cup. "You boys have fun?"

"Yep," Henry says, snatching his drink and disappearing from sight. Footsteps bound up the stairs a moment later.

Mom shakes her head lightly. "Thanks for bringing him with you."

"Of course. We had a good time," I assure her. "Did your auction go okay?"

My mom works for an art gallery downtown and has since I was a child. Every once in a while, they host events for the public—pop-up shows, charity auctions, and the like. My mom is the one in charge of making sure the events go off without a hitch. She's still dressed in a black-and-white wrap dress and heels, telling me she likely beat us back by only minutes.

"It was great," she says, putting the orange juice back in the fridge. "I dare say we had a record turnout." She lets out a big gust of air before leaning against the counter, as if this is the first time all day she's had a chance to slow down. It probably is. "How'd Rebecca seem?"

"Good," I tell her, although I'm sure my mom has made her fair share of calls to Rebecca to check in. "She has a few friends already, and she likes her classes. I think she'll be fine."

My mom nods, sighing. "Good. That's good. And, uh, you have that research thing, right? How's that going?"

I open my mouth to tell her about it when Henry yells down the stairs. "Where'd my chips go?"

"Back in the pantry where they belong," Mom calls back.

"Did you move my headphones?" he asks.

Mom lets out a breath, pushing off of the counter and heading out of the room. Her voice gets quieter the further away she walks. "They're in your desk drawer, Henry. If you'd cleaned your own room like I asked, you'd know exactly where to find them."

Henry retorts something I can't quite make out, and I nod, looking around at the empty kitchen.

"Yep," I mutter. *Seems about right.* Raising my voice, I call out, "See you guys later!"

"Bye, hon," my mom calls back.

Slipping out of the house, I close the front door and head to my car. There's a pinch in my chest as I buckle in, but I brush the sensation off. It's not disappointment if it's expected, is it?

My phone pings with a text, a welcome distraction.

Christian: Where are you, Specs? It's Saturday, which means you should be on your second energy drink by now, doing your smart brainy thing while I (not at all creepily) stare at your ass. Have you been kidnapped? Are you listening to David Attenborough without me?

A smile creeps onto my face, my pulse kicking.

Me: On my way home now.

After only a pause, I add...

Me: Should I cue up the next episode?

Christian's response comes through before I've even turned the ignition.

Christian: I'll bring the popcorn. Can Arthur eat popcorn or should I bring him regular corn?

Christian: Never mind. I'll bring both. Hurry your ass up, Specs!

Grinning, I start the car and head for home.

Chapter 10

CHRISTIAN

"Shit, shit, motherfucking *shit*," I hiss, sucking the blood off the pad of my index finger before I wrap it in one of the Band-Aids I keep at my sewing table. I pick up the pin I dropped. "Keep your pointy end to yourself."

Luckily, the pin doesn't stab me this time as I secure the pleat in place.

"Fucking better," I mutter.

A flash of movement in my periphery has me turning my head. Emil is standing inside his bedroom, hand in the air. He stops waving and holds up two ties.

With a huff of laughter, I pick up my phone.

Me: The blue one. Why so spiffy?

Emil reads my text, shoots me a thumbs up, and then throws aside the red tie. He wraps the blue one around his neck, securing it in place before picking up his phone again.

Specs: We're starting preliminary questionnaires for the research project. I need to look presentable.

Me: Well, you look like a hot professor I would've fucked if I'd gone to college, so I'd say mission accomplished.

Emil looks as if he snorts, but then he shakes his head.

Specs: No need to flatter.

I frown.

Me: It's not flattery if it's the truth. You look great, Specs. Knock 'em dead.

He grimaces.

Specs: Christ. I hope not.

I'm not sure what to make of that response, but Emil gives a wave before turning and disappearing from sight. I get back to work, pinning the pleats I already ironed into place so I can sew them down.

The skirt I'm working on today is red and similar in style to the black one I'm wearing. I like the design—it's fun and flirty and shows off my legs. The red will be a little more bold, but I'm sure I won't have a problem finding an excuse to wear it.

I take a break midafternoon, making myself a late lunch as I bop around the kitchen to some eighties music. I suppose I have my mom to thank for that. We may have our differences, but our taste in music isn't one of them.

The thought is accompanied by a pang. I haven't spoken to my mom in years, and most of the time, I'm perfectly okay with that. But there are times, like now, where a nostalgic sense of *what if?* has me thinking of picking up the phone. *What if* we could get along? *What if* she could accept me?

What if she didn't see me as a reminder of all she lost?

It's fruitless wishing for something I know will never come to pass, but I suppose it doesn't stop me from yearning for it all the same.

I don't pick up my phone, instead heading back into my bedroom. My grandmother's apartment—*my* apartment—isn't huge, but the bedroom is a rather decent size in comparison. It's why my sewing table is set up in here, providing me, serendipitously, a perfect view of Emil's place.

I retake my seat in front of Bernie and spend the next couple hours finishing the skirt. I go slow, making sure each detail is perfect. The time passes quickly, though, and when I happen to catch movement, once again, at Emil's, I realize it must be... Yep, five-thirty on the dot.

I grin and grab my phone.

Me: What class do you come from Monday afternoons?

I've never asked for specific details about his classes before, but now I don't hesitate. Emil unravels his tie, setting it on the end of his bed before pulling his phone from his pocket.

Specs: Behavioral Neuroscience.

He continues to undress as I type out a response, and I get a little caught up in watching him. How this man can be so casually confident at times yet bashful at others is fascinating.

Refocusing, I send my message.

Me: What is that, Specs? Talk nerdy to me.

He plops onto the end of his bed, back hitting the mattress and phone held over his face. I have the sudden urge to be closer. Would it be weird if I just...went over there? Probably not, right? We've hung out a few times.

As Emil types his response, I slip my feet into shoes, lock up my apartment, and head next door. His lengthy reply comes through as I'm walking up the stairs inside his building.

Specs: It's basically the science of why we do what we do. How our environment impacts our brains, which impacts our behavior. Humans so often feel as if we're driven by our emotions and feelings more than logic, but it's all the same thing. It's all neural processes. And our brains are more adaptive than we realize. They change based on our individual experiences, and those changes

then affect our future experiences, like a circuit. When we understand how and why those changes occur, we can help people break out of their cycle and reroute their neural processes into healthier thoughts and behaviors.

Holy shit.

Me: What's it called when you're attracted to intelligence?

Specs: Um... Sapiosexual?

Me: Hold that thought.

I knock on Emil's door, and he appears a moment later, phone in hand. He blinks at me owlishly before swinging the door wide, apparently having accepted my random drop-ins, which is good news for me.

"I didn't understand half of what you said," I admit, stepping inside, "but that was hot as fuck, Specs. I like the way your brain works."

He huffs a small laugh, nudging his glasses up his nose before closing the door. "I think it could use a bit of rerouting."

I make an unhappy noise as I toe off my shoes. "No. You're lovely. Now how *do* you reroute neural processes?"

Emil follows me into his bedroom, giving me an odd look as I jump onto his mattress. I don't think it's a look of displeasure. His forehead scrunches when he's upset about something, like when he gets stuck on a problem for one of his classes. This is more like he's trying to decode the situation. He had the same look on his face the first time I snuggled him to death while we watched TV.

"Specs?" I prompt.

He seems to shake himself loose, walking closer and sitting on the edge of the bed. "Yeah, uh. It's like... You know streams?"

My lips quirk. "I'm familiar with them, yes."

He rolls his eyes slightly, another behavior I've become accustomed to. He's berating himself for the question. "Water follows the path of least resistance down a stream. If you want to change that path, you need to carve out a new one. So you take a stick..."

He looks around, hopping up to grab a pencil and then coming back to the bed. I scoot over as he smooths his hand over the comforter, flattening it. He uses his arm to press a large divot into the fabric, and then he drags the eraser side of the pencil off from that line, drawing a much thinner one.

"You use a stick to create a new path. But you need repetition," he says, dragging the pencil along the thinner line again and again until it starts getting wider. "Repetitive conditioning reroutes the water, but not until the pathway has been carved out enough. The stream not only needs a big enough trough to support it, but it also needs an outlet at the end."

"And what's that?" I ask.

Emil blinks at me, the smallest of smiles curving his lips. "Hope."

My heartbeat hitches and then races ahead as Emil runs his hand over the comforter, smoothing it back out. His hair is falling messily over his forehead, his glasses have the effect of making his eyes look even bigger than they are, and the fact that he doesn't seem to realize how absolutely astounding that simple, one-word answer was has me shaking my head in disbelief.

"What is it you want to do with your degree?" I ask.

He looks at me in something akin to surprise. "Oh. Um, research."

I nod, leaning back onto my elbows. Emil's gaze drops to my stomach, his throat bobbing once before he looks away.

"The same kind of research you're doing now?"

"Probably not the same exact topics, but yeah, same idea," he answers, fidgeting with the pencil in his grip. "There's so much to learn. So much to understand about behavior, psychology, the way our brains work. I just want to be a part of it."

"I can see it," I tell him.

"What?"

"You in a white lab coat. Those glasses on your nose. Making some grand discovery and shouting 'eureka!'"

He huffs a laugh. "Maybe someday."

"Definitely someday."

Emil shifts, poking the comforter with the end of the pencil. "Can I ask you a question?"

"Another, you mean?"

He snorts. "Yes, another. Smartass."

I shoot him a grin. "Go for it."

"Why do you spend so much time in front of your window? Is that where your TV is or something?"

My lips quirk. "What, I can't be sitting there simply because it has the best view in the house?"

It takes Emil a second to realize what I mean, and then he huffs, cheeks reddening. "Yeah, no. There's another reason." Before I can express my disapproval for the way he so easily dismissed himself, he takes another guess. "Is it your computer?"

"It's a sewing machine," I answer. "That's what's beside the window."

"I..." He makes an aborted sound. "Seriously?"

"Is that so hard to believe?" I ask, amused by his apparent shock.

"It's just..." His eyes trail over me almost absentmindedly. "I had it in my head that you were this eighty-year-old grandma. I guess I wasn't that far off the mark."

My mouth falls open slowly. "You thought I was *eighty*? And you were doing the things you were doing in front of me? What if I had a heart attack, Specs?"

He barks a laugh, eyes twinkling. "Would've been a good way to go, I presume."

I huff, shaking my head. "Okay, we're gonna circle around to that later, but back up a second. What's wrong with sewing? It's not only for grandmas."

"Sure," he says with a shrug.

"Specs..."

"No, it's a great hobby. Very...hip," he finishes, voice choked.

I swing upright and crawl his way. "Hip?"

His eyes widen. "What are you..."

"I'll have you know," I say, grabbing his wrists and tugging until he lands flat on his back, "that this *hip* hobby is responsible for the miniskirt I'm wearing."

Emil's eyes ping down to said skirt. He swallows harshly. "You made that?"

"Mhm. And the white one. And a red one I finished today. Not to mention many, many others you haven't even seen yet. So tell me again," I say, leaning down until my face is hovering right above his, "how *hip* sewing is."

His eyes dart between my own, his chest brushing mine as it rises and falls. "So hip," he breathes, the tickle of air from his words making me realize exactly how close we are. Our mouths, inches apart. Our bodies, connected at multiple points. His pulse is feathering beneath my grip, and my own heart starts to race as Emil watches me steadily. For once, he doesn't look away. As if he's waiting. Waiting on *me*.

Sucking in a breath, I sit back, chuckling as I let Emil's wrists go. "I can't believe you thought I was eighty."

He huffs a laugh, blinking as he sits up. His hand brushes my knee, and tingles race over my skin as his fingers skim up my thigh until he reaches the hem of my skirt. He pinches the fabric between his thumb and index finger, rolling it gently.

"It's really good, Christian," he says, voice soft. "Remarkable, really."

"You think so?" I ask, smiling a little shakily.

"Yeah." His eyes meet mine for an extended moment before he lets the fabric go. "Have you made anything else?"

I clear my throat. "Uh, yeah. Shirts and some formalwear."

He nods, quiet for a moment before he says, "I, uh... I have some studying to do."

"Of course," I say, making to scoot off the bed. "I'll go."

"You don't have to," he says immediately, a blush rising on his cheeks.

I pause. "I won't distract you if I stay?"

His eyes slip down my body again, drifting over my legs, lingering on my skirt, and then skittering away. "Maybe a little. But it's fine."

I should go. I really should, but...

"If you're sure."

"I'm sure," he says, sliding off the bed. He grabs a textbook and his laptop before returning, setting both in front of his pillow and lying flat on his stomach. Without a word, he sets to work.

After a moment, I lie down and pull out my phone. The sound of tapping keys is a steady presence next to me as the minutes pass, almost as soothing as the whir of my sewing machine.

I could get used to it.

The scary part is, there's a little piece of me—one I long thought extinguished—that *wants* to.

Chapter 11

EMIL

I'd like to say I'm more prepared this time when I step onto set for my second live stream video with Christian. And in some ways, I am.

I'm expecting the heady rush of anticipation that sweeps over me. I'm expecting my brain to go somewhat offline. I'm even expecting the tinge of fear that this euphoria will, someday, pass, and I'll go seeking a more dangerous hit.

That last one is something I've talked to my therapist about. She's assured me I am, in fact, in control of myself, even when I feel anything but. That's what those exercises in restraint are for. Proving to myself I can step back.

But it's still something that sits at the periphery of my mind. Because how am I possibly going to find someone who understands this facet of my life? That this is something I crave, possibly even need? That there are limits I have when it comes to my exhibitionism, and those limits aren't something I feel confident about enforcing when I'm heavily under the influence of my own drug?

It's a lot.

But today isn't about my nonexistent love life. It's about sex.

Which brings me back to what I *am* prepared for. And that's the sight of Christian strolling into Studio 3 in that little black miniskirt he apparently sewed himself. I'm prepared for the way everything in me curls tight like a spring waiting to unload. I'm even prepared for the smirk he flashes me, as if he can't quite help himself.

Vixen, indeed.

"Hey," he says, coming to a stop in front of me.

How was this man lying on my bed just last night? It seems unreal because Christian is, quite honestly, stunning. And I'm still not sure I understand what it is he wants from *me*.

"Hi," I answer, trying not to squirm, even though my dick is hard and I'm having trouble not touching the person who I know will spend the better part of the next hour working me into an even more frenzied state than I'm already in. *Christ*.

"Are you okay doing a scene today?" Christian asks, eyes skimming over me.

I huff a small laugh, perfectly aware he's likely cataloguing my red cheeks and strained expression and trying to determine whether it's *good* strain or bad. "You take consent seriously."

"Yeah, I do," he answers, offering me a smile. "So?"

"I'm good."

"A little horny?" he asks quietly. And now the fucker is *toying* with me.

"You dick."

If only I truly hated it.

Christian laughs, light and airily. "You can have my dick later, Specs. If you want it."

Fucking fuck. Like I ever wouldn't want it.

I clear my throat. "Hey, Christian?"

He cocks his head, a lock of silky black hair falling in front of his face. "Yeah?"

"I'm not sure if you know this about me, unless you've happened upon one of the few videos in which it's been recorded here, but I used to swim in high school."

"Okay?" he says slowly.

"I wasn't all that great at it. I didn't win much or anything, but I enjoyed the rhythmic motion. I probably would have joined a team in college if I wasn't busy with so many other things. But every once in a while, I like to go to a local pool and swim. I've kept up the practice."

Christian waits, clear curiosity on his face as I slowly get around to my point.

"I can hold my breath for over two minutes," I tell him. "Which means you can keep your cock in my throat for *two minutes*."

I see the precise moment my words saturate his brain. How his pupils blow and his nostrils flare and his posture gets ever so slightly more rigid. I won't lie. I get a perverse sense of satisfaction causing that reaction in him. Knowing I've shocked him.

"Something to consider," I say, shooting him a wink as I head toward our bed for the day. I hear a laugh behind me and smile to myself.

"All right!" Jerome yells, coming through the door in a flurry of his usual energy. "We're nearly ready to roll. Felix, Vixen, all good?"

"Yep," I say, a little calmer this time as I settle on the bed, although no less turned on. Maybe it should embarrass me that so many people can clearly see my arousal before we've even begun. But again... It's never been *embarrassment* for me.

"Ready," Christian says, joining me on the bed.

Jerome confers with the cameramen, of which there are two today. One to monitor the static shot and another for the moving close-ups. Other crew members are scattered around the room, getting final details set before we begin.

I sneak a peek at Christian. At his skirt and the bulge front and center beneath the fabric.

As if he feels my eyes on his person, Christian spreads his legs wider. I curse as the fabric tents a little more obscenely.

"How *do* you hide that thing?" I say, thinking of Alex's comment from weeks ago.

"My dick?" Christian asks, sounding amused. "I don't usually walk around with a raging hard-on, Specs. This is all for you."

My eyes flash up to his, a bolt of arousal sending heat through my core.

"Thirty seconds," Jerome yells.

Christian clears his throat. "Do you want me to take the lead again?"

"I should be a little more coherent this time, but yeah, if you wouldn't mind."

He nods, swinging his legs lightly. His arms are braced behind him, and his hair is down today, falling in its usual tousled style.

"Ten," Jerome calls, switching to hands as he counts us down. The room falls silent.

I lean a little closer to Christian, keeping my voice at a whisper. "For the record, I *do* want your dick, Christian. Any-and-everywhere you can put it."

"You cheeky little—" Christian cuts off a second before we switch to a live feed and smiles for the camera. His hand slips behind me, curling beneath the curve of my ass as he starts to talk. My pulse skyrockets, but he sounds unaffected, voice light. "Well, well, if it isn't our favorite at-home viewers. Hello, all you naughty dogs. I'm Vixen, and this is Felix. Are you excited to watch us get down and dirty today?"

Comments flood in, seemingly more than last time, although I'm not sure I can trust my observational skills from that day.

"Oh, I like that idea, AnonymousHottie," Christian says, looking my way. "He said there wasn't enough kissing last time. What do you think, Fe? Wanna make out with me?"

My answer is giving Christian's arm a tug. He comes easily, falling over me as my back hits the mattress. I don't know if it's because this is work or I know what's expected of us, but it's so much easier to do exactly what I want while we're on this set. And what I want is Christian's body on mine. His lips on *mine*.

I wrap my ankles behind his ass and tug him to me as my hands sink into his hair. The ever-present awareness of the cameras keeps me from blocking his face, but I don't hesitate to pull him closer, even as Christian is already on the move. Our mouths lock, our groins connect, and I moan, already keyed up and horny and having no qualms about showing it.

Christian rocks his hips against mine, the unmistakable hardness of his cock dragging against my own. I can feel his bare ass beneath my heels as I try to drag him closer, and I wonder at what the viewers are seeing right now. Christian's ass under his skirt? The skimpy underwear that's barely concealing him?

The thought threatens to unravel me because any reminder of the audience has my mind wanting to sink into that wonderful, hazy surrender. But Christian's lips keep me rooted. His kiss is more frantic this time, and I have no doubt mine is the same. This isn't the lazy post-coital bliss we shared after our first scene together. This is raw and hungry, *anticipatory*, and it's not just me, right? Christian wants this, too. Maybe for his own reasons, but you can't fake genuine interest like what I feel pouring from his lips.

Christian doesn't kiss like the rest of my coworkers.

The sound I make as Christian drags his mouth down to my neck is needy as fuck, but I don't care. "Ch—" *Shit*, I almost said his name again. "Christ. Vixen, would you get this shirt off?"

My hands tug at Christian's top, and he laughs against my neck, nipping gently before leaning back to pull it free. Long, lean muscle is revealed, as well as the sparkling jewelry at his navel. He makes quick work of my shirt next, and then his hands are on my chest, thumbs circling my nipples as I hiss and arch up against the touch. He whips his hair to the side before coming back in, mouth pressing kisses to my neck and jaw and finally my lips as his thumbs circle and circle and *circle*.

My moan is loud. But painfully real.

Christian smacks away from my mouth, a wicked gleam in his eye as his gaze flashes to the tablet beside us. "Mm. I agree. He does like that. I think I could probably make him come from this alone."

He punctuates his point by leaning down and, ever so lightly, flicking his tongue across my nipple.

I bite my lip. *Hard*.

"Should I see how close I can get him?" Christian asks the viewers.

The consensus must be yes because he gives me a grin before pulling his hair up into a poofy little bun and securing it with the band around his wrist. I don't know why that simple act is as goddamn sexy as it is, but as Christian slinks down my body, his mouth poised above my chest and a few tendrils of his hair falling around his face, I'm not sure I've ever seen anyone as utterly enchanting as him.

My exhalation must alert him because his eyes meet mine a moment before his lips wrap around my nipple. There's mischief there, that's for damn sure. But there's also something soft and almost excited, so I hold my tongue about Christian torturing me—*again*—and let him have his fun.

The first suck of his mouth has my legs falling flat against the mattress. The next, tongue included as it presses up against the underside of the bud, has my hands flying above my head. I grab a pillow, toss it away, search for something more stable. One hand finds the headboard, and the other holds on to the goddamn sheets as Christian treats my nipple like the end of my cock and sucks for all he's worth.

His name on my lips is more a plea than anything. The way he holds tight and flicks his tongue back and forth is a *nuh-uh, we're not done yet.*

"You're... evil..." I pant.

Christian's hand slips down beneath the band of my jeans, fingers teasing the head of my cock.

"Evil," I insist. *"Don't fucking stop."*

He huffs a laugh against me, swirling his tongue, and I damn near shoot off the bed. Christian's mouth slips to the other side of my chest as his fingers leave my cock, landing on my pec instead. His thumb rolls over my nipple, wet now from his spit, and the way he circles it, rubbing firmly in the same pattern as his tongue, has me wondering if I really could come like this.

"Vixen."

He hums, popping off the bud, only to tug down my pants and suck my cock into his mouth. I curse, and he pops off again, returning to my chest. He sucks my left nipple into his mouth and then my right. And then, eyes on me, sinks back down to my dick.

"Oh my God, oh my God," I mumble, squirming, hips shifting, hands trying to find a better hold as Christian repeats the circuit twice. When I realize I can grab *him*, I do just that, my fingers tangling in his hair as I roll him onto his back. His eyes widen, a grin on his face that I swiftly kiss away.

He groans, but I pull back, breath puffing out of me.

"Fuck my goddamn fucking mouth," I tell him firmly.

His eyes spark with something fierce, lips looking bright against his pale skin. "If that's what you want," he says slowly, "then get on your knees, Fe. Before I make you."

I scramble backwards, and Christian pushes himself up, his hair a riotous mess and his eyes wild. He looks like a predator, and I don't know what it says about me that I trust him implicitly even with that gleam in his eye, but I do. I trust him, and I don't move a muscle as he rises fluidly to his feet atop the bed and slides his fingers through my hair.

My pants are hanging around my thighs, but I don't bother shifting them. I probably look like a needy mess, exactly how I feel. The thought of people seeing me like this has my cock throbbing without touch.

Christian doesn't remove his black miniskirt. He simply tightens his grip in my hair. "Take me out."

My hands fly under the hem of his skirt, fingers mapping the front of his barely-there thong before I grip the material and tug. The tiny scrap pools around his feet.

"Get me wet, Fe."

Bunching up the front of his skirt, I don't hesitate. I take him into my mouth, sucking hard, moaning at the taste and feel of him. Christian's eyes slip shut as I bob my head, soaking him with spit and popping off to lick his crown.

"Still, now," he says hoarsely, that dark gaze back on me, the wild glint still there, yes, but also a tenderness that has me opening my mouth wide without hesitation.

Christian readjusts his grip to my jaw and the back of my head and starts to thrust. He fucks my mouth shallowly, "*Fe, Fe, Fe,*" falling from his lips with each glide of his dick along my tongue. It doesn't take long before he's going deeper, his cockhead easing into my throat. When he pulls all the way out, I know what to expect. I inhale deeply through my nose, and as soon as I'm done, Christian's dick is back in my mouth. He slides as far as he can go, and this time, he stays put.

I nearly come right then and there.

"Do you have any idea," Christian pants, hips flexing in tiny increments, "how incredibly sexy you look right now, Fe? The way you're wrapped around me tight, taking my cock down your throat as if you're starved for it."

He pumps his hips a little harder, grip tight. My pulse is hammering, head fuzzy, but it's not from lack of oxygen. I hold still, eager to take everything he'll give me.

Christian's neck arches back as he slides his cock in and out of my mouth an inch at most, denying me breath like I all but dared him to do. He looks regal. All long, irresistible lines. The masculinity of him. The femininity.

"You're remarkable, Fe," he breathes, when I'm sure that's *him*. "Look at the screen. Look at what they're saying about you."

My eyes flit to the tablet that's sitting just behind Christian. The text is large enough I can read it, and the comments make my dick throb. I don't dare touch myself, not wanting this to end.

"Mm," Christian hums, his cock still burrowing into my throat, his pace careful and measured. I have maybe thirty seconds left. "You're perfect, and I don't care how many of them are watching. I don't care whether or not they wish you were theirs. Because right now? Right fucking now, it's *my* cock in your throat. Right now, Fe, you're *mine*."

My hands squeeze Christian's hips, and he pulls out immediately. I suck in a harsh breath, feeding my lungs and trying to steady the quick beat of my heart.

I meet Christian's gaze, unflinching. "Then show me."

Chapter 12
CHRISTIAN

Alarms blare in my head as I register the words I let slip. The ones that felt oh so real.

You're mine.

Emil is looking up at me in utter rapture, and no matter how hard I try, I can't break his gaze. Can't figure out *why* this man has me in his clutches. He has since the moment I first saw him spread out on his bed, glasses crooked and dick in hand.

I want him. *I want him*, and I'm having a hard time remembering why I can't just have him.

Emil lets go of my hips as I step back, and my skirt falls haphazardly over my cock. I force myself to turn toward the tablet as I sink down to the bed, hoping I didn't mess up the shot when I stood up in the first place. I don't worry about it right now. I slow my breaths and focus on work.

"You get two choices," I tell the viewers, aiming a smirk their way. "One way or another, I'm fucking Fe. Hands and knees? Or on his back?"

Comments pour in, and there's no way I can do an actual count, but I skim them nonetheless, not sure which option I want them to pick. Part of me is desperate to see Emil's eyes. The other... The other part of me knows that's dangerous.

I idly take stock of one of the cameramen moving around me and the boom operator nearby, but it's amazing how easy it is to block it all out. I wonder, for Emil, if it's something he's always aware of. If it skims along his skin like electricity.

Decision made with the help of our viewers, I turn back to Emil, who's still kneeling, his cock out, lips puffy and red.

"Have you ever been fucked by a man in a skirt, Fe?"

His eyes never leave mine. "Ask me again in five minutes."

I bark out a laugh. *This*. This is why I can't resist the man before me. He makes me feel light. He makes me *happy*.

"Hands and knees, Fe," I say hoarsely. "I'm gonna fuck you like I own you. *You're* going to take it and plead for more. And they're going to watch *every single second*."

Emil's eyes shutter, and he blows out a breath before snapping into action. As I grab a condom, he shucks off his clothes. Once nude, he flips onto his hands and knees and presents his ass. His forearms meet the bed, and he drops his cheek to the sheets, back arching. He looks like a man ready to be taken. Ready to be *owned*.

I try to tell myself this is just sex—just playing, just our job—but the fiery heat flowing through my veins doesn't let me believe it. Not fully. I wasn't supposed to develop feelings. I didn't *want* to want more.

But I do. And I don't know what to do with that.

Emil barely flinches when I bring lubed fingers to his ass. He leans into it, muscles relaxed, his entire body languid. My finger slips in with ease.

"More," Emil says instantly.

A smile pulls at my lips. "What did I tell you? Begging already."

I slip in two.

"Be confident...later," he huffs out. "Once your cock...is in me...making good on your promise."

I twist my fingers, and Emil curses. "You don't think I can make you feel just as good like this?" I goad, adding a third digit.

"You said...you'd own me," he replies, hips rolling back against my fingers as I fuck him looser. "So give me your goddamn cock, Vixen. Pin me to this fucking bed, and *own* me already."

Jesus fucking Christ.

I breathe a silent apology to my skirt as I get up on my knees behind Emil, knowing the fabric will need a damn good cleaning after this. I press the tip of my cock to Emil's asshole, hand holding tight to his hip.

"Come *on*," he urges, his glasses askew as he looks back at me, his cheek rosy bright. "Come on," he says again, softer but no less vehemently.

"Whatever you want, Fe."

Emil's breath whooshes out of him as I ram forward. His body accommodates me, making way, muscles throttling my cock as I sink balls-deep. I shift, grinding more than fucking, and Emil mewls, his fingers flexing against the sheets.

"Better, Fe? Is this what you wanted? You wanted to be filled and fucked and owned for all to see?"

His answer is a garbled moan. I keep grinding, waiting for some of that resistance to give way. I know Emil has expert control over his body, but I still don't want to hurt him. Couldn't bear it. I glance over my shoulder as I take stock of everything around us. The crew is silent as they work, and no cues are being given, so I stroke over Emil's ass cheek as I read the live chat.

"Gorgeous, isn't he?" I ask the viewers. My skirt is rucked up, still falling over my own ass but not obscuring Emil's. I pull out just a little and then push back in, letting them see my cock sinking slowly into Emil's body. "He feels perfect. *Perfect*, Fe."

"You'd feel better if you moved," he answers, the cheeky fuck.

I grin, snapping my hips forward. He groans.

"BigApple14 wants me to give you a creampie, Fe. What do you think? Should I flood your ass with my cum?"

"After...you *fuck* me," he huffs, angling his hips to take my cock deeper. "Or are you just planning to talk me to orgasm?"

I muffle a laugh, unable to hide my grin as I smooth my hand up and down Emil's back. When I reach his tailbone, I stroke over the swell of his ass. "Hold on to something, Fe."

"What am I supposed to—"

His question ends abruptly as I fuck into him exactly like I promised I would. As if he's *mine*. Emil scrambles to grab hold of the sheets, his face sinking into the bedding, his glasses getting knocked away. He takes every single thing I give him, and, for minutes, that's all there is. Emil's ass. The slap of skin on skin. His moans and my spoken encouragement—telling him how good he feels, how sexy he looks, how those watching can see exactly how well he takes my cock.

I fuck him until his panting breaths become uneven. Until he starts losing purchase, his legs shaking and arms trembling. I fuck him until he slips down to the bed, my own body following, my hips pressing him into the mattress as my lips find the nape of his neck. My fingers thread through his, holding tight as I roll my hips, sinking inside his body again and again.

"*Vixen*," he groans.

I let go of his hand to tug Emil's hip into the air, giving me the space to grab hold of his cock. One of the cameramen sinks to his haunches feet from the bed as I jerk Emil off.

"Do you feel it, Fe?" I rasp, my teeth near his earlobe. "Can you feel the way your body belongs to me?"

He groans.

"I want you to come," I tell him. "And I want you to do it now. I want you to lose yourself all over my fingers and think about the people who are coming with you, so turned on, they can't help it."

He inhales sharply, his eyes flying open and his body starting to clamp down on me. I grind against him, letting my hair conceal my face as I drop my lips to his ear, speaking at a whisper.

"Come on, my little exhibitionist. Show yourself off like the beautiful work of art you are."

With a hoarse cry, Emil coats my fingers. I jerk his cock as it throbs in my fist, working him through his orgasm. Only once he groans in oversensitivity do I stop, pulling back and hoisting his hips up as I slip entirely from his body. Emil gets his knees under him, his breath ragged but his eyes bright as he looks back at me. I strip off the condom—knowing I have approval to do so for this purpose—and stroke myself to that look in his eye. Right before I come, I kiss Emil's asshole with my cock.

My cum pools on his still loose hole, ropes of it unleashing until I'm utterly spent. Back bowed the way he is, it stays there, creamy white and practically begging for me to push it inside of him with my fingertips. I don't. I rub my thumb against his taint, up into my release, teasing his rim for just a moment before pulling away. I bring my thumb to Emil's lips.

"Taste."

His mouth wraps around the digit, tongue swirling as he gathers my cum into his mouth.

"Do you like the flavor of me on your skin?" I ask cheekily.

He releases my thumb, his eyes on me but squinted ever so slightly, as if I'm blurred in his vision. "Vixen."

"Mm?"

"Maybe you should try for yourself."

I let out a pained laugh. "Fuck, Fe."

"Yes, you just did," he snarks, not moving as he smiles at me over his shoulder.

Shaking my head, I lean back in, grabbing Emil's ass cheeks and bringing my tongue to his hole. He groans, a sound of pure satisfaction. Dutifully, I lick the cum from his skin.

It tastes like us.

"That was hot as fuck," a voice says the moment I push into the break room. Alex gives me a grin. "You two have chemistry for days."

I huff a laugh, swiping my damp hair out of my eyes. "You were watching?"

He nods, completely unabashed by that fact. There's a drink in his hand with a straw poking out of it and his phone is in the other. "The chat went haywire when you called him yours, you know. People are speculating that you're a couple."

I hum, my insides doing a very complicated dance as I grab a peach tea from the fridge. When I turn back around, Alex has a brow raised.

"Quite the defense," he teases.

"We're not dating," I say, even though I'm realizing that, *maybe*, I want us to be.

"But you two *are* chummy," he replies. "Makes me wonder."

It's then I realize Alex, at the very least, and the rest of our coworkers at most, aren't aware that Emil and I knew each other before I started working here. On one hand, I understand why Emil hasn't said anything if his secret exhibitionist habits are, in fact, a secret.

But, on the other hand... There's a part of me that wonders if he's ashamed of *me*. Of whatever sort of relationship we've shared over the past three plus months, nearly four now. Does he not want people to know we're neighbors and...friends?

"Chemistry," I answer, popping the cap on my tea. "Like you said."

"Sure, sure," Alex answers, scrolling through his phone, even though I'm fairly certain it's a ploy to make me think he's not observing me. When Emil himself walks into the break room, hair freshly wet from his own shower, Alex's eyes ping his way. "Hey, boo."

"Hey," Emil says, grabbing a bag of chips. He hovers for a moment before coming over to sit near me and Alex.

I can't help but take him in, even though I just spent the better part of two hours in his presence. His dark brows are set in a line, as if he's thinking about something with that clever brain of his. His cheeks are still a little red from the heat of the shower. And he's perched at the edge of his seat as if attending a lecture, which I'm guessing is more due to habit than any soreness in his ass.

Compared to Alex, who exudes sexual energy, it'd be hard at a glance to guess Emil is as wild and uninhibited as he is. I wonder if that's intentional on his part or if he's simply used to hiding himself away.

The thought has a frown pulling at my lips, but Alex's voice redirects my attention.

"*Soo*," the small blonde says, "how's our favorite crustacean doing?"

"He's fine," Emil mumbles, rolling his eyes as he opens his chips.

Alex snorts, but then he explains, for my benefit, "Emil is a crab daddy."

Before I can figure out whether or not I should say anything, Emil pipes up. "He knows. He's met Arthur."

Alex's head turns my way slowly. "Is that so?"

I shrug, although that tightness in my chest releases. Maybe Emil isn't ashamed of us, after all.

"Although, really," Emil continues, sounding as grumbly as I've ever heard him, "why you feel the need to announce that to everyone is beyond me, Alex."

Alex gasps. "*Emil*. You should be *proud* of your shell-baby. What would Arthur say if he could hear you?"

Emil levels Alex with a flat expression that has me stifling a laugh. "Nothing, Alex. He'd say nothing. He's a crab."

Alex sniffs. "A crab with feelings."

Emil shakes his head, but Alex goes on in a rush.

"Oh! Christian, has anyone invited you to Sublime yet? It's our go-to club on Friday nights. Emil hasn't been in *ages*. Maybe you can drag him along."

"I'm sitting right here," Emil mutters.

"I'd be up for that," I say, giving Emil a swift grin. "Maybe I could wear that red skirt I was telling you about."

Emil sucks in a breath. It's quiet, and I would have missed it if I hadn't been looking directly at him. But the reaction has my pulse hitching all the same.

"That, uh... Yeah. I guess that'd be okay," he says.

Alex looks between the two of us. "Interesting," he whispers.

Emil tucks back into his bag of chips, and even though Friday is days away, I'm already planning ahead. And if the outfit I have in mind is designed to drive a certain bespectacled neighbor of mine wild, well...

That can be my little secret.

Chapter 13
EMIL

"Thank you, Mrs. Park. That was the last one. We're all set for today."

The elderly woman across from me nods, sitting back in her chair. She's wearing a soft ivory cardigan, and despite being in a nursing home, she appears to be both spry and intelligent.

"I'll be back in another week to—"

"Specs?"

My words cut off, and I look up in surprise at Christian, who's standing beside our table in the recreation room.

"Christian? What, uh...what are you doing here?"

"I could ask the same of you," he says, leaning down to give Mrs. Park a hug. "Hey, Grandma."

Oh. *Oh.*

"Hi, sweetheart," Mrs. Park says in return, patting Christian's—her *grandson's*—cheek. "I wasn't expecting you today. You know Mr. Reed?"

"We're neighbors," Christian says, eyes meeting mine. "He lives across the alleyway."

"What a coincidence," Mrs. Park says.

A coincidence.

Christian's lips twitch into a smile. "Mm."

"We were just finishing up," I tell Christian, who looks at the papers in front of me. I slip them back into the folder.

"Finishing up with..." Christian says slowly.

"I'm doing Mr. Reed's experiment," Mrs. Park replies.

"It's not my research," I hasten to remind her, as well as make sure Christian understands. "But, uh, yeah. Your grandmother is one of the participants in our study."

Christian's brow furrows, but Mrs. Park starts to stand, so he offers an arm. "Here."

She accepts the support, even though she seems steady on her feet. "Thank you, sweetheart. Why don't you walk me back to my room, and then you can come catch up with your friend here."

I give Christian a nod. "I'll wait. Have a nice day, Mrs. Park."

"You, too, dear," she says. "I'll see you next week."

Christian heads out of the room with his grandmother, and in the relative quiet that follows, I realize exactly how hard my heart is beating. I'm just putting away the last of my things when Christian returns. He plops into his grandmother's vacated seat, arms crossed on the table in front of him and an open, if not befuddled, look on his face.

"Explain," he says simply.

I never told Christian the specifics of the research study I'm involved in, but I see no problem doing so now. "We're studying the effects of cognitive training in relation to de-mentia."

Christian sits straighter in his seat, as if he's been zapped. "My grandma is showing signs of dementia?"

I pull in a quick breath. "Oh, no. No, no, no," I rush to say. "Shit, Christian, I'm sorry. No, she's not. She's in a participant group of individuals without dementia."

He lets out a gust of air, forehead plopping onto his arms. "Jesus, Specs."

I curse again—quietly, mind you, considering where we are. Telling my nerves to fuck off, I reach forward and thread my fingers through Christian's hair.

"Sorry," I say again. "I didn't mean to freak you out."

He hums, rolling his head enough to look at me. His hair is falling over his forehead, and I brush the long strands to the side. It takes me a minute to realize I've repeated the motion several times.

"Sorry," I repeat, pulling my hand away.

Christian sits upright. "What'd I tell you about that, Specs?"

You have my permission.

"Right," I say, clearing my throat, forcing myself not to say *sorry* in response.

"Mr. Reed?" he asks, a wry twist to his lips.

I huff a laugh. "Yeah. Guess we never really exchanged last names, huh? Yours, though... Jerome said it's Ducat."

He gives a small nod. "My mother's surname."

"Right. That makes sense. Um... Your grandmother is really nice. Smart."

"She is," Christian says, a soft expression on his face. "She's the most important person in my life."

Wow. "Um..."

"I find it strange," he says.

"What's that?"

Christian leans forward. His eyes, so dark they look nearly black, blink at me once. The liner at the edges makes him look sharp and impossibly beautiful.

Or maybe that's just Christian.

"I find it strange," he repeats slowly, "that if you hadn't moved in next door, if you hadn't left your curtains open, if

I hadn't accepted a job at Elite 8 Studios... We still would have met. We would have met right here, right now. Don't you find that strange?"

My heart thumps wildly.

Christian simply hums. "You have class soon."

"I, um... Yeah, I do."

"Which one?"

"Interpersonal Skills and Group Therapy," I answer.

"But you don't want to be a therapist," he says, more statement than question.

"Still need to learn the skills."

He nods, looking lost in thought for a moment. "Can I take you out tonight?"

"Out?" I say in surprise. "Where?"

Christian huffs a small laugh, mirth in his eyes. "Someplace quiet. Trust me?"

I do.

I nod, and Christian offers me a smile. "Six o'clock, Specs. Be ready."

With that, Christian stands, presumably to go spend time with his grandmother. And me? I watch him until he's out of sight, my heart continuing to race.

I try to tell myself it has nothing whatsoever to do with the man upsetting my quiet and comfortable routine.

I'm not sure I buy it.

The knock at my door is expected, but I jump nonetheless. I close the top of Arthur's terrarium before pushing to my feet.

"Here we go, Arthur."

My hermit crab doesn't respond.

The distance to my door seems to last forever. My feet shuffle forward, and no amount of telling myself this is just Christian and there's nothing to worry about settles my nerves. I don't understand why he wants to spend so much time with me. All I do is study and talk about psychology, and, sure, I have sex in front of cameras. But that's the most exciting thing in my life. Everything else is just...

"Specs," Christian says. "I can hear you thinking. Open the door."

Puffing out a breath, I do. Christian appears in front of me wearing a smile and a pair of loose black pants that cinch at his ankles. His shirt is white, understated, but it complements his frame as if it were made for him. *It probably was.* His hair is down today, his eyes look like onyx pools, and I'm fairly sure I've never seen anything lovelier.

"Hi," I manage.

His smile twists, and he holds out a hand. "Ready to go?"

Pulse thrumming, I accept his palm, closing the door behind me. "Where are we going?"

"You don't like surprises, do you?" Christian says, leading me down the hall. He lets go of my hand to open the stairwell door, waving me forward.

"What gave me away?"

Christian snorts. "You're a very interesting blend of predictable and unexpected, Specs."

I don't know what to say to that. It doesn't sound like a bad thing.

"I think you'll like this," he says as we step out onto the sidewalk. "It's only a few blocks away."

I nod, and Christian offers his hand again. I take it.

Christian tells me a little bit about the rest of his day while we set off along the busy street, including the fact that he set up an Instagram account for his Vixen alter ego. I don't have one for Felix, but several of the guys at the studio keep up a social media presence.

When I ask to see it, Christian pulls out his phone with ease. My feet stutter to a stop when he flips the screen my way. The picture—his only so far—is of him standing in front of a mirror in the locker room wearing nothing but a skirt. Well, not nothing. There's also a silver chain around his middle, a drop pearl hanging in his belly button. I just about swallow my tongue, my mind so helpfully supplying the mental image of *other* pearly white things that could be pooling in that divot.

"Shit," I murmur.

"Do you like it?" Christian asks, a hint of cheekiness in his tone.

"Very nice...smile."

He laughs as I duck my head, both of us well aware I wasn't fixated on his smile. We resume walking, and, when we reach a flora-covered gate I've never noticed before, Christian comes to a stop.

"We're here," he says.

There's a plaque on the front of the gate that reads, "*All welcome. May you find peace.*"

"What is this?" I ask.

Christian opens the latch. "A meditation garden."

My brows pop up, and he huffs a small laugh.

"I can feel your skepticism from here, Specs."

"No, it's just..."

Christian gives my hand a squeeze. "This place is special. You'll see."

Unable not to, I follow Christian as he steps down a winding, narrow path. Trees flank both sides of us, making it feel as if we're traveling through a natural tunnel. When we reach a clearing, I come to an abrupt stop. Christian chuckles, stepping to the side so I can see better.

It *is* a garden, but... At its center is a perfectly circular, manicured lawn with spiraling stone pavers. Along the sides are impeccably tended-to bushes and flowers. A butterfly flits above some bright red petals. At the far side of the lawn is a bench stationed in front of a small pond. A couple ducks are floating in the water, and just past is a brick building, the entire side of it painted with a mural of wildflowers below a sunrise.

I had no clue this was here.

Christian gives my hand a tug, a smile on his face. "Come on, Specs."

I follow Christian along the smooth pavers, both of us stepping stone to stone. The path leads around the lawn to the center and then back out again in the opposite direction until it reaches the pond. It would have been quicker to simply walk across the grass, but... I don't think that's the point.

Christian lowers himself onto the bench, and I sit beside him. We're both quiet for a minute, watching the ducks swim around in front of the brightly painted flowers across the water. The setting sun in the mural makes it feel as if we're suspended in time, even though everything is moving and alive around us.

When I look over at Christian, I find him already watching me. "Well?" he asks.

"It's nice," I say. Even though it's so much more than that. "How'd you find this place?"

"My grandma," he answers, lips lifting into an almost melancholic smile. "I used to come here with her a lot." He huffs a laugh when the ducks start chasing one another. "Earlier this year, in the springtime, there were ducklings here. I wonder if these are them, all grown up."

"Could be," I say softly, following his gaze. "Animals often return to the places they know are safe. It's ingrained in us. Instinctual. Humans, ducks, we seek safety without conscious thought. We're all just trying to survive in this world the best way we know how."

Christian hums. "What'd you call that? The tenacity of life?"

My head whips his way, breath hitching. "Um, yeah. I did."

Christian nods, a soft smile on his face as he looks out over the pond. He remembered that?

My heart pounds heavily as I try to focus on the nature spread out in front of us, but a question circles around my mind again and again. It's no surprise to me when it finally finds its way out.

"Why'd you bring me here, Christian?"

He lets loose a breath before shifting his gaze my way. "I don't really know, Specs. That might seem like a cop-out, but it's the truth. I...like you. And I like this place. It's quiet. It brings me comfort. I guess I just wanted to share it with you."

I nod, unable to speak. One of the ducks splashes, honking once, the sound almost joyous, despite its crass nature. Christian chuckles beside me.

"Thank you," I finally respond.

"Yeah, Specs. Thanks for being here."

Sadness hits when I realize it's entirely possible Christian's grandmother *can't* come with him anymore. I wonder, briefly, about the rest of his family. Whether or not he has any. It doesn't feel like the right time to ask.

After a long while, Christian's gaze lands on the side of my head again. "Ready to go?"

I swallow and nod. "Yeah."

Christian stands, and I follow suit. We start walking the stones again.

"Want to grab some food on the way back?" Christian asks.

"I, uh... Sure?"

"My treat," he adds, shooting me a smile. "It's customary, after all, to take a guy out to dinner before you fuck."

My foot misses a paver, and I catch myself on the next, heart thrashing about inside my chest. It takes me a good, long moment to realize he's talking about our scenes. Our *scenes*. Not...*us*.

The wink Christian sends me over his shoulder sure doesn't help settle my pulse, though.

Is it possible to develop an arrhythmia because of a painfully attractive, thoughtfully sweet neighbor?

"Um, we've already fucked," I point out, if for no other reason than to have *something* to say. "Also, I don't think you're supposed to say 'fuck' in a meditation garden."

Christian laughs, a sound that has a smile sneaking onto my face. "I won't tell if you don't."

"Deal."

When we reach the end of the spiraling path, Christian stops. "Well, Specs? What's the verdict? Did you find your inner peace?"

I'm not sure what I found inside this garden, but I can't deny I feel lighter than I did before.

"Inconclusive," I tell him. "I think I'll need to gather more evidence."

Aaand shit, am I flirting? Was that flirting?

Christian's eyes light in a way I'm coming to recognize as familiar. Like he's got a secret I should know but can't quite figure out. "Mm. I think that can be arranged. Now how do sandwiches sound?"

"Perfect," I tell him truthfully.

With a grin, Christian heads back down the narrow path out of the garden, me at his heel. It's not until much later, when I'm lying in bed with a book out in front of me, Christian long since having gone back to his own apartment, that a thought flashes to life inside my head, so blindingly bright I nearly pull a neck muscle from the whiplash.

Was...was that a *date*?

Chapter 14

CHRISTIAN

"Holy shit," Emil says, his eyes wide. He bumps up his glasses. "Um."

It's Friday night. Club night. Emil and I agreed to share a ride to Sublime, which is why I'm at his door. But based on my neighbor's shell-shocked expression, it seems as if I've still managed to surprise him.

"You like the outfit?" I tease, striking a pose.

He blinks at me.

I'm wearing the red skirt, like I promised. The hem ends mid-thigh—not that far below my ass, to be honest. My black boots add a couple inches to my height, the stilettos adorned with pointy silver studs. And my shirt is a fine white mesh that's soft to the touch and see-through enough for my belly chain to be visible. I added a touch of red on my eyelids to wrap it all together.

Emil blinks again.

"Good, Specs? Or should I go change?"

"No," he says quickly, coughing once. "Um, no. It's good. Although now I feel a little underdressed."

"You look great," I tell him honestly. He's dressed casually in jeans and a simple long-sleeved shirt, but the clothes fit him well, and the light oatmeal-colored top suits his complexion.

Emil rolls his eyes a little. "Yeah, okay. Come on in. Are you thirsty?"

I tsk as I follow him through the door. "Do you always do that?"

"Do what?" he asks.

"Brush off compliments instead of accepting them?"

Emil stops still, looking at me in something akin to shock before shaking his head and continuing on into the kitchen. "Um, yeah," he answers, opening the fridge door. "I do, actually."

I cock my head as Emil hands me a bottled water. "Why?"

He huffs a laugh, closing the fridge and leaning against the counter. He doesn't look at me when he says, "I guess because I'm not used to hearing them. And it's easier to avoid getting attached to something nice than coming to expect it only to be disappointed by its absence."

It takes me a second to say anything, my chest aching at that response. "Why would it go away?"

He shrugs. "People aren't always permanent, Christian."

"I'm not going anywhere."

He shrugs again, looking off toward Arthur's terrarium. "You never know. I had to leave my last apartment because they found asbestos in the basement. Things happen."

I take a step closer, my breath shuddering. "And you think, if one or both of us ends up moving, we'll stop being friends?"

His eyes ping to mine for only a second. "I don't know what to think."

His answer stings, but how can I blame Emil for being uncertain about...*us* when I haven't given him any indication

I'm planning on sticking around for good? Not just here, in this neighborhood, but with *him*. I want to be around him.

I haven't said that, though, have I? I've barely been able to admit it to myself.

I've seen what romantic attachments do to people. Seen what happens when you lose the person you love.

I guess, in a way, I can understand perfectly why Emil is so scared of losing something he's never really had.

"Well," I say softly, clearing my throat. "I think you look nice, Specs. I always do, even when your hair is rumpled and you drool on your pillow."

His mouth falls open. "I don't *drool*."

I hold my thumb and forefinger a half inch apart, as if to say *a little bit*.

Emil, indignant, shoves my shoulder. I laugh as I catch my balance, Emil's hand helping to steady me, even though he was the one to unbalance me in the first place. His eyes drop, gaze trailing over my legs and up my body as if he can't quite help himself. With a shake of his head, he lets me go.

"Well...maybe you should stop stalking me," he mutters, walking past me to grab his keys.

I hum, unperturbed. "You could always close your curtains. But you like it, don't you, my little exhibitionist? You like me watching you, whether you're sleeping, studying, or fisting your cock."

Emil freezes, his shoulders going ramrod straight. He lets out a breath before turning. "Christian."

"Mm?" I ask, pulse kicking.

"You can't say stuff like that when we're out."

"No?"

He shakes his head, the motion slow, his brown eyes looking almost hazy as he blinks once. "No. Because if you tempt me,

I'm going to try to get you to fuck me where everyone can see. And that can't happen. Okay? No matter how much I beg for it."

My inhale is sharp, my cock thickening as the mental image of Emil begging enters my mind. Emil on his knees. Emil's lips wrapped around my cock. Emil pleading with me to fuck him already, to get my dick inside his ass before he loses it and asks someone else to do it.

"Christian," he says, snapping me out of my reverie. He takes a single step closer, expression serious. "I'm not kidding. You have to promise me. Because I'd do it, but I *can't*. I can't, okay? It could seriously fuck up my future, and the risk isn't worth it. So you need to promise me, no matter when, no matter what I say, you won't let me do that in public. *Ever.*"

I swallow roughly. "I understand, Specs. And I promise."

He breathes out, nodding as he slips his wallet into his pocket. His jeans, I notice, are pulled much more snugly against his crotch than they were a moment ago.

"Ready?" he asks.

Christ. I'm not sure I am, not after that. But I nod, setting down my untouched water, and the two of us head out the door.

Sublime, as it turns out, is like every other club in Las Vegas. Loud. Lit up. And brimming with energy.

We head right to the VIP balcony above the dance floor. Several of our coworkers are already here, and Emil and I find a couch to share as a couple servers move about in skimpy shorts. With a pinch in my gut, my thoughts flit to Noel. I haven't heard from him in over a week.

A tap on my arm shifts my focus. "Want a drink?" Emil asks.

I lean closer so he doesn't have to shout. "Trying to loosen me up, Specs?"

Emil does that thing where he looks at me for an extended beat, as if he can't fathom the idea that I'm flirting with him. He can be so blunt and demanding at times, and yet subtlety seems to fly right over his head.

"I'd love a drink," I tell him before he can get stuck too far inside his thoughts. "Jack and Coke?"

"Interesting choice," he says, catching one of the server's eyes and holding up his hand.

"Why's that?"

"Bold but sweet," he answers. "Kind of like you."

I open my mouth but lose my tongue.

"Hey, Miles," Emil says to the server who stops in front of us. His crotch ends up inches from my face.

"Hey, Felix," the guys practically purrs. "And Vixen. *Damn*. Must be my lucky night. Nice to meet you, gorgeous."

I shake Miles's proffered hand, ignoring the up-and-down he gives me. "Pleasure."

"Could we get two Jack and Cokes please?" Emil asks.

"You got it, cutie. Be right back with those." Miles blows a kiss before walking away, hips swaying.

Emil, I notice, doesn't watch him go.

"Are you going to dance with me tonight?" I ask.

He swallows, his light brown eyes looking darker than usual in the dim club. "I don't dance."

"No?" I cross my legs, and Emil's eyes drop, following the motion. "Could I convince you?"

"You could likely convince me to do just about anything," he mumbles.

I hum, liking that answer a lot, even though I probably shouldn't. "I'll go easy on you," I tease.

"You're capable of that?"

I bark a laugh, and Emil's lips twitch into a grin.

It doesn't take Miles long to return with our drinks. He sets them on the table in front of us, eyes lingering appreciatively before he heads off. As Miles collects empties from Alex and his boyfriends, Emil picks up his glass.

"To getting me to dance," he says.

I grab my drink, clinking my glass against his. "To being brave and trying new things."

Emil nods, but I don't explain the words were meant more for me than him.

We take our time sipping our drinks, but once they're gone, I raise an eyebrow. Emil stands with an exaggerated sigh. I grin, and the two of us head down to the dance floor. Emil gets a lot of attention as we move through the crowd, likely being recognized by those who follow Elite 8 Studios. People seem respectful, though, and I wonder if that's because of the heavy presence of bouncers nearby.

We stop in the middle of the dance floor, surrounded by people but in a bubble all our own. Emil looks uncomfortable and unsure, so I step closer, looping my arms over his shoulders and swaying us side to side.

"Um," he says.

"Dance with me, Specs."

His hands find my waist. "You want to dance like this?"

"Why not?"

"No one else is slow dancing," he points out.

"Who cares?" I say, moving us in a slow circle as EDM pumps through the speakers.

Emil's fingers tighten on my waist before he starts to relax. He says something I can't quite make out, so I lean forward.

"What was that?" I ask, my lips brushing his ear.

His hands smooth around to my lower back. "I said you're really tall tonight. I mean, you're always tall, but right now, with the heels..."

His words trail off, and I smile to myself before leaning back enough to catch his eye. "Do you like the stilettos, Specs?"

He blows out a breath. "Like is not the right word."

"No?" I ask. "What is?"

After a long beat, he answers, "Enraptured."

My heart thumps. "What?"

"You're beautiful without adornment, Christian," he says, each word cutting through the din around us. "It doesn't matter what you're wearing. But in your skirts? In those heels? You shine from the inside. And seeing that? I'm enraptured."

Holy shit.

I focus on my breathing. On the simple in and out as Emil guides me in a circle, him leading our dance now. I don't know what to say, and part of me wants to run. I want to run *far* and *fast*, but I can't.

I can't.

Emil doesn't seem to need me to say anything. He lays his head on my shoulder, his hands warm on my back. It's not often that I feel delicate, but I feel it now in Emil's arms. I hate it. And I don't.

Clearing my throat, I say, "I was led to believe you'd be a horny troublemaker tonight, Specs. And instead, you're turning out to be very cuddly."

His lips brush my neck, almost a kiss. And then his hips press against me, and... *Oh*.

"I'm trying *very hard*," he says.

I huff a laugh, grabbing ahold of him to grind us together. "I can feel that."

"Christian," he groans, breath hot on my neck.

With Herculean effort, I let him go. "Should we grab another drink? Cool down a bit?"

He nods, his forehead against my shoulder, before he takes a step back.

I grab Emil's hand, and the two of us make our way off the dance floor, reconvening with our coworkers up in the VIP lounge. It's my first time seeing Teddy and Kipp together, and I can't help but chuckle at Kipp as I sip my second drink of the night. He's telling a story, hands waving wildly as he all but sprawls over his husband's lap. Teddy, for his part, has an arm around Kipp's waist and a serene, calm smile on his face.

When there's a sudden cheer that goes up around the room, I follow the gazes of my coworkers to the entrance of the lounge. A chiseled specimen of a man waves from beside a guy with blonde hair who tugs his beanie down as if trying to hide.

"Do we know them?" I ask Emil.

He huffs a laugh, his breath so close it's as if his lips are back on my skin. "The dark-haired one is Cas. He used to work at the studio as Himbo. Next to him is Jason, his boyfriend. He's a nurse."

"Ah," I say, nodding as Alex launches himself at a rather startled-looking Jason. Just behind them, another man appears, a massive grin on his face. Miles the server latches onto him immediately, hand on his arm.

"And the one being stroked by Miles?" I ask.

Emil snorts. "That's Jason's Brad."

My eyebrow pops up, and I look at Emil in amusement. "Is that like a growth one acquires?"

Emil starts to laugh, covering his mouth, but it doesn't hide the sparkle in his eye. "You could say that."

After Alex throws himself bodily at each of the newcomers, he leads them our way. "And this is Christian," he's saying. "He's new."

"Whoa," Brad breathes, his eyes landing on my stomach. He smacks Jason's arm without even glancing over. "Look, Birdie. *Look*. You could get a necklace for your stomach! I didn't even know that was a thing."

Jason looks as if he wants to sink into the floorboards. "It's really nice jewelry," he says to me, seeming to smile apologetically. "And sorry about Brad."

Brad says something else to Jason that I miss. When he reaches for Jason's shirt, Jason smacks his hand away without missing a beat.

"Hi, I'm Cas," the last man cuts in. "Nice to meet you."

"You, too," I answer, giving Emil's old coworker a smile.

"Hey, Emil," Cas adds, coming over to his side of the couch. "How've you been?"

"Good," Emil says. "How's the physio program going?"

"Oh, it's great," Cas replies, but I don't hear the rest because Brad plops onto the cushion next to me.

"Is that, like, permanently attached?" he asks. "Or can you take it off to shower and stuff?"

"It comes off," I tell him, lips twitching. "It's held in place by a navel piercing."

"Ah. Cool, cool," Brad says. "I thought about getting a piercing once 'cause this girl I was dating said it'd feel good, but I dunno, man. I think sticking a needle through my dick would be painful as hell."

Jason sighs, shaking his head.

"If you want to know about dick piercings," Alex interjects, "ask my Ginger Bear. He has five."

Brad chokes on absolutely nothing. "Holy shit. Finn!" he shouts, jumping from the couch and heading toward the tattooed redhead. "Can I see your dick?"

"Oh my God," Jason mutters.

Emil's hand on my leg pulls my attention. Cas is gone now, and Jason is following after Brad, saying something about *oblivious straight best friends*. Emil's eyes look a little hazy. I know he hasn't had enough alcohol to be drunk, but it'd be easy to assume as much with the way he's looking at me.

"Specs?" I ask, pulse jumping as his hand slides further up my leg.

"I think we should dance again," he says.

"Is that a good idea?" I check, considering he specifically asked me not to let him get overtly horny in public, and right now...right now he looks very horny.

Emil nods. "I don't like to dance with people, Christian. But I like it with you."

I pull in a breath. How am I possibly supposed to say no to something like that? Specs has me wrapped around his finger, and he doesn't even know it. He could ask just about anything of me, and I'd say yes, just to see that trust in his eyes. Just to have his attention on me, the same way he so ardently hoards mine.

There's so much I want when it comes to this man. Things I've never wanted with another person before. But most of all—above all else—I want *him*.

It takes me a moment to understand what that icy feeling coursing through my body is. Fear. It's fear.

Emil's fingers tangle with mine. "Christian," he says softly, my name quiet beneath the noise of the club. "Please dance with me."

"Yeah, Specs," I answer, the warmth of his hand chasing out the cold. "Let's dance."

Chapter 15

EMIL

Christian looks drop-dead gorgeous tonight.

Frankly, he looks gorgeous all the time. But tonight, he's like a jewel. A ruby, maybe, with all the red. And it's not just me. Guy after guy has tried approaching Christian to no avail. Each time, he's brushed off their advances and sometimes, quite literally, their hands. Just a minute ago, when one guy touched his ass, Christian spun around, said something I couldn't make out clearly but that sounded a lot like *hands off unless you want to lose them*, and then he turned back around and looped his arms over my shoulders with a smile.

Christian hasn't once tried to move my hands away, not in all the time we've been at the club. Not even now, when my fingers not-so-accidentally skim the soft underside of his ass cheek as we spin in a slow circle beside Alex and his boyfriends. He simply raises an amused eyebrow my way.

It makes me feel bold, and I trace the swell of his ass, feeling the curve of it, uncaring if anyone notices my hand beneath his skirt.

"Are you being naughty, Specs?" Christian asks, leaning close.

In answer, I let my other hand slip between our bodies, over the front of Christian's skirt.

This time, he does catch my hand. But still, he doesn't push me away.

"Specs," he says, my name a gentle admonishment. "You told me not to let you do that."

"I told you not to fuck me," I counter, inhaling Christian's scent from his neck. It reminds me of wintergreen.

He chuckles, something I can feel more than hear. "I think it's time to go."

"What? Why?" I groan, wanting to stay right here where I can touch Christian all I want and he lets me.

His lips skimming my ear perk me up as much as an electrical zap. "Because I made you a promise, Specs, and I intend to keep it. And right now, you're acting like you're two seconds away from pulling out my cock here on the dance floor."

God, that sounds good.

"Come on," Christian says, stepping back, my hand in his. He says something to Alex, who waves at me wildly, and we head for the exit.

There are a few people out on the sidewalk waiting for rideshares. It doesn't take long for our own to arrive, and I follow Christian into the backseat of our car, trying my very best not to stare at his ass as he gets situated. It's a losing battle. When we pull away from the curb, the thumping beat of the club continues to pulse in my ears, everything still a little muddled, as if I'm swimming underwater.

Christian eyes me. "Okay, Specs?"

I nod, head feeling heavy.

"You're not drunk," he says, almost a question but not quite. His next word is a whisper. "Horny?"

I groan, and Christian laughs. It's a light sound, not mocking, so I laugh with him.

"I'm messed up," I mutter, letting my head fall back against the seat.

Christian grabs my hand. "No," he says firmly. "Not in the least."

Neither of us says anything more, mindful of the driver in the car with us, but I'm positive not everyone gets a raging hard-on from the idea of pleasing another man in front of a club full of people. I would have dropped to my knees right there and worshiped Christian's cock if he'd let me. It would have been so *good*. Thrilling. I wouldn't have cared about the repercussions. Not until later.

There's a reason I rarely ever dance. Rarely ever date.

How do I know who I can trust?

"Specs," Christian says, pulling my focus. "Whatever you're thinking, stop. There's nothing wrong with you."

I swallow and nod, but I'm not sure I believe it.

When the driver drops us off outside our apartments, Christian heads toward my building without a word. I follow, my bravado faltering now that the haze has passed and we're back in the real world where I'm just Emil, nerdy psych major who prefers solitude apart from his hermit crab and the company of his books.

Although that hasn't been the case lately, has it? Christian has been nice company, too.

My neighbor stops outside my door, waiting for me to unlock it. I do, and we head inside together. I flick on the lights as Christian unzips his ridiculously tall boots. I try not to stare, instead making my way over to check on Arthur.

I can sense Christian as he walks into the room behind me. He hums, drawing my eye.

"I've seen these before but never really paid attention," he says, stopping in front of the art on the wall behind the couch. There are three frames. "Are these brains?"

"Yeah," I admit a bit sheepishly, crossing the room to stand beside him. He's looking at the leftmost piece.

"It's lit like a city or something."

"Yeah, uh, it's a representation of the portions of our brain that light up in response to fear."

"Seriously?" he asks, looking over at me with wide eyes.

I nod, pointing to the one next to it. The middle one. "That one is pleasure."

Christian examines it for a long moment. "It's so different," he says, almost in awe.

"Yeah, it is."

"And this one?" Christian asks, stepping over to the third.

I clear my throat. "That one is love. See this here?" I tap a portion that's lit. "That's the midbrain's ventral tegmental area. Its primary function, above all else, is the assessment of need. It's what drives us to eat and drink to stay alive. People like to think of love as this wild, intangible thing, lust-driven and passionate. But look."

Christian looks over at the brain map for pleasure again.

"It's not the same," I point out. "When you fall in love...that person becomes a necessity. Your brain lights up the same way it does when you eat or drink or breathe air. That person—*loving* that person—is something your body has adapted to and now views as essential to your survival. And that..." I huff a laugh, shrugging. "I don't know. I guess that's more romantic to me than passion ever could be."

Christian is quiet, and when I look over at him, he's staring right back. "That's remarkable, Specs."

"Is it?" I ask, knowing I tend to enjoy this stuff vastly more than the average person.

He hums, looking back at the neural representation of love. He stares at it for half a minute before looking at the electrical activity for fear again. Christian swallows, something passing over his face I'm not sure how to decipher, but then he shakes his head and says, "I like these. They're very you."

"Cerebral?" I ask with a chuckle.

He tilts his head. Appraising. Thoughtful. "Pretty," he answers. "Smart and pretty."

My pulse takes off like a shot.

"I had a scene with Alex this morning," Christian says, throwing me for a loop. He heads toward the hall, and I follow.

"Um, yeah?"

I knew Christian would be filming with other guys at the studio, of course. And sure, maybe I already checked the schedule and saw he was slated for a scene with Alex. I was curious, sue me.

Christian nods, flipping on the light in my room. When he doesn't say anything more, I start to worry.

"Was it *bad*?" I ask.

"Oh, no," he says quickly, shooting me a small smile. He takes a seat on the edge of my bed, crossing his long legs and leaning back on his arms. His skirt rides indecently high up his legs. "It was fine. Just...different, I guess. He's very exuberant."

I huff a laugh. Sounds like Alex.

"It was scripted, too," Christian says, his leg swinging. "It felt more like a production, you know? Like I was acting. There was a lot of '*Ooh, baby. Faster, yes. My God, you're so tight.*'"

I snort, and Christian grins.

"But even so," he goes on, expression turning almost pensive, "it was just sex, you know? It wasn't... Well, it wasn't the same as my scenes with you."

For a moment, I forget how to breathe. "Sex with me is more than sex?" I ask.

It takes Christian a few seconds to answer. His leg keeps swinging, but his face...his face goes through a myriad of emotions, the last of which is resolve. "Yeah, Specs," he finally says. "I guess it is. At least, it feels that way to me."

"Oh," I say, unable to produce a single other word. *Wow*. That's... My head spins. *Say something!* "Um... Thank you?"

Christian's lips twist into a smile, his expression smoothing into something fond and familiar. "Can I stay here tonight?"

Holy—

"Yes," I squeak out. "Um, sure. That'd be fine."

He nods, dropping his foot back to the floor and standing. "Do you have face wash I can use?"

"Uh, yeah. In the cabinet behind the mirror."

"Thanks," he says, walking from the room.

I stand there. Staring at the empty doorway. Contemplating my life.

I get changed for bed while Christian is in the bathroom. It doesn't take long for him to return, his makeup gone and his face looking freshly washed. Some of his hair is a little wet, too, as if it got dampened during the process.

"Do you have something I can wear?" he asks, tugging his see-through shirt off over his head. His belly chain shifts as the fabric rolls over it, but then it settles once more along the curves of his stomach. He folds his shirt before setting it on my desk. "Specs?"

"Um, yeah," I say, heading to my dresser.

"Can I have the bottoms with the crabs?" he asks, a soft sort of amusement in his voice. "They're my favorite."

My cheeks flame, more at the knowledge of Christian knowing what I wear at night—having seen me through the window, of course—than embarrassment over the print on the pajamas. I grab them from the drawer, grateful that they're clean. "Here you go."

"Thanks," he says, unceremoniously unzipping and dropping his skirt.

I swallow my tongue. And my moan.

Christian pulls the pajama bottoms on, covering his skimpy black thong. He sets to work taking off his jewelry next, and I get caught up in watching the process. The way he handles the silver chain is mesmerizing.

"Not the most comfortable to sleep in," he says, catching my eye.

"Sure," I manage. "Does, um… Does it ever get caught during sex?"

He huffs a small laugh, setting the neatly rolled chain on his folded shirt and then picking up his skirt from the floor, adding it to the pile. "It can happen, yeah. The tug isn't pleasant."

"I can imagine," I mutter, making a mental note to be extra cautious next time Christian wears one during our scenes.

"Ready?" he asks.

My mouth pops open. "For?"

He cocks his head slightly, a small smile on his face. "Bed, Specs."

Oh God. Right. Bed.

"Of course," I say quickly. "Um, did you want a shirt?"

"No, that's okay," Christian says, throwing back my sheets and climbing onto the mattress. He sinks into place opposite my normal position, and something about that makes my head reel. "Coming?"

"Yep."

I hit the light, and then I carefully scoot into bed next to Christian. He still smells like wintergreen, all fresh and light. I set my glasses aside before trying to close my eyes.

"Hey, Specs?"

"Yeah?" I answer, voice quiet.

"I've never slept in a bed with anyone before."

The admission shocks me. "No?"

"No. Would it bother you if I were the big spoon?"

I huff a laugh, part disbelief, part giddy nerves. "That'd be fine."

Christian hums, a sound I've gotten used to hearing from him. The next second, he's rolling me onto my side and slotting into place behind me as if it's the most natural thing. His arm comes around my waist, our legs fitting together like magnets, and then he lets out a breath, his nose brushing the back of my head.

Slowly, I cover Christian's arm with my own.

"I think I like this," he says.

"Yeah," I whisper.

It feels as if his lips press a soft kiss against my hair. "Night, Specs."

"Goodnight," I say, my pulse skidding along as Christian breathes quietly behind me.

What does it mean that we're sleeping together? That Christian says sex with me doesn't feel casual?

I don't know what to make of it, but my heartbeat settles, my eyes slip shut, and I sink into the same sense of calm I feel anytime I'm in Christian's arms.

As I drift to sleep, I can't help but wonder what parts of my brain are lit like Vegas lights.

Chapter 16

CHRISTIAN

It takes a fuzzy moment as I wake to remember where I am. But the sight of Specs sprawled so casually in front of me clears up the confusion fast.

We're not tangled like we were when we fell asleep. Emil is on his back now, his head turned gently to the side, but my arm is slung over his chest, as if I wanted to keep him close, even in my sleep.

I watch him for a moment, feeling a strange—but not un-welcome—sort of disconnect. For once, I'm not across the alleyway while my neighbor is sleeping. I'm right here with him.

I don't dare move, don't dare shatter the moment, but Emil shifts before long, letting out a soft sigh. I pull my arm back, wondering if... *Yep.* Emil raises his arms above his head, stretching and letting out a soft groan, his hands flexing into fists.

I bite my lip.

He pauses mid-stretch, and I can see the moment he real-izes he's not alone. His eyes fly open, and his head turns my way slowly.

"Hey," I practically whisper.

Emil tugs his arms down, instinctually reaching for his face before seeming to remember he's not wearing his glasses. He grabs them off the nightstand, sliding them onto his nose before blinking at me a few times. "Um, hi."

"Told you," I say lightly. "Just like a cat."

He blinks again before snorting. It feels like a lifetime ago that I called him out for his feline behavior. Back then, I didn't even know Emil's name. He was my kinky neighbor, my sorta friend, but not *more*.

"I, uh," Emil says, clearing his throat. "I need to use the bathroom."

When he doesn't make a move, I ask, jokingly, "Do you need a hand?"

His eyes widen before he huffs a laugh and throws back the covers. They smack me in the face, and I pull them down, catching the side of Emil's smile before he's out the door.

Sassy kinky neighbor.

As Emil takes care of morning necessities, I get out of bed and find a shirt. Hopefully, he won't mind. I take a whiff of the collar, humming happily when I find it smells like him. Clean laundry, mostly, but also something that's simply Emil.

Dressed, I head into the living room and sit down in front of Arthur's terrarium. It takes me a minute to find the crab, but eventually I see a tiny peek of orange among the fibrous material at the bottom of his tank. A leg, maybe.

"I don't have an extra toothbrush," Emil says from the hall, startling me somewhat, "but you can use my toothpaste if you want."

I shoot him a smile. "Thanks, Specs."

He nods and disappears into the bedroom.

"Arthur," I say quietly. "Can you keep a secret?"

The crab doesn't budge.

"I kinda like your daddy," I admit. "But I don't know what to do. I've never had a boyfriend before."

Arthur has no response.

"It's scary, you know? When I stop to think about it, it freaks me out. But...when I'm with him, it doesn't feel scary at all. He's a man who dotes on his hermit crab. How can that be scary?"

Arthur still doesn't reply. With a sigh, I pick myself up off the floor, gaze catching on the pictures on the wall. The three brain maps.

I don't want my choices to be based on fear. Specs said we're all just trying to survive. That all of the chaos in this world is proof of that fight. He also said to trust my gut.

Well, my gut is telling me there's more to living than survival. And am I really living if I keep myself relegated to a safe, *easy* existence like my mom did after my dad died? She won't let herself be happy. Not truly. She grieves the life she could have had, ignoring the one she's been given. She's surviving, but she's not *living*.

I don't want to end up like that. Yes, I'm scared. Scared of failure, of loss, of heartbreak, even. I'm scared I might not be enough for Emil in the end. That I might disappoint him, the same as I have my mother.

But *fuck*, if Specs can be brave enough to admit, even indirectly, that he's scared of me leaving, I can be brave enough to tell him I don't want to. Is it really so hard? It shouldn't be.

I head to the bathroom before Emil can emerge from his room. Using my finger, I brush my mouth until it's minty fresh. Then I step back into the hall, on a mission.

I find Specs in the kitchen, sifting through the contents of an open cupboard. He looks mildly alarmed as he spots me strutting his way. Before he can speak, I stop in front of him and open my mouth.

"Can I kiss you?"

He makes an aborted sound. "Now? Here?"

"Yes and yes."

"I, um... Yeah," he finally answers.

I breathe in, my chest swells, and I take Emil's face in my hands.

His lips are soft, just like I remember, but we're not in the studio. We're not in front of the cameras. This is just me and Emil, kissing for no other reason than because we want to.

It doesn't surprise me when Emil's hands fist my shirt, pulling me closer. I bump into him, bump *him* into the counter. He moans, a soft sound, but there's no doubt in my mind it's real. And only for me.

When I pull back, Emil blinks his eyes open, and I carefully adjust his glasses on his nose. "Can I take you on a date?"

He inhales. Exhales. "Another one?"

That startles a laugh out of me. "Have we been dating without me knowing it?"

Emil licks his lips and says, "The garden felt like a date. Last night felt like a date."

I can't even argue it. "Can I take you on *another* date, then?"

His lips twitch. A small smile. "I guess that would be okay."

"Well, shit, Specs. Don't sound so damn excited about it."

"Shut up," he grumbles, pushing me away before pulling me close again. We bump together, and he stares at my chest, working his lip between his teeth as his fingers twist in my shirt. *His* shirt. "It's been a while since I've dated."

"Yeah?" I ask, caging him against the counter. He doesn't seem to mind.

"I had a boyfriend before I started working at Elite 8," he says, continuing to toy with my shirt. "We were pretty vanilla, which was fine, but, uh... There was this one time I blew him in the car. We thought we were alone, or I wouldn't have. But we got caught, unintentionally, by a couple guys getting into the vehicle next to ours. Dane was mortified. But I..."

He huffs a laugh, and it's not hard to guess.

"You liked it," I say.

He nods. "So much. It was like this jolt to my system. I came in my pants, Christian. No one even touched me."

Damn. That's hot.

"After that," he goes on, "I couldn't get it out of my head. I kept trying to engage Dane in semi-public places, but he adamantly refused. We broke up shortly after that. Not really *because* of that. We weren't a great fit. But that was when I got a little reckless."

"What happened?" I ask softly, smoothing my fingers along his sides. For whatever reason, it seems like this is a story Emil needs to tell. And I'm happy to listen.

"I started having sex in clubs," he says. "In the bathrooms, mostly, but, uh... There was this one time when it was right in the hall. Plenty of people saw us, and I didn't even care. I loved it. It was like a drug."

"It's nothing to be ashamed of," I say gently.

He shakes his head, eyes meeting mine. "That's the thing. I'm *not* ashamed of it. Not in the least. But I'm on my way to getting my doctorate in psychology. I want to go into research, and I can't have a record, Christian. It could seriously affect my options."

"Whereas porn is legal," I say, making the connection.

He nods, eyes imploring me to understand, but I already do. "It's safe," he says. "And it's consensual for everyone involved.

I couldn't...couldn't trust that someone I started dating would understand how much that matters to me. Because when I'm in that place, that hazy, intoxicating place, logic shuts off and *want* overrides everything else. I'm not in control of myself. At least, I don't feel that way."

"Which is why you warned me last night."

There's a beat of silence before Emil says, "It's why I *trusted* you last night."

My pulse kicks, and Emil tugs me closer, his arms wrapping around my back.

"Christian... Before I even knew you, the very day after I moved in, you wrote me a letter. You saw me through the window, and you cared about *my* consent. You could have kept watching me, and I would have been none the wiser, but you didn't do that. I've trusted you since the beginning. I never have to worry when I'm with you. I know I'm safe."

I swallow roughly, my throat tight. "Specs... You'll be my first."

He cocks his head slightly. "Your first what?"

"Boyfriend."

His eyes pop wide, but all he does is tighten his arms. We're already flush, but the added pressure is nice. "Christian," he says softly.

"Mm?"

He leans close, tilting his head up so his lips are near my ear. "I'll go easy on you."

I bark a laugh, and Emil pulls back, grinning at me.

"Fuck, Specs," I mutter, tracing the shape of his mouth with my eyes. "My brave exhibitionist."

He snorts. "My beautiful voyeur."

There goes my heart again, thumping loudly, the beat impossible to ignore. "I was never much of a voyeur before you," I tell him truthfully.

He breathes out. "And I may be the one with boyfriend experience, but I don't really know what I'm doing, Christian. I'd never even cuddled on the couch until you."

"So I guess we're kind of in this together, huh?"

"That *is* the implied intent of dating," he says, lips twisting. "You do it together."

"You're such a little shit," I say fondly.

He laughs, lifting his chin in a proud display or a bid for a kiss; I'm not sure which. "You like it."

In answer, I drop my mouth to his. He sighs against me, hands flattening on my lower back. In no hurry to be anywhere else, I keep Specs pressed against the counter, and we kiss and kiss and kiss.

"So we have a couple different species of hermit crabs available," the pet store employee tells us as she leads Emil and I down a row of glass fish tanks. "You got your last one here?"

"Yeah, I did," Emil answers. Despite being nervous when he asked if I'd come with him to get Arthur a tank mate, Emil seems determined now as we stop in front of a selection of hermit crabs. He points to the ones that look like Arthur. "He's a *Coenobita clypeatus.* I think I'd like to get one about the same size."

"That's a good idea," the employee says. "You'll want an isolation tank for the first thirty to sixty days. What size is your terrarium?"

"Thirty gallons," Emil says.

"That's great," she chirps. "Plenty of space for two young crabs. Do you know the process for isolation and introduction?"

As Emil and the employee discuss the logistics of adding a crab to his terrarium, I bend down and watch the little crustaceans. The ones in this tank are itty bitty, like Arthur, with bodies in varying shades of orange. It's hard to imagine that Arthur could, one day, be the size of a baseball.

"What do you think of the one on the rock?" Emil asks, bending down next to me. "He's pretty cute, right?"

I glance over at my brand-new boyfriend as he bites his lip. "Adorable."

He nods absentmindedly, eyes sweeping the tank. "What if I choose wrong?"

I knock his shoulder gently with my own. "What does your gut say, Specs?"

He looks at me, letting out a breath. "For some reason, it's saying the one on the rock."

"Then that's the one you should get."

He nods again before standing upright. "Um, we're ready."

The employee helps us gather everything Emil needs for the isolation tank before loading his new hermit crab into a transportation carrier for the short trip home. Emil glances over at me and the crab in my lap every available chance as he drives.

"He's fine," I assure him for the tenth time.

Emil nods, but his tension doesn't dissipate until we're pulling into the parking lot behind his building. Between the two of us, we manage to bring everything up to his apartment in one trip. Emil sets to work outfitting the small tank, adding substrate and rocks and various bowls for water and food, while I continue to assure him his new crab is alive and well.

"Okay, it's ready," Emil says some time later.

Ever so carefully, he transfers the new hermit crab into the terrarium, a mini replica of the one Arthur resides in. We both watch, and Emil holds his breath as the new crab immediately burrows out of sight.

"Yeah, good," he says, blowing out a breath and nodding. "He'll need some time to destress, possibly molt. This is good."

I give Emil's shoulder a squeeze. "You're a good crab dad, Specs. Everything will be fine."

He snorts, but there's relief in his eyes when he looks my way. "Thanks for helping me do this."

"I'm not sure I did anything."

He shakes his head, resituating so that his leg is pressed against mine. We've barely been apart all weekend, but I like it. The closeness. Spending time with Specs.

"You're here, Christian," he says softly. "That's everything."

My gut swoops, the briefest sensation of free fall. It's so simple. And so big.

Is this what people mean when they say they're falling?

Slowly, I edge my pinkie over until it touches Emil's. He loops his own over top of mine and lays his head on my shoulder. Locked together, it's all too easy to make a vow.

If Emil needs someone to be there for him, I'll show up. Time and time again.

Chapter 17

EMIL

"Well, well. Look who it is. You've got some explaining to do, mister."

I let the door to the studio close behind me, wondering how in the hell Alex knew I was coming. "Were you waiting here for me?"

He scoffs, but he doesn't deny it. "You and Christian."

"Um," I say, skirting past the blonde menace to head down the hall. "Yeah?"

"Don't *yeah* me, Kent. What the hell is going on? The way you two were looking at each other Friday night... You can't tell me that was nothing."

I give Marco a nod as we pass in the hall. Luckily, when I enter the break room, Alex hot on my heels, the only other person present to witness my interrogation is Dixon.

Turning, I face the firing squad. "We're dating."

Alex's mouth falls open before he recovers. "Since when?"

"Saturday."

I can see his wheels spinning. "You, the guy who never dates, are going out with your coworker whom you've known for all of a few weeks?"

"Um..."

"Kent," he warns.

"We've known each other longer."

Silence falls, and Dixon snorts.

"You, hush," Alex says to our coworker before addressing me. "Define 'longer.'"

I sigh, knowing there's no way out of this. Alex is going to pry the truth from me, either slowly or by force. Might as well save myself the struggle.

"Christian lives next door to me. We met, or rather started texting, four months ago after he caught me jerking off through the windows of our respective apartment buildings. He applied for this job without knowing I worked here, and now...here we are."

Alex doesn't say a word. Not a single one.

"I think you broke him," Dixon mumbles before taking a sip of his latte. "Bravo."

"You..." Alex says before pausing. His eyes light. "*He's* the one you're always texting."

"You solved it, Lois," I say, taking a seat at one of the tables. I swing my bookbag to the ground as Alex sits across from me.

"Why were you hiding it?" he asks, expression and tone gentle if not a little confused.

Because our relationship, at the time, was based around the fact that I'm an exhibitionist who gets off on my neighbor watching me pleasure myself?

"Um..."

"Not everyone is as open with their lives as you are, Alex," Dixon points out.

"'Scuse you. Like that's a bad thing?" Alex retorts.

Dixon levels him with an unimpressed glare. "Pudding pop, darling, my little tater tot, there are things no person needs to know. Like how many cumulative dicks and fingers their coworker's ass can take."

Alex turns to me with a grin. "The answer is two plus three."

I blanch.

"And we're porn stars," Alex says, returning his attention to Dixon. "Like any of the intimate details of our *assets* are secret. Must I remind you where your tongue has been?"

"Jesus Christ," Dixon grumbles. "Why did I engage?"

I grab my bag, slipping from my seat while my coworkers are distracted.

"Grumpy Bear," Alex says, "just because you're allergic to sharing your own feelings doesn't mean everyone in class is."

"How in the hell did we get from DP to *feelings*?" Dixon asks in concern.

Nearly there...

"Because," Alex says proudly, "when my boyfriends share their *dicks* with me, I feel—"

The door to the break room closes behind me, thankfully blocking whatever *that* was. Dixon's responding groan comes through loud and clear.

"Don't even wanna know," I mutter, heading toward the locker room.

The space is empty when I arrive, and I stash my bag inside my locker before grabbing my shower supplies. Having come from a meeting with Nicole and Lucy about this week's allocation of research-related duties, I haven't yet cleaned up for my scheduled scene. I do that now, my mind, unsurprisingly, flashing to Christian.

As if my thoughts conjured the man himself, his voice rings out. "Specs?"

"Yeah," I call back. "It's me."

I'm nearly finished rinsing off when the shower curtain shifts to the side and a somewhat blurry Christian appears in my vision.

"What are you—"

Christian's lips fitting to mine bring my words to an abrupt halt. He backs me into the tile wall, his naked body pressing against me as he flings the shower curtain shut. A moan spills from my lips as his leg slots between my own.

I break our lip-lock to suck in a breath and finish my question. "What are you doing?"

"Kissing you," he says, his hand roaming around to my ass, lips at my neck. "Was that not obvious?"

"Oh my God," I mutter, shifting my cock against his hip as he sucks tiny kisses up to my ear.

"Mm. My horny exhibitionist," he murmurs, as if he wasn't the one to barge in here and all but tackle me. His fingers slide between my ass cheeks.

"Christian," I groan, my brain doing its best to rally. "We...we have a scene. We should save..." I lose my words to a moan as his fingers find their target, the tip of one digit pressing in.

"I won't make you come," he says before his mouth is back on mine.

I let Christian sweep me away, his finger teasing as his tongue destroys. Why this gorgeous man wants *me*, of all people, as his very first boyfriend, I can't figure out. But I trust him. And I want him, too. So I grab his hand, giving it a push, and Christian slips his finger in deeper.

I ride the digit as our tongues duel, his hand cupping my ass, his leg beneath my balls. It feels as if he's cradling me from all sides, and I realize I feel that often with Christian—surrounded, protected. Secure.

When I know I can't last much longer, I give Christian's hair a tug. "Stop."

He does immediately, his finger stilling and his head dropping to my shoulder. For a moment, we both simply...*breathe.*

I curse when his finger slips out of me. "What, uh...what was that for?"

Christian leans back, catching my eye. At least, it seems that way. With my farsightedness and astigmatism, it's impossible to see him clearly without my glasses.

His thumb travels along my lower lip. "I just wanted you all to myself for a minute. Is that okay?"

Fucking hell.

I nod as my heart pounds.

Christian grabs my shampoo. "Okay if I use this?"

I nod again, and a blurry but stunning Christian proceeds to wash his hair in front of me. I squint as best I can, trying to make out the details of his face and body, but they're lost to me for now. Christian's chuckle lets me know I've been caught.

"Do you ever wear contacts?" he asks.

"No. I tried them once, but I didn't like how they felt."

He hums. "The glasses suit you."

"You think so?"

"I do," he says, his arms in the air as he rinses the shampoo out of his hair. He lathers his body next. "They just fit you, you know? You're my Specs."

Oof.

"I think you might be bad for my heart," I say. *Aloud.*

"What?" Christian asks around a laugh.

I step closer, pulling his wet body against mine. "When we're on that bed, I want you to finger me open."

Christian's cock bucks against my hip.

"I want you to do it slowly," I say, "until I'm all but begging for your cock. I want you to take your time, make me incoherent, and only once I threaten bodily harm do I want you to fuck me into that mattress. You're going to do it hard, and you're going to do it fast, because I'll be too keyed up to tolerate anything else. You're going to show them, Christian. You'll show them who I belong to."

Christian's hand snakes into my hair, a shaky breath leaving his lungs as he pulls my head back gently. "Fuck, Specs. I think I'm infatuated with you."

I run my hands up the sides of his slender waist. "The feeling is entirely mutual."

He reaches over, shutting off the water. "Let's go."

After getting dressed, Christian stands in front of a mirror and blow-dries his hair. It doesn't take long. He adds a touch of product after that gives it an effortlessly tousled look, and then he turns his sights on me. I let Christian dry my hair, too, sitting on the bench seat in front of the mirrors, my fingers tracing over the grooves of Christian's hips and the dainty jeweled bar in his navel. When I lean forward to press my lips to the bulge in his pants, the blow-dryer turns off.

The next twenty minutes are a blur of scene setup and anticipation that thrums heavily through my veins. My head has already shut off, cognition having given way to baser wants, but I trust Christian to watch over me, my ever-present sentinel. My voyeur turned protector.

When I hear Christian addressing me, I snap back to consciousness, as if awaking from a dream. I realize we're already filming.

"Come on, Fe. I need my hands on you."

Not about to argue, I let Christian push me onto my back. He tugs off my pants and underwear, then my shirt, and rolls me to my stomach. I go like putty, his to command.

"Gorgeous," he mutters, the word for our viewers but also for me.

I lift my ass higher, getting up on my knees, and Christian's finger, cool and wet, circles my rim. He presses it inside of me, and I moan.

"Look at you, Fe," he praises, sliding that finger in and out, using a *come hither* motion that stretches me with every pass. "Your ass was made to be cherished. To be spread open and worshiped. You're a sight, and I get to show you off."

I nod frantically, breath hitching. "Please. More."

He presses in with two fingers, his other hand traveling along my taint. When he moves his hands in tandem, as if trying to bring the fingers of both hands together, I damn near shoot out of my skin.

"Oh fuck, *fuck*."

Christian chuckles, a dark yet warm sound. He continues to stroke me in the same way, the added pressure on my prostate making me concerned I might not *last* long enough for Christian to fuck me. But he gentles the motions before long, his hand on my taint running up over my ass cheek. His fingers continue fucking me leisurely.

"I like seeing you like this," he says.

"Like...what?" I huff between breaths.

"At my mercy," he answers.

"Oh, fuck you."

He laughs, knowing full well I love it. *And asked for it*. "No thanks. I'll be doing the fucking today."

"*Vixen*."

"In time, sweetheart. I'm not done playing."

I groan, but Christian continues to take his time, avoiding my prostate as he fingers me open. Two fingers slowly become three. He presses downwards as he moves, the tugging pressure on my rim damn near driving me mad.

"Come on," I moan. "I'm ready."

"Not quite," he says, his free hand cupping my balls. He rolls them in his palm, squeezing gently.

"*God*, fuck, Vixen."

"Mm."

"You—"

His hand slips along my cock, a single smooth stroke before his palm caresses the head, rolling, rolling, like he's chalking a pool stick.

"Need..." I garble.

"You need what?" he asks, giving me another full stroke on my cock as his fingers press deep into my ass.

"I need you to fuck me before I smother you with this pillow."

I toss it over my shoulder in demonstration, and Christian laughs, letting me know I probably hit the mark. His hand leaves my cock, smoothing over my backside as his fingers slowly retreat out of my ass.

"There it is," he says smugly. I feel him shuffle closer before his body blankets mine. His lips press to my ear, voice much too soft to be picked up by the boom. "The cutest threat to my person I've ever heard."

"I meant it," I whisper back.

"I know."

And with that, Christian lifts off of me and flips me onto my back. With quick efficiency, he sheathes his cock in a condom and tugs my legs up and into place around his hips. His hand settles under my ass as his other positions his cock, and *finally*, he's pushing inside of me.

I arch into it, accepting the stretch, marveling at how this feels just like the other times we've fucked. Familiar, almost. Right. As if, from the get-go, I really did consider Christian mine. And I was his.

The realization makes me feel almost unbearably vulnerable. But the sensation only lasts for a moment because Christian, having seated himself fully, bends forward and catches my lips. He punches his hips at an angle that has me crying out, and then he swallows down the sound, fucking me harder, damn near mercilessly just like I asked him to. I lock my ankles behind his ass and sink into the bedding, unable to do anything but.

I don't even realize I'm rambling, but when Christian's lips drop to my neck, I can hear the, "God, yes. Please. Yes," pouring from my mouth. Again and again, I plead, and again and again, Christian delivers. I feel like I might just burst apart, and when it hits me that *yes*, I'm about to, I gasp, "Coming."

Christian pulls back quickly, and I don't have time to mourn the loss before his hand is wrapping around my dick. "Come on. Paint yourself, beautiful."

And fuck, that's all it takes.

I come across my stomach and chest, my entire body seized tight. Christian groans, as if pained, and I realize it's because he's trying desperately to stave off his own orgasm.

As soon as I slump flat, I wave him forward. "Come on, come on."

He seems to get the hint because he pulls out and crawls up over my chest. I strip his condom as Christian falls on his hands above my head, and with his cock positioned over my face, I stroke. I barely have time to blink before he's coming across my cheeks and lips, his release hot on my skin. His accompanying moan is quite possibly the most satisfying sound I've ever heard.

As soon as Christian slumps, I let go of him. He scoots down my body, his eyes running up and down the mess on my skin before he barks a bright and joyous laugh. In a display of superb cheekiness, he brings his fingers to his lips and blows a chef's kiss.

"Perfect. A true masterpiece," he says.

I feebly kick at his leg. "You dick."

Laughing, Christian falls back over me and licks my lower lip. He drags his own cum up to my mouth, kissing me soundly, letting me taste his flavor. I'm pretty sure I can taste his smile, too.

It's not until there's a distinct and loud throat clear that the two of us break apart, both of our heads whipping to the side. Jerome is standing next to the camera, his eyebrow raised. The light is no longer blinking red.

"Gentlemen," our boss says evenly. "Once you're both cleaned up, a word."

Chapter 18

CHRISTIAN

"Are we in trouble?" I ask Emil the moment we're alone.

He winces. "I don't know. I doubt it. But, uh...we kind of checked out at the end there."

Understatement. I completely forgot about the cameras until Emil was clamping down on my cock and I remembered I couldn't come inside his body. But then we were kissing again, and...

"Shit," I mutter, holding the door to the locker room open.

Emil, clad in a robe, walks in ahead of me. "He won't be upset about the two of us," he says. "Dixon and Niko are dating."

"But they're not messing up lives."

"Not yet," he says with a shrug. "But live recording is always going to come with risk. It's not like anything *bad* happened. We just..."

"Got a little caught up in one another?"

"Yeah," he says softly, shooting me an almost shy smile. Admittedly, the fact that Emil isn't freaking out over what happened makes me feel better. "We should get cleaned up."

I nod, and Emil and I head for separate showers, not wanting to keep Jerome waiting.

When we get to our boss's office, the man himself is inside, looking at something on his computer. He waves us in, gesturing toward the seats in front of his desk. He doesn't keep us in suspense for long.

"I'm fairly certain," Jerome says dryly, "that I just watched two of my employees making love during a live broadcast. Somewhat filthy, kinda *rough* love, mind you. But love nonetheless. Is there anything I should know?"

I glance at Emil, whose eyes are wide.

Jerome sighs, leaning forward. "We don't have stipulations against fraternization in this studio, but I expect when you're here to work, you do your job. Which means paying attention to cues, not getting lost in each other's eyes for twenty goddamn minutes, got it?"

There's no heat in Jerome's words, despite the swearing.

I nod quickly. "Understood. Won't happen again."

Emil mirrors the sentiment next to me.

"Good," Jerome says, sitting back in his chair. "Now, if any adjustments need to be made to your partnering or scene preferences, that's information I should know."

When Emil and I share another glance, Jerome sighs.

"If you require monogamy," he says drolly. "Or...I don't know...if receiving facials from anyone but your beloved is now a limit."

Emil chokes next to me. "Um...no," he says hoarsely. "I'm good. No changes."

"Vixen?" Jerome asks.

I shake my head. "All good."

"Okay, then," our boss says, letting out a mighty breath. "In that case, get out of here. Let me know if anything changes. And I expect professionalism the next time you're on that set."

We both nod and scoot hastily out of our seats.

"And congratulations," Jerome calls as we reach the door. "I'll send you the tape for the wedding."

As the door clicks shut behind us, Emil bends over and grabs his knees. "Oh my God. Holy crap. That was so much worse than I expected."

I huff a laugh as Emil blows out a breath. I didn't think it was too bad.

"He said *beloved*," he mutters. "*Jerome.*"

Not only that, he said *making love*. Did we really look that smitten?

"His concern was kind of sweet," I note.

"Sweet?" Emil says incredulously, standing upright.

"I mean, he didn't even yell," I point out as the two of us head back down the hall. "It seemed like he just wanted to make sure we were both comfortable with our current work arrangements now that we're in a relationship. That's pretty respectful, actually."

"Yeah, I guess," he mumbles. "Still felt like a weird sort of sex talk with a parent."

I snort, not disagreeing.

Emil pushes the door to the locker room open, and we head inside. Teddy is standing near the lockers, and a shower is running.

"We'll need to be more careful," I say quietly.

Emil nods. "Yeah. Do you think we can find a way to keep emotions out of it while we're here?"

I hum, stopping with Emil near his locker. "Honestly, I don't know. It's been different with you from the start, Specs. I'm not sure I can turn that off."

He blushes, a sight that has my chest warming.

"We'll need to stay more focused then," Emil says, grabbing his bookbag from his locker. "No more slip-ups."

"Agreed," I say, watching Emil's profile as he swings his bag onto his shoulder.

He closes his locker door, pausing when he sees me staring. "What?"

"I don't know," I admit, not sure how to explain the pressure in my chest. "Guess I just like watching you."

Emil snorts, nudging his glasses up. "Creeper."

"*Your* creeper," I say happily. "You have class?"

"Yeah. Are you coming over later?"

"You bet." I hesitate for only a moment before adding, "I still want to kiss you when we're here at the studio. Can I do that?"

His lips twitch. "You better."

Grinning, I tug Emil in. He comes willingly, his bag knocking into my hip as our lips meet. He smells like eucalyptus from his soap, and I inhale deeply, wondering why I can't seem to get enough of this man. Now that I can kiss him anytime I want, I never want to stop. I want our mouths planted together, his lips mine to devour. I want to feel his body against me and hear the soft sounds that pour out of his throat every time I skate my fingers along his skin. I want to curl myself around him late at night after the sun has gone down and earn those smiles he gives me when I do something right.

I never wanted a boyfriend, not before. But with Emil, everything feels right.

I pull back before I'm tempted to drag Emil somewhere private and show him how I feel. He looks a little flushed, and it's reassuring to know I'm not the only one affected. I give his shirt a tug, straightening it. "Have a good class, Specs."

"Um, yeah."

He walks out of the room in a bit of a daze, and I smile to myself.

Teddy catches my eye, raising an amused brow. "Guess Kipp was right," he says, shutting his locker.

"About what?"

His lips twitch. "He bet me the two of you were an item."

"And you took that bet?"

The twinkle in his eye only grows. "Sure did. The prize was well worth it."

I cock my head. "Yeah? What did Kipp want for winning?"

Teddy's smile turns smug. "Let's just say...it'll be a toss-up whether his ass or my hand is more sore in the end."

A laugh jumps out of my mouth, and Teddy winks. *Damn*, I guess Emil isn't the only kinky one around here. Although, frankly, I don't think anyone can compete with Specs.

My dirty little exhibitionist. My boyfriend.

Mine.

"Noel, hey."

"Hey, Christian," my friend says, dropping into a seat across from me at the coffee shop we agreed to meet at. He looks rough, his clothes a little rumpled and eyes tired. I frown.

"Everything okay?"

"Long night," he answers, which only has my concern growing. It's midafternoon.

"When's the last time you slept?"

He stops to think about it, which tells me enough. "The night before last? I spent the morning at a hospital."

I jolt. "Shit. Noel, what happened?"

He groans, scrubbing over his eyes before slumping against the edge of the table. "Max got fired."

"What?" I ask in alarm. "What does that have to do with being at the hospital?"

"He broke up a fight and ended up with stitches," Noel answers. Seeing my face, he adds, "He's *fine*. It was two stitches right here." He taps his temple. "No other injuries, and he already got discharged. But *shit*, Christian, our boss didn't even care."

"No, I don't suppose he did," I say, my voice hard. *Fuck*.

"It wasn't even Max's fault," Noel says, almost as if he's pleading with me to understand. "The customer started it. Max just stepped in to break up the fight. It wasn't his fault."

He sounds so dejected, and I reach across the table to squeeze his arm. "You should get out of there, Noel. A club like that should have hired security, but there's none. The owner doesn't care about the safety of his employees, only about profits."

Noel nods. "I know you're right. And it's only going to get worse now that you *and* Max are gone. But what else am I supposed to do?"

"Anything you want."

"You know the world doesn't work like that, Christian. I have no skills other than serving drinks."

"Noel, there are so many other bars or clubs you could work at. *Better* ones. Or, hey, what about a coffee shop?"

He huffs a laugh, looking around. "It would be kinda nice to work during the day."

"See?" I say, giving his arm a prod. "You have choices. Just...please consider them."

He nods again before sighing. "I'm gonna grab a muffin or something. I'm kind of hungry."

"Of course," I say. "I'll be here."

Noel slides off his chair and heads to the counter while I sip my tea, gut churning. I knew Knee Highs was bad news from the moment I started working there, but Noel and I got close fast, and I didn't want to leave him behind. Plus, I figured I could hold my own, so what would be the harm?

But when you have someone running the place who doesn't care about what happens to his employees, people are bound to get hurt. Like Max.

I don't want the same to happen to Noel.

When Noel returns, he has a large blueberry muffin on a plate. He slides into the seat across from me and starts removing the wrapper. "*Soo*, how's the whole porn star thing going? You haven't said much about it."

I huff a laugh. "I'm far from a star."

"You know what I mean," he says, rolling his eyes. "Tanner said you seem to be settling in fine."

"Yeah, it's been great," I say truthfully. "I, uh... I'm seeing someone."

Noel perks up, looking energized for the first time since coming into the coffee shop. "You are? What's he like?"

"Smart," I say instantly, a little smile taking over my face. "Cute. Sexy. He's gentle but can be pushy, too. He's shy and bold, sweet and fucking filthy. He hates taking compliments but dishes them out in the most sincere way. And being around him is like...like the sun after a storm, you know? He's bright. *Good*."

Noel looks at me curiously.

"What?" I ask.

"It's just...you really like him, don't you? I've never heard you talk about anyone like that."

I twist my cup of tea between my palms. "Yeah, I really do."

"He doesn't mind the porn?" Noel asks, picking off a piece of his muffin and popping it into his mouth.

It's a valid question. But... "Considering he's my scene partner, no, I don't think he minds."

Noel coughs, his hand stopping the spray of crumbs. "Holy crap. That's—" He clears his throat, thumping his chest once. "It's like some sort of modern-day fairy tale."

I huff a laugh. "Ah, yes. The classic *porn stars falling madly in love* story."

He shakes his head. "Shush, it's romantic. Who is he?"

"Would you know if I told you his name?" I ask. When Noel looks down at his plate sheepishly, I realize...*yes*, he would. "Noel, do you have a subscription? Have you watched *me*?"

His cheeks redden, and he mumbles, "My cousin works there. I'm *supportive*."

I snort, not minding in the least if he's seen my videos. "It's Felix."

He nods, expression thoughtful as he chews the last of his muffin. "Huh, yeah. I can see that. He's hot, but not in, like, a *bench you over his head* sort of way."

"Yeah," I say softly, lips twitching as I imagine Emil hulked up like a gym bro. "Speaking of buff men... Are you ever going to tell Max you like him?"

Noel coughs again.

I reach across the table, giving his arm a squeeze. "He has no clue, Noel. He thinks he makes you nervous."

"He *does*," Noel says. "Have you seen the guy?"

"Yeah, but it's a good sort of nervous, and we both know it. You should tell him," I encourage. "You spent the morning at the hospital with him, right? He would have sent you away if he didn't want you around."

"You really think so?" he asks, voice quiet.

"I do."

"I'll think about it," he murmurs. But then he yawns, loudly.

I give his arm another squeeze before letting go. "We should get out of here. You look beat."

"Yeah. Probably not a bad idea."

Noel and I return our dishes to the counter before heading for the door. He promises to keep me updated about Max and the club, and I promise the same of Emil and the studio. On my walk home, my thoughts flit to my boyfriend. He'll be back from class soon, and I'm pretty sure we've got a date lined up that involves him, me, the couch, and our favorite nature documentarian. I wonder what Arthur and his new friend would like to eat for dinner tonight. Maybe some strawberries?

It hits me, as I'm a block from my apartment, that I'm making plans that involve someone other than just me for once. A few someones, if you count tiny, adorable hermit crabs, which I do.

I don't hate it.

I don't hate it one bit.

Chapter 19

Emil

"Have you picked a name yet?" Christian asks, his thumb distracting me as it glides over the skin near my belly button.

"A name?"

"For your new hermit crab," he says, chuckling.

"Oh. Right. Um, not yet."

He hums, the vibration of it feeling almost like a purr. Before I can rub back against him like a cat myself, my phone rings. I pick it up, seeing my brother Henry's name on the screen.

"Hello?" I answer.

"Hey," he says simply.

I scoot up, and Christian lets me go, rolling onto his back as I sit beside him. "What's up?"

"So, I was wondering..."

My brother goes quiet, and I look at the time. It's a school night, but early still. If he's calling, there's a reason. "Want me to pick you up?"

"Yeah. Can we go to that arcade by your place?"

I huff a laugh. "I actually moved, but yeah, we can still go there. Be ready in fifteen?"

"You got it," Henry says and clicks off the call.

I turn toward Christian. "Want to play some arcade games with a fourteen-year-old?"

"Your brother?" he asks. I nod, and he grins, but the expression falls quickly away. "Should I go change first?"

"What? Why?" I say, glancing at his outfit. He's wearing a skirt today, which isn't a surprise. But unlike some of his bolder, *shorter* options, this one is long and black, with a bit of a flare that makes it billow out when he walks. He paired it with a t-shirt that has a somewhat distressed, vintage feel. It's a casual look, perfect for the arcade, so I'm not sure why he would want to change. "You look great. You don't need to be fancy for this."

He cocks his head slightly. "The skirt, Specs. Would your brother be offended by the skirt?"

I nearly laugh but stop short fast. Christian doesn't know my family. His concern is justified, as shitty as that fact is. And since I'm fairly positive Christian isn't in the habit of hiding himself for anyone else's benefit, the idea that he's willing to do that just to make a good impression with my family is sweet yet tastes like a bitter pill.

"I don't want you to be anyone but who you are," I tell him seriously. "My brother will like you because I like you. Don't change."

Not your clothes. Not anything.

Christian's expression softens, and he sits up at the same time as he leans forward, snagging my bottom lip between his teeth. It's a kiss, yes, but there's bite to it. It feels very much like a claim. "All right, Specs," he says against my mouth. "Ready when you are."

I nod, we disentangle, and after putting on our shoes, Christian and I head out the door.

Henry is sitting at the top of the porch steps when I pull up to my parents' house. He hops up and sticks his game inside his pocket as he comes jogging over to the car. He opens the door and drops onto the backseat with all the finesse of a teenager.

"Do Mom and Dad know I'm stealing you?" I check.

He nods, hair flopping over his forehead. "Yup."

"Okay, then." I back out of the driveway, waiting until we're going forward to make introductions. "Henry, this is my boyfriend Christian."

"Hey," Henry says.

"Nice to meet you," Christian replies.

"You didn't have a boyfriend the last time I saw you," my brother informs me.

I snort. "No, I didn't."

"I'm telling Bec," he says, pulling out his phone.

Christian raises a brow, but I shake my head. "It's fine," I tell him more than my brother, knowing the text has likely already been sent.

It doesn't take long to get to the arcade near my old apartment building. The parking lot is fairly empty tonight, and Henry bursts from the car before I've even turned off the ignition.

"Never stops, that one," I say wryly.

Christian looks amused.

We catch up with Henry inside of the arcade. The pinging and clanking of various games echo off the walls as we walk up to the attendant, neon lights giving the place a futuristic feel befitting the theme. Henry is engrossed in his phone as I fork over enough cash to get us a small bucket of tokens. When my brother finally pulls his face out of his game, he notices Christian's skirt.

"Are you nonbinary?" he asks my boyfriend.

"I... No, I'm not," Christian answers, seemingly taken aback by my brother's bluntness.

"He/him, then?" Henry asks.

"That's right."

"Okay. Me, too," my brother says, grabbing the bucket of tokens and hustling away.

Christian looks at me, eyes wide. "Kids these days, am I right?"

I bark a laugh, grabbing his hand and twining our fingers together. "We're all woke."

He snorts, and I tug him along after Henry, curious what my brother wants to say to me that he hasn't yet worked up the courage for. He's at a Skee-Ball machine, and I take up position next to him, letting go of Christian's hand to send a ball flying.

For a while, we simply play, hitting all of my brother's favorite games and a couple of my own. Christian doesn't seem as familiar with them, but he joins in, smiling the whole while. He even manages to beat my brother on the dance pads, a sight that has me wanting to drag Christian back to the club to see what he'd look like *really* letting loose. We only slow danced together, and I didn't realize it at the time, but I think I was missing out. Christian is sexy as fuck, which, sure, I already knew. But *damn*. Maybe he'd show me some of his less PG moves later.

When Christian heads off to grab us all drinks, I catch Henry glancing at me. I know that look.

"Want to talk about it?" I ask, taking a seat at a nearby table.

He sits across from me and shrugs. "It's nothing."

I wait him out.

"It's just... I think Mom and Dad are disappointed in me."

His statement hits my chest with all the blunt force of a hammer. "What makes you think that?" I ask, my own old wounds flaring beneath my sternum.

"I don't know," he says with a huff. "I'm not a big deal like Julian or out saving the world like Eloise. I can't play an instrument like Bec, and I'm not smart like you. I'm just me, which isn't much."

"Hey," I say sternly, catching Henry's eye. "Just you is worth a hell of a lot, okay? It doesn't matter what you do with your life or whether or not you follow anyone else's footsteps. You're important to me, to Bec, to Mom and Dad, and to Eloise and Julian. You're important to your friends and people you probably don't even know. You're important, point blank. And being smart in your own way doesn't make you not good enough, Henry. You could never be a disappointment."

Even as I say it, I wonder why I have such trouble believing the words myself. But I don't linger on the thought while Henry is sitting in front of me, looking so uncharacteristically down.

"I don't want the things everyone else wants, Emil," he says. "Sometimes I feel like I'm missing some important piece. Like something was left out during manufacturing, and now I don't function the way I'm supposed to."

"Are you unhappy with who you are?" I ask.

"No," he says, and I can tell he means it, which is a relief. "I like myself. But that doesn't change the fact that I'm different."

From the corner of my eye, I spot Christian approaching. He stops a few feet away from the table, drinks in hand, likely having caught on to the fact that Henry and I are having a serious conversation. But before he can back away, Henry notices him. Christian walks the remaining distance to the table and sets down our drinks.

"Should I come back?" he asks.

Henry shakes his head and grabs his soda. Christian mouths *sorry*, but I give a little headshake. It's not his fault.

Christian takes a seat, and, much to my surprise, says, "I'm different, too."

Henry lifts his gaze off the table. "What do you mean?"

Christian fiddles with the straw in his drink before saying, "I never knew my dad, but my grandma told me about him. He worked in construction when he and my mom met. Before that, back in high school, he played football. He was the hypermasculine type, you know? And all my mom seemed to see when she looked at me were the ways I was different from him. She had a box she expected me to fit in, and I never did. My grandma, though, she also told me my dad was kind and sensitive. Sometimes I wonder what he would have thought of me, but I'll never get to know that."

I set my hand on Christian's arm, my heart aching. It's not difficult to read between the lines. His dad is gone, one way or another, from Christian's life. He shoots me a tiny smile, a *brave* smile, before going on.

"I haven't fit in many people's boxes, Henry. I'm gay and femme. I wear skirts but have body hair. I'm vocal when some people expect me to be meek. And it took me time to be comfortable with all that. Being different isn't *bad*. The important part is whether or not you're happy. So fuck anyone who doesn't get that, and if your parents aren't proud of the person you are, then that's on them, not you."

For a beat, Henry simply stares at Christian, his eyes wide. I stare, too.

Christian turns to me and winces. "Too much? I probably shouldn't have said fuck, huh?"

I shake my head, huffing a laugh as my heart beats a fast staccato inside my chest. "No. It was perfect." Christian gives me a relieved smile, and I turn to my brother. "Henry?"

His gaze meets mine.

"I'm proud of you all the time," I tell him, meaning it. "I thought that the last time I saw you. You're strong and independent, you think for yourself, you care about your friends and family, and you *are* smart, whether or not you think it. Didn't you tell me you figured out a cheat for your game that lets you map the best spots to mine precious gems based on loot drop rates?"

"Yeah," he says quietly.

"See? I don't know anyone else who could write code like that at fourteen. You're your own person, and I'm really proud of that person. And Christian is right. If Mom and Dad can't see all that you are, that's on them." I speak past the lump in my throat to add, "But I don't think they're disappointed in you."

"You don't?" he asks.

I shake my head. "I think they just forget sometimes that we need to hear the things they think in their heads."

He nods, looking down.

"Want me to grab some more tokens?" I ask, looking inside the empty bucket. "We could stay a while longer. It's only..." I check my phone and cringe. "Eleven."

Henry huffs a small laugh. "It's past my bedtime."

"Yeah, well, Mom and Dad can be mad at me for keeping you out."

"Thanks, Emil," he says, voice quiet but a little lighter. "I'm ready to go home, though."

"All right," I say before giving Christian's arm a nudge. *Thank you*, I mouth.

His lips twist into a smile.

The three of us leave the same way we came, Christian in the front passenger seat of my car and Henry in back. We're quiet on the drive to my parents', but Henry is back to playing his game, so he must not be too upset.

When I park, Henry opens his door.

"Hey, Henry?" I say before he has a chance to climb out. "Thank you for calling me."

"Yeah, Emil," he responds. "You're always easy to talk to."

With that, he scoots out the door, leaving my chest swirling with a mixture of happiness and something foreign and a little hot. I watch Henry make his way inside before turning to Christian.

"Would you give me five minutes?" I ask.

He nods slowly. "Of course."

"Thanks," I say, opening my door.

My feet carry me toward the house on autopilot, that burning in my chest propelling me forward. The front door is unlocked, and I step inside, not bothering to toe off my shoes. I don't see Henry in the living room when I pass, and he's not in the kitchen, either. But my father is.

"Emil?" my dad says, looking up from his laptop, which is sitting in front of him on the kitchen table. His glasses are perched on the end of his nose, and he lowers his head a little to see me over them. "Did you see this article?"

I step around the table to get a look at what he's talking about. It's a medical journal, this particular article co-authored by my brother Julian, the cardiac surgeon. Julian, the *big deal*, as Henry called him. The firstborn who followed in our father's footsteps, even going so far as to work in the same hospital where our dad is a surgeon still.

"I saw it," I tell him.

He hums, the single sound full of so much appreciation and parental pride that I snap, just a little.

"Henry thinks he's a disappointment to you and Mom."

My dad looks at me sharply, plucking his reading glasses off his nose. "Pardon?"

"Henry. Your youngest son. He thinks he's a failure. He's *fourteen.*"

"Why on Earth would he think that?" my dad asks, sounding genuinely perplexed.

"Really?" I say a touch hotly. "You have no idea?" I wave my hand at the laptop. "Maybe because you can't go a day without spouting off about Jules's successes?" I point at the fridge next, where there's a picture of Eloise and her wife next to one of Rebecca holding her violin. "Maybe because in last year's Christmas card, Mom gushed all about her activist daughter's win against big oil and her youngest daughter's solo exhibition that was 'art in its purest form,' but Henry got a single line about how he's growing up and in high school now?"

My dad blinks at me.

"Do you really not see it?" I ask, my voice betraying me by wobbling. "How is he supposed to know you care when you never *show* it?"

"Emil," my mom says quietly from the doorway. I hadn't even heard her approach.

I turn, speaking to the both of them. "Don't assume, just because he never says anything, that Henry knows you're proud of him. He's hurting, and neither of you can see it."

With that, I walk out of the kitchen and through the front door. My blood is pumping, my face is hot, and righteous indignation continues to course through my veins as I stomp down the steps toward my car. I don't think that was the con-structive conversation my therapist has been encouraging me to have with my parents, but it felt fucking good nonetheless, even if it was for Henry's benefit and not mine. Even if my own hurt and anger are still roiling inside of me like a pot left unchecked.

It doesn't matter. For once, I said the words my parents needed to hear. My brother deserves someone in his corner, and I'll always be that for him.

If only I knew how to stick up for myself.

Chapter 20

CHRISTIAN

When Emil returns to the car, he's practically vibrating. He shuts the door with a bang and pulls his seatbelt into place with jerky movements.

"Okay?" I ask, even though it's obvious he's not.

He nods once, swiftly, and backs down the drive.

"Did something happen?" I say carefully. I've never seen Emil angry before.

He doesn't answer me for a good block. "I yelled at my parents."

My eyes widen. "You yelled? Damn, Specs. I would've paid to see that."

He huffs a laugh, which makes me feel marginally better. His eyes meet mine before he refocuses on the road. "I'm sorry about your dad."

My gut pinches, but I shrug it off. "He passed before I was born."

"Still," Emil says, reaching over like he wants to comfort me. It's a little clumsy, his hand hovering in the air for a moment, but finally, his palm lands on my thigh, and he squeezes once. "Sorry about your mom, too."

"What do you mean?" I ask, taking his hand in my own, positive I'm supposed to be the one reassuring *him* right now, not the other way around.

"I'm sorry she wasn't what you deserved," he answers.

My breath punches out of my lungs. How can such a simple statement mean so much?

"Pretty sure tonight isn't about me," I say gently.

He huffs. "Deflecting."

"Thank you, Mr. Psych Major," I tease. "How about when you start accepting compliments, I'll accept conversations about my familial baggage?"

"Touché," he mutters, lips twitching as he takes a turn.

I eye his profile, gaze running over the planes of his face in the dim interior of the car. I want to ask about his parents, but maybe it's not the best time with Emil driving. So, instead, I point out something else on my mind. "You," I say seriously, "have the most gorgeous eyebrows."

"What?" he asks in surprise, head whipping my way for a second.

"They're perfect," I say, tracing the one nearest me with my finger. "They give away your mood sometimes. Like when you're *thinking* serious versus when you're being *studious* serious. Or when you're *embarrassed* happy versus *excited* happy."

He glances at me again, a befuddled expression on his face.

"There," I say. "*Embarrassed* happy."

"I...don't even know what to say."

"You could say, 'thank you, I'm so glad you like my eye awnings.'"

Emil barks a laugh, looking at me again. "Thank you, Christian, for being the weirdest, most wonderful boyfriend."

"Nuh-uh," I say, tugging his hand up to my mouth and nipping the tip of his finger. "Now *you're* deflecting. You wrote off my compliment by calling me weird."

He puffs a breath through his nose. "I also called you wonderful."

"*Specs.*"

"Fine," he groans. "Thank you."

I lean over and smack a kiss against his cheek. "You're welcome."

Emil has a little smile on his face for the rest of the drive home. But once we park in the lot behind his building, his tension returns.

"Okay?" I ask.

"Actually, could, uh... Could I come over to your place tonight?"

My heartbeat trips. "Yeah?"

There's his *shy* happy smile. "Yeah. If that's okay?"

"Of course, Specs. Need to grab anything from your place first?"

"Might as well since we're right here."

I nod, and Emil and I head up to his apartment. He feeds Arthur and checks on the new hermit crab, who Emil thinks is molting, considering the little fella hasn't reappeared or eaten in days. I'm not sure how much he can determine with the crab burrowed out of sight as he is, but Emil seems satisfied after looking into his tank.

I follow along as Emil packs a very small bag, consisting of a change of clothes and a few toiletries. With that in hand, we lock up and head the short way down the street to my building. Emil looks around as we climb the stairs, as if he's wandering into a brand-new world.

"How's it feel being on the other side of the curtain?" I ask.

Emil huffs. "Let me in, and I'll tell you."

Grinning, I unlock my door and throw it open. Emil steps in ahead of me, his head on a swivel.

"Whoa," he says quietly.

"Pretty great, right?"

Although small, the apartment is beautiful. My grandma picked a bold, bright teal for the walls, and on the far side of the room, she hand-painted a massive cherry blossom tree in full bloom. The building is old, so it has some character you don't see in most modern apartments around here, like crown molding on the ceilings and gold fixtures in the kitchen and bathroom. Even the light plates are gold.

Emil walks around, taking it all in. I could probably update some of the furniture, like the dated, floral couch, but I haven't yet been able to bring myself to change a thing.

When Emil reaches my open bedroom door, he looks back at me.

"Go ahead," I tell him with a chuckle.

He walks inside, glancing at my bed. His eyes sweep over to the closet next, and then he spots the sewing table. He heads that way.

"That's Bernie," I tell him.

His eyebrows pop up.

"The sewing machine," I explain. "She's a Bernina. Hence, Bernie."

Emil makes a soft sound, his fingers tracing ever so lightly over her surface. I feel the motion like a caress, and my dick perks, which is just... *Huh*. I don't know what that is.

He sits on the chair in front of the table, looking out the window. "There it is. My bed."

"Looks better with you in it."

His lips twitch. "Want me to go over there so you can double-check?"

"Nuh-uh," I say, stepping closer. "Not this time, Specs. Tonight, you're all mine."

He meets my gaze, hand lifting to give my skirt a little tug. I step between his legs, and he starts bunching up the fabric.

"What'cha doing, Specs?"

In answer, he lifts the material up to my waist. My dick strains against the front of my underwear as Emil leans forward, skimming his cheek over my hardening cock. I mutter a curse.

His eyes lift to mine, mere millimeters separating the two of us.

"Anything you want, Specs," I tell him, knowing it's the truth.

His request is simple. "Watch me."

"As if I could look away."

Emil blinks slowly before leaning forward and mouthing my dick, his exhalations hot through the fabric of my underwear. I suck in a breath and reach above his head to swipe the blinds shut, mindful of Emil's request to keep these sorts of activities private when we're outside the bounds of the studio. Emil quickly finds the zipper on the side of my skirt, and the fabric falls to my feet. His fingers curl in my skimpy briefs next, and he tugs them down.

"I haven't had a chance to do this on my own terms," he says before wrapping a hand around my cock and licking the head.

"I'm at your disposal," I rasp out.

A smile curls his lips. "So selfless."

My rebuttal is silenced by his mouth sliding forward. The heat of him surrounds me like an embrace, smooth and wet, the pressure exquisite.

"Would..." I huff out a breath as Emil's cheeks hollow. "Would I sound like an asshole if I told you you're the most beautiful cocksucker?"

His laughter is quite possibly the sexiest thing I've ever heard. *Or* seen. Because it's accompanied by his lips wrapped around me tight and a sly gleam in his eye that tells me he knows *exactly* how good he looks while doing this.

"Gorgeous," I say again. He deserves to hear it. "Can I fuck your throat, Specs?"

Emil goes still, looking up at me through thick lashes, his answer clear.

I thread my fingers through his hair, punching my hips forward slowly. The sight of my cock sinking between Emil's lips has my gut tightening alarmingly fast. His hands flex on my hips, thumbs pressing against the sensitive skin near my hip bones. I jerk, seating myself fully inside his throat, and Emil gives me an encouraging moan.

"Fuck," I mutter, setting a slow, steady pace as I fuck Emil's mouth. His eyelashes flutter, and the reminder that he can deepthroat for two full minutes floats into my mind. But I don't want to test the limits of Emil's breathing. Not right now. Knowing what he's capable of is heady enough. "You, Specs... You're breathtaking."

Brown eyes blink up at me, tear-filled and wanting. He gives my hips a squeeze, and I stop, letting Emil take over again. He grabs the base of my cock as his mouth sets to work, his head bobbing up and down, his tongue flicking over my slit on each pass. I grunt, my stomach clenching beneath his fingertips.

"Fuck, Specs."

He moans, his eyes never leaving mine. When he starts sucking rhythmically and pressing my balls up against my body, rolling them as if encouraging them to tighten and release, I damn near shout. He sinks down on me again, strong suction as he pulls off, his tongue flicking, his hand squeezing and working my base, and—

"Coming," I warn him.

He looks victorious, and a second later, I shoot down his throat. He swallows around me, gentling his suction once I'm spent but keeping his lips wrapped around me like the gift they are. As soon as I pull from his mouth, I drop down, taking those lips with my own. Emil's tongue greets mine, and he shares my taste with me. I suck it down, wanting to imprint it on my memory: the combination of him and me. *Us.*

Sitting back, I crouch in front of the chair Emil is perched on. He's still hard.

"Stroke yourself for me, Specs."

It's a request, not a demand, but he doesn't hesitate. He unzips his pants, pulls out his cock, and starts working himself over furiously as I watch. I tug up his shirt and take his nipple into my mouth.

Emil cries out, his hand in my hair holding me in place. I flick his nipple in time to his strokes, and when Emil's quick breaths let me know he's about to come, I pop off, twist the bud between my fingers, and bend down to wrap my lips around the head of his cock.

It's all over from there. Emil spurts into my mouth with a surprised gasp, his groan quickly following. His hips jerk off the chair, and I keep working his nipple between my fingers, my tongue soothing his dick until he slumps.

"Fucking fuck," he mutters, breathing heavily, his glasses askew on his nose. The sight has something warm tumbling through my chest, and I smile to myself as I set them to rights. "Thanks."

I huff a laugh. "Mhm. C'mon, Specs. Let's wash up."

Emil follows me to the bathroom, where we clean our hands, brush our teeth, and snort-giggle like schoolkids every time we catch each other's eye in the mirror. There's a blush on Emil's cheeks that's incredibly endearing, considering it wasn't there while I was fucking his face. In the bedroom, Emil strips down to his briefs while I pull on my favorite silky pajamas. When he climbs onto my bed and sinks down against the rumpled comforter as if letting the weight of the world off his shoulders, I can only stop and stare.

I wouldn't call Emil a high-strung person. But there's often a tension lining his frame that seems to be a part of his everyday existence. I didn't even notice it until after we first had sex, when that tension was entirely absent. But as soon as he got off that bed and wrapped a robe around his body, it returned.

I think there's a pressure Emil lives with, something he's maybe used to and doesn't think much about. It's a bookbag slung over his shoulder even when nothing is there. It's the high expectations he's set for himself and his attempt to always reach a little bit further. It's the worry he's falling short, perhaps, which I'm starting to think has to do with his family.

We're all living with our own weights, measures we've set for ourselves or had placed upon us. But seeing Emil so relaxed on my bed, as if he's able, at least for a little while, to let it all go... It rocks me to my core. I'm not sure what I did to deserve that.

"Hey," I say softly.

Emil turns his head as I climb in next to him, his eyes remaining closed. I grab his glasses off the pillow, placing them on the nightstand so they won't get crushed. Emil barely moves as I settle beside him and run my fingers through his hair, but he offers a soft, sleepy smile.

"Can I ask you something?"

He nods, reaching for me. I scoot closer, and he wraps a leg around me, the simple gesture making my heart stutter.

I almost don't want to open my mouth, but I do. "Your parents?"

Emil sighs ever so slightly, his eyes finally opening. His gaze looks a little unfocused as he finds my face. "They're not bad people," he says, and the statement hurts. The fact that he has to preface whatever he's going to say with that? It makes me think Emil is used to defending them, even inside his own head.

I give him a small nod, and then, in case he can't see it, add, "Listening."

"I don't think they mean to play favorites," Emil says. "But there are five of us. Julian, Eloise, me, Rebecca, and Henry. Henry and me...we're the ordinary ones in comparison to everyone else. I don't... I don't want my brother to feel like I did growing up. Like I was invisible. Forgotten."

"Specs," I say quietly.

He shakes his head, grabbing me and tucking his face against my chest. His words are spoken over my heart. "I know they love me. Henry, too. But it still..."

He swallows, as if saying this aloud is hard for him. I rub his back, my fingers drifting lightly over his skin. He relaxes against me when I scratch the area between his shoulder blades, so I keep it up.

"It still hurts," he finally says, "when the people who created you, the ones who raised you, don't seem to see who you are."

I have to blink my eyes a few times. "Yeah, Specs. I get that."

He nods against me. He knows.

"Your grandma," he says, his own question evident in his tone. "You said she's the most important person in your life."

"Yeah," I say, clearing my throat. "She's always been in my corner, for as long as I can remember."

"I'm glad you have her."

"Me, too."

Emil exhales, and I know it's late, past midnight at this point. He'll need to be up early for class. But there's one last thing I need to say.

"Specs?"

"Mm?"

"You're far from ordinary."

He goes still, body and breath both. "You think?"

I squeeze him like my own life-sized pillow. He smells clean, and I don't know whether or not I'm imagining it, but I swear there's still a hint of *us*, too.

"Specs," I say, amazed this man can't see what I do. "I *know* so."

Chapter 21

EMIL

A textbook sits open in front of me. An empty energy drink is beside my arm. I've been studying for my Behavioral Neuroscience exam for so long I'm not even sure what time it is. Early evening, I think?

I rub my eyes, the words in front of me starting to blur together. When my phone pings, I nearly jump. Setting down my half-chewed pencil, I pick up the device to find a text from my brother.

Henry: Did you say something to Mom and Dad?

Shit. I blow out a breath and text back.

Me: Yeah, I did.

There's a bit of a pause before his response comes through.

Henry: Thanks, Emil.

The tension in my chest uncorks.

Me: Of course.

They must have talked, then. I hope, for Henry's sake, my parents do a better job of showing him they care.

I cut a glance out through the window. The blinds in Christian's bedroom are open, but he's not there. He mentioned going to visit his grandma today, so he's probably still at the nursing home.

Usually, I have no problem studying all hours of the day or night by myself, the room around me quiet. But today, I can't help but wish Christian were here, lying beside me, tapping away on his phone and occasionally chuckling in that soft way he does. It's alarming how fast I got used to his presence, and how, now, everything that was once *optimal studying conditions* feels sterile and cold.

With a huff, I close my textbook and head into the living room. Arthur is hiding at the moment, as if he, too, decided to thwart me in my attempt to find company. With the new crab firmly underground and me left with nothing but my own thoughts, I sit down and open Christian's Instagram.

He's been posting photos every few days as Vixen, most of them suggestive in nature yet somehow still classy. He doesn't show enough skin to need censorship, but the pictures have heat rushing through me regardless. I'm not surprised to see the massive following he's grown in only a few short weeks.

Curious, I click on the most recent picture. Comments are all over the place. People telling him he's hot. Others saying lewd things. A few asking if he's available. There are a couple replies mentioning *me*. Or, well, Felix.

I heard from Alex that our fanbase went a little wild after the teensy tiny screw-up in our live. Frankly, I'm glad they suspect we're dating. We *are*, as outrageous as that seems to me. Christian is so incredibly beautiful, and the fact that he somehow wants *me*? I still don't get it, but if I could, I'd lay the rumors to rest so everyone knows, once and for all, that the man is taken.

And *fuck*. I'm what—jealous now? Am I? No, not jealous. *Territorial*. That's what I'm feeling.

I've never wanted to stake my claim on someone before, but with Christian, all of what I thought I wanted is being thrown out the damn window. That's as scary as it is exhilarating. Like, for maybe the first time, I jumped without double and triple-checking my parachutes, and now I'm soaring through the air, not a single thought in my head apart from what it feels like to *fly*.

"Someone needs to remind me I'm not a bird," I say to my hidden hermit crabs.

Neither answers, not that I expected them to.

The knock at my door is a welcome interruption. There's only one person it's likely to be. Only one person who drops by unannounced but always welcome.

There's a grin on my face when I pull the door open. It quickly falters. "Christian?"

"Hey, Specs," he says gently.

"What are you..."

Christian holds out the takeout bag in his hand. I grab it, and he sweeps into the apartment. After kicking off his shoes, he beelines for my bedroom, and I follow, at a loss.

Christian sets a small vase of white flowers on my desk, turning it until he's satisfied, and then he starts carefully and deliberately dotting my room in tealights.

I finally find my voice. "W-what are you doing?"

He gives me a soft smile, his hair falling in front of his eyes before he swipes it away. "Date night in."

"What—"

"You have an exam tomorrow," he says, setting the last of the tea lights on my desk. "Which means you need to study. And since I'm apparently clingy, something I did *not* realize about myself, I'm giving you an excuse to keep me around."

I don't even have time to explain I *wanted* him around—that I always want him around—before he goes on.

"The candles are cinnamon scented because it's supposed to help with focus and memory retention," he says. "But if you don't like cinnamon, we don't have to light them. And I brought food because you need to eat."

"And the flowers?" I ask, voice hoarse.

Christian looks nervous almost, his hand ruffling through the hair at the back of his neck. "Um, the flowers are because it sounded nice. I...I've never bought someone flowers before."

Time of death: precisely now.

I set the bag of food down before approaching Christian. It only takes a couple steps to reach him. Without a word, I wrap my arms around his middle and hug him tight.

I've never been particularly good at physical affection. Ironic, really, considering my day job. But piece by piece, Christian has been making it easier for me to take that leap. To seek comfort. To give it. To trust that it will be returned and not a transient thing.

Unsurprisingly, Christian's arms wrap around me immediately, his gentle wintergreen scent familiar and calming and right.

"So, uh," he says quietly, giving me a squeeze. "The cinnamon is okay?"

I huff a laugh and lean back. "It's perfect."

He looks relieved. "Okay, good. Hungry?"

I give a nod and let my considerate-as-fuck boyfriend go. While he spreads a spare sheet out on the bed, I grab a lighter for the candles. The smell of cinnamon wafts through the room as Christian unboxes our food. Korean, he tells me, with pork bulgogi because he knows I like it. I do.

With the ambiance set for a far more romantic study session than I've ever had, Christian and I settle beside one another on the bed and eat our food.

"Christian?" I ask some time later, my pork mostly gone.

"Mm?"

I don't really know a way to ask this other than to just do it. "Do you have any dreams? Things you want to do in life or, I don't know, a dream job? I know you kind of fell into porn, and I realize I've never asked what you'd do given the choice."

He hums, nodding as he finishes chewing his food. "I don't know. For a long time, I just wanted to get out, you know? I wanted my own life."

He doesn't say "away from my mom," but after hearing about her the other day, I'm guessing that's what he means.

"It took me a while to realize I was...in stasis," he says, setting his chin in his palm. "I was getting by. Going through the motions. I think if I could choose, I'd do something with sewing. I've always enjoyed it. I like expressing myself through clothes. I like the process of creating something new. I like shopping for fabric and seeing the potential in the cloth...making it come alive. So, yeah, I think that's what I'd do."

"Why don't you?" I ask, hoping I'm not overstepping.

Christian offers me a wry smile. "Bills, I guess? I can't just throw myself into something that has the potential to earn me nothing without a backup. Maybe, if I can get enough saved, I could try. But... It's complicated. If I sold clothes online, there's so many regulations and laws I'd have to follow. I don't even know the half of it."

"But it sounds like you know some," I point out. "That's a start. I could help you figure out the rest. Or at least try."

He cocks his head slightly, the tiniest movement. "Why would you do that?"

Why?

"Because you're my boyfriend, and I want you to be happy? And even if you weren't...*mine*, I'd still want to help." I try to figure out how to explain it to him. "Christian, you've...you've been there for me from the start. Maybe it was a weird sort of support when you were across the alley, texting me while I jerked off—"

He huffs a laugh.

"—but you were *there*. And even now, helping me find a friend for Arthur, and bringing me fucking candles and bulgogi to help me study? I..." I shake my head, somewhat in disbelief. "Honestly, Christian, I don't even know how you're real. But if you are—and not just a figment of my sleep-deprived, study-addled brain—then you deserve someone who's there for you, too. I want to be that person, okay? I know you have your grandma, but... Well, you have me now, too."

His lips hitch up at the corner. "I do, don't I?"

"Yeah," I say firmly. "You do."

Christian's smile is so vulnerable, softening the already youthful lines of his face. It makes me feel unbearably fond, and I clear my throat lest I throw myself at him.

"On that note," I say slowly, "if you ever wanted to, like, post a picture of me? I'd be okay with that. I told you I'm not active on social media anymore because I don't really trust myself not to get caught up in the thrill of an audience and post stuff I really shouldn't. But, uh... If *you* wanted to, I'd be good with that."

Christian is silent for long enough that I start to worry. But then he says, voice soft, "You want me to share a picture of you, Specs?"

"I mean..." I shrug a little. "Only if you want to. But if you *do* want to, then you know... You have my permission."

His smile is slow. "Emil."

"What?"

"You..." He shakes his head, lips twisting. "You're adorable, you know that?"

"I..."

"Take off your pants."

"What?" I squeak.

He snorts a laugh. "I'm taking a picture. And you know everyone loves that ass of yours, so take 'em off, Specs. That way I can show *you* off."

Blood rushes south *fast*.

Christian chuckles as I roll to my back and unceremoniously shuck off my jeans. He pushes our food containers out of the way, as well as my textbook, and once I roll back onto my stomach, pants-free, his hand smooths up over my tailbone, lifting my shirt.

"Perfect," he says softly. "Now just turn your head a little this way. Yeah, like that. But don't look at the camera."

My heart pounds, and Christian's palm shifts, pressing down on my lower back. He hums as my ass lifts the tiniest bit.

"Hot, Specs."

Fuck.

He backs up, making a soft, satisfied sound. A second later, there's a click. He takes a couple pictures before lying next to me. With his face an inch away from mine, we stare at one another, and his phone clicks again. Then, he's kissing me.

It's soft, and it's gentle, and for the briefest of moments, I feel it again, that sensation of soaring through the air.

When he pulls back, I make a sound of protest, but Christian merely chuckles.

"Don't give me that face, Specs. No funny business tonight. I came here with every intention of being good."

"Good is overrated," I mumble.

Christian grabs his chest. "Be still my heart. My boyfriend is a rebel. Next, you'll be telling me textbooks should be shelved by color, not alphabetical order."

I snort, my insides doing funny things. "That would be sacrilege, and you know it."

"There's the man I know," Christian says happily. "Now put your pants back on, Specs, or I won't be held accountable for my actions."

I'm oh so tempted to keep them off just to see what *would* happen, but Christian is right. I really do need to study for this exam. *Funny business* can wait.

Christian cleans up the remains of our meal as I pull my pants on and get to work. When he comes back into the room, he flops down next to me, phone out. He shows me the screen. "Okay?"

I look at the photo that's ready to post. It's clear I'm on a bed at home, not in the studio, but Christian took the shot in a way that the background details are blurred. Even my face is obscured slightly, the focus on my ass. It's a good picture, subtle somehow. Below, the caption reads, "In one of my favorite places."

If he posts this, it'll be obvious he's with me outside of work. That I'm half-naked. That I'm someone important, considering he's never posted photos of anyone else on his account. Christian's fans will recognize who I am. It's a clear message.

Vixen and Felix. Him and me.

"Yeah," I say a little hoarsely. "Post it."

With a smirk, Christian does. Once done, he bumps his shoulder lightly into mine, leaving it there. I try to focus on my class notes, but my mind is otherwise occupied.

"Is this bedroom really one of your favorite places?" I ask. Frankly, I like his bedroom better. His apartment has more character than mine. It feels like a true home, lived in with memories baked into the very walls.

Christian huffs a small laugh, although I'm not sure what's funny. "*You*," he says, shaking his head a little. "You are, Specs."

Oh.

Oh, fuck.

Christian has a smile on his face as he scrolls through his phone. My heart is racing, and for the longest moment, I can't look away.

I'm one of his favorite places.

If I am a bird, I pray to a higher being I don't believe in that Christian is one, too. Because for a man who's never been in love, who's never dated or had a boyfriend before me, Christian has masterfully stolen my heart.

And if I'm the only one climbing, the only one soaring through the clouds, it's going to hurt a hell of a lot to realize my heart is still back down on Earth.

Chapter 22
CHRISTIAN

I had it in my head that relationships meant pain. That they meant inevitable loss.

I know my preconceived notions were skewed because of my mother. Because of what *she* lost. She never bothered to explain to me the parts that made it worth it. Why she was with my father. Why she loved in the first place.

All I knew was the aftermath. And it wasn't pretty.

But everything with Emil feels like *life*. That's the best way I can think to describe it.

He's good, and he's smart, and there's this vibrant glint of hunger in his eyes that fascinates me. Hunger for knowledge. Hunger, sometimes, for *me*. When I'm with him, I can almost believe there's no *after*. That the *now* is all that's important.

Which is why I find myself stalled in front of a bolt of fabric I've walked past time and time again, thinking, for the first time, of buying a few yards. Emil is standing next to me, looking at a distressed denim. After a moment, he notices I'm not moving.

"You like that one?" he asks.

I nod, running my fingers along the outer edge of the fabric, where the embroidered flowers become thickest before ending. It's an extravagant pattern, meant to be a showstopper. I've never had a reason to buy it before, not considering the ridiculous cost. But last week, after acing the exam I knew he would, Emil helped me look into some of the regulations for selling clothes. And now...now I can't stop dreaming up these designs in my head. And every time, I think about this fabric. About what it could be.

"You should get some," Emil says. "It's gorgeous."

I look over just in time to catch his encouraging smile. When I hold up the tag so he can see the cost, his eyes widen a bit.

"Okay, so that's kind of expensive..." he starts.

"That's the cost for one yard," I clarify.

Emil makes a choked sound. "Shit."

"Mhm."

He nudges up his glasses before touching the fabric, his fingers drifting over the flowers delicately. The same as when he touched Bernie, I feel a flash of heat rush through me. Maybe because I want those fingers on me? Maybe because I know what they can do. I know how much Emil seems to love my skirts. How he likes to drag them out of the way and tell me to watch him while he drives me wild. How, sometimes, he likes me to fuck him in them.

I grab the bolt of fabric and tuck it under my arm. Emil gives me a grin.

Before heading to the cutting counter, I grab a few other supplies. A long zipper. Some tulle to create volume. Since the base of the fabric is white, I stick with that, already envisioning a simple yet structured crop top to complement the skirt.

"When's the awards ceremony?" I ask Emil. Nathaniel mentioned it to me, saying they'd appreciate for all of the performers to be there, even though surely I won't win anything, new as I am.

"Right before New Year's," he answers.

Plenty of time.

When we reach the counter, I set my haul on top. It physically hurts, watching the employee cut into the embroidered fabric, knowing the cost of such a cut. But it feels good, too. Like growth, maybe. Healing.

"I, uh... I've been meaning to ask you..." Emil says, a hint of nerves in his voice.

"The answer will probably be yes," I tell him before thanking the employee who hands over my fabric, along with the slip to pay up front.

Emil huffs a laugh. "Are you that certain I won't ask for something outlandish?"

"That certain I simply can't refuse you."

He flushes at that, a sight that has me feeling smug. It takes Emil a moment to finish his original question. "I was wondering if you'd come to Thanksgiving with me?"

"At your parents'?"

"Yeah. Uh, it's usually our biggest get-together during the holidays. Immediate family, plus aunts and uncles, cousins."

I take a slow step toward him. "You want me to meet your family, Specs?"

Emil's lips lift into a small smile when he sees my own. "Shut up," he grumbles without heat. "Yes, I do. Would you come? Your grandma would be welcome, too, if you think she could make the trip."

Emil looks a little startled when I back him down an aisle filled with fabric. He glances over his shoulder, walking backwards until I press him against a few bolts of chiffon. The fabric settles like colorful, billowing clouds on either side of his body. My kinky, angelic nerd.

He doesn't protest when I bring my lips to his. I'm all too aware of Emil's own restrictions when it comes to being in public, so I keep it light, and I don't grind up against him the way I want to. But he still clings to me, hands fisting my shirt, trying to pull me closer.

When I break away from his lips, I lay my cheek against his. "Yes, I'll go to Thanksgiving with you, Specs. I'll ask my grandma, too."

I can feel his smile against my face.

When Emil and I finally make it to the register, I hand over my fabric slip and the other notions I grabbed. "There goes a month's worth of groceries," I say quietly.

Emil winces, hand landing on my lower back. It's a simple touch, but those simple touches from Emil are big. "At least you'll look gorgeous. I mean, you *always* look gorgeous, but you know what I mean."

He rolls his eyes at himself, and I chuckle.

After paying, we head to Emil's car. Since he already packed some study materials in his bookbag before we left, we head straight over to my place after parking. Emil sprawls out on my bed, getting comfortable like he does at home. He lays a book out in front of himself, powers on his laptop, and pops open a bag of pretzels.

I unload supplies for my skirt while he studies. I have large wooden hangers with clips in my closet, so I hang the embroidered fabric up on one of those to prevent wrinkles. Next, I add the tulle to the pile of fabric on the floor—I really need to get cubbies to organize it all—and then I pick out a length of muslin to draft the skirt pattern.

Emil looks up as I'm spreading the material out on my foldable cutting board. Since it's a little wrinkled, I plug in my iron.

"What's that?" Emil asks.

"This fabric? It's called muslin. It's a cheap, plain cotton, so it's good for scrap material."

He hums, watching me for a moment before going back to his work. I like having him here in my space, even when we're focused on different things. It feels nice. Comfortable.

Time moves swiftly as I work on patterning my skirt. The *shht, shht* of my scissors cutting through fabric is a familiar soundtrack amongst the tapping of Emil's keys. Emil looks up again as I'm standing in front of my mirror, the muslin draped around my waist. There's a pincushion strapped to my wrist for easy access.

I can practically feel his curiosity.

"What is it?" I ask.

"It's just... Isn't that usually done on a mannequin?"

"A dress form," I correct. "And yes, but I don't have one. They're expensive."

He makes a soft sound. "Do you ever prick yourself?"

I raise an eyebrow, and Emil shakes his head, lips twitching into a smile.

"You know what I mean," he mumbles.

"Sometimes I do," I admit.

Emil shuffles around, sitting upright and leaning against the wall. He sips his energy drink as he watches me work, seemingly taking a break from his *own* work.

"I saw your scene with Dixon," I note, shifting a few pins around. "The one you did at the end of last week."

"Yeah?"

"Mhm. That was hot as fuck, Specs. I couldn't take my eyes off you. Pretty sure Dixon could have been wearing a tutu, and I wouldn't have noticed."

Emil snorts, but then his gaze goes kind of distant before latching back onto me. I don't miss the way his eyes rove over the makeshift skirt I'm wearing.

"Are you imagining me in a tutu?" I ask.

He flushes, licking his lips.

I grin. "I'll wear a tutu for you, Specs."

"Shit," he mutters, shaking his head as if clearing his thoughts. "I don't know why that's so hot, but it is."

"Have you always been attracted to femme guys?" I ask, curious.

"I actually, um..." He huffs a small laugh. "I'm not sure I have a physical type. My last boyfriend was a big guy. Wore flannel. You two look nothing alike."

"Huh."

"Have you always liked nerds in glasses?" he retorts.

"I sure as fuck like one," I answer, trying to think back on my usual go-to type. True, I haven't often gone for hypermasculine men—the big, macho types—but I've also never been drawn to anyone the way I am to Emil. Yes, I thought the glasses were cute from the get-go. The way they make his eyes a little bigger, vulnerable almost. I like the softness of his body and the way he feels tucked up against me. And, admittedly, I do love his ass.

But it was that time I first met him in person inside Studio 1 that I felt a *swoop* of something more in my stomach. I don't know what caused it. Emil's goodness? His gentle grace? The way he looked at me as if he already knew me and liked what he saw?

I'm attracted to Emil physically, that's undeniable. But I've liked the look of a lot of guys and not once wanted more. So maybe my type is whatever it is inside of Emil that drew out my bravery. The thought makes me smile.

A soft sound draws my attention back to Emil.

"What is it?" I ask.

"Nothing," he answers slowly. "Sometimes you just...you say the most perfect things."

"Yeah?" I say, walking over to the bed. I'm careful as I climb onto the mattress, making sure not to disturb any of the pins in the fabric around my waist. Emil draws his knees up as I approach, spreading his legs and giving me room to fit in between them. I knee-walk closer, curling my palms against the sides of his neck, thumbs at his jaw. "You like being my one and only, Specs? You like being the only person I see?"

He lets out a small breath, his eyes fluttering closed. "You know I do."

I kiss the side of one perfect eyebrow before bringing my lips to his, brushing our mouths together ever so gently. "Good. Because I'm not giving you up. Your ass is on my Instagram. That shit's official."

He huffs a laugh, his eyes opening. They don't stay that way for long, slipping closed again when I take his mouth with mine. He parts his lips, and I sweep my tongue inside, blood igniting. He tugs me closer, instantly eager, *always* eager, and I shuffle forward, cursing the skirt pinned around my waist.

I'm about to tear the fabric off when my phone rings. I groan, knowing there are only a few people who would call me out of the blue.

"Hold that thought," I say, pulling back from Emil's lips. He looks a little dazed as I sit on my heels and grab my phone off the nightstand. It's Noel. "Hello?"

"Uh, hey, Christian," my friend greets, the background noise in the call nearly drowning out his voice.

"What's going on?" I ask, his tone putting me on high alert.

"I, uh... *Shit*. It might be nothing, but I'm at work right now, and there's this guy who's giving me the creeps." I turn my volume up as Noel continues, the heavy beat of the club making it hard to hear him. "He hasn't *done* anything, not really, but..."

"You have a bad feeling," I fill in, talking loudly, too, so he can hear me.

"Yeah. I'm probably being ridiculous, but last week, he asked me out. A *couple* times. I said no, but he keeps coming around. And I swear I saw him in the parking lot the other night. I almost felt like...like he was waiting for me? Which, again, probably ridiculous."

"It's not," I assure him. "Always trust your gut, Noel."

My eyes ping to Emil, his words from what feels like a lifetime ago flitting through my head. *"How do we know if the choices we're making are the right ones?"* His answer was simple. *"I think you just have to trust your gut."*

"Noel, did you tell anyone about him?" I ask.

"Yeah," he says. "I told our boss, but he didn't seem concerned."

Of course not.

"I'll be right there," I tell him, eyes on Emil. "Don't leave the club, okay?"

"Thank you, Christian," he says in clear relief.

When I hang up, Emil is already closing his laptop. "Where are we going?" he asks.

We. My heart kicks.

"My friend Noel might need some help," I explain. "He works about twenty minutes from here."

Emil nods, pulling out his phone. "Name?"

I rattle it off, and Emil's fingers fly over the screen as I climb off the bed, quickly unpinning the muslin around my waist. I pull on some pants as Emil's phone and my own start pinging in rapid succession.

"Who are you texting?" I ask.

"The crew," he answers simply.

By the time I'm dressed, Emil is waiting for me. He hands me my phone, and my throat closes up as I look at the screen. Emil started a group chat with our coworkers.

Specs: Need help. Knee Highs on The Strip.

Dixon: OMW.

Niko: We're twenty-five minutes out.

Alex: Rowan is bringing his bat. Ignore the knicker-bockers. We were doing...a thing.

Teddy: Leaving now.

Kipp: I'm in the chat!

Alex: Porn stars assemble, bitches! Yeehaw!

"Come on," Emil says gently, giving my arm a tug. "Let's go."

Blinking the moisture from my eyes, I nod, and we head out the door.

My foot taps the floor of the car as Emil drives us across town. I text Max on the way, certain he'd want to know what's going on with Noel. He doesn't answer right away, and I can only hope he gets my message soon. The drive seems to take forever, but after exactly twenty minutes, Emil parks beside the club.

I see a lot of familiar faces as we walk through the front doors. A few of my old coworkers wave, and I return their hellos, but I don't stop to chat. I head right toward the bar where Noel is standing. He heaves out a sigh when he sees me coming.

"You okay?" I ask as soon as I'm close.

He nods. "Yeah. I'm probably being paranoid, but I just can't shake the feeling that something is off."

"Where is this guy?"

He cants his head behind him. "Black shirt. Near the wall."

My gaze sweeps the area. "Sitting alone?"

Noel nods.

I give his arm a squeeze as Emil subtly takes the guy's picture. "Don't go anywhere alone tonight, okay? We'll be here until you're ready to leave."

Noel nods, looking grateful.

"Oh, and this is Emil," I tack on. "My boyfriend."

Noel holds out his hand, even as his cheeks pink. "Nice to meet you."

"Likewise," Emil answers.

"You guys want anything to drink while you're waiting?" Noel asks.

"Actually," I say slowly. "You might want to get a tray of waters ready. There are a few others coming."

"There are?" Noel asks, head cocked. "Who?"

A smile twists my lips. "Friends."

Chapter 23

Emil

"I say we crush him," Alex says, grinding his fist into his palm.

"He hasn't done anything yet," Finn says calmly from beside him, the big bear of a redhead threading his fingers through Alex's hair. His other hand is around the back of Rowan's neck.

"Yet being the key word," Alex retorts, eyes narrowed. "And stop trying to pet me into submission, Ginger Bear."

"As if that would ever work," Finn replies, voice fond as he continues to play with Alex's hair.

Alex harrumphs but looks pleased.

"Dude's suspicious," Dixon says.

"See!" Alex cries. "*Thank you*, Grumpy Bear."

The guy in question hasn't once left his table near the back of the club. He's gone through a couple drinks at this point, but instead of paying attention to the dancing entertainment, his eyes, more often than not, have been following Noel through the club.

"I don't trust him," Christian says.

"Me neither," Kipp puts in. He's sitting on Teddy's lap, even though there's an empty seat at the table. "Couldn't we just call the cops?"

"And say what?" Alex replies. "There's a guy we don't like the look of who's sitting politely inside a club and making googly-eyes at our friend?"

Kipp scrunches his nose. "You have a point. Wasn't he loitering in the parking lot, though?"

"Noel thinks so, but he's not positive," Christian answers.

Kipp deflates.

"Maybe we've got it wrong, and he's just lonely," Niko says, popping the top few buttons on his shirt and standing. "Be right back."

"Jesus Christ," Dixon mutters.

"What's he doing?" Alex asks in alarm.

Dixon heaves a sigh. "Flirting."

We all watch as Niko saunters over to the man's table. He leans his hands on the surface, grinning as he says something to the guy. The guy's expression is like stone as he shakes his head once. Niko says something else, but the man clearly isn't interested. With a shrug, Niko turns around and heads back our way. The guy's eyes immediately seek out Noel.

"Yeah, no," Christian says. "He's got a target."

Alex curses.

We all fall silent as the stranger waves Noel down. Christian's friend approaches at a steady pace, looking uncomfortable but trying to hide it. He picks up the man's empty glass, the two exchanging words. The guy must order another drink because Noel nods and heads back toward the bar.

"I don't like this," Teddy mumbles.

"If he so much as flinches, I'm getting the bat," Alex practically growls.

"Whoa, slugger," Niko says calmly. "Let's cool it a little. The last thing we need is you getting arrested for battery."

Kipp snorts. "*Bat*-ery. With a bat. Get it?"

"There will be no battery or getting arrested," Dixon grumbles. "There's nine of us—ten, including Noel—and only one of him. *If* this guy acts up, we'll ask him to leave. Simple as that."

"Ask?" Niko says, lips curling into a smile as he rubs Dixon's arm.

"Tell," Finn declares, to which Dixon nods his agreement. Alex gives them both a grin.

"Couldn't we just do that now?" Kipp whines.

"Hold up," I say, squeezing Christian's arm. "He's back."

We watch as Noel sets a new drink down on the guy's table. The man smiles, picking up the glass. And then he tips it down Noel's front.

Christian makes to jump out of his chair, but my grip on his arm stops him. "The fuck," he hisses.

"It's just a drink," I say. "It was probably an accident, right?"

Noel wipes his shirt as the guy seems to apologize. Noel shakes his head, holding out his hand in a clear *I got it* gesture. He sets his tray on the table before heading along the back of the club toward the hall.

"Where's he going?" Alex asks.

"Employee room," Christian says quietly. "To change. At least, that's what I'm guessing."

"Okay. So that's not so bad," Alex says. "Even if that was on purpose—"

"Guys," Rowan says. "Where'd he go?"

Heads whip back toward the table. The man in the black shirt is gone.

Christian curses, looking around frantically. Alex stands on his chair.

"There," Niko says, pointing toward the back hall as the guy disappears around the corner.

Everyone is out of their seats in a second.

I lose my grip on Christian's arm as he all but runs toward the back hallway of the club. He deftly evades the crowd and rounds the corner before I can catch up. My pulse sprints as I hear him shout, "Hey!"

Teddy turns the corner ahead of me, surprisingly fast for such a big guy. I vaguely remember he's a runner. When I make it into the hall, I see a flash of dark hair as Christian barrels through the slowly closing door at the back of the club, his momentum pushing it right back open again.

"Fuck," I mutter, racing after him.

I've never in my life been more grateful for the men at my back.

My ears ring as I follow Teddy out into the alley behind the bar. I hear Christian yell, "Let him go!" followed by a grunt. There's no overhead light back here, only a faint glow from the street, so it's hard to make out what's happening as Teddy rushes into the fray. But there appears to be a scuffle, and my stomach drops even further toward my feet.

"Hey!" Finn bellows, running past me. "I'm calling the cops."

That seems to be enough to catch the guy's attention—either that or the near dozen of us that have spilled into the alley—because less than a second later, there's a sound of alarm from Noel, and the guy is taking off.

"Yeah, you better run!" Alex shouts.

"Holy fuck," I breathe, rushing to where Noel is sprawled on the ground. "Are you okay?"

"Oh my God," he says, taking my hand and rising shakily to his feet. "Did...did that just happen?"

Finn is talking on the phone, and Teddy is assuring Kipp he's fine, but my attention is on Noel as Christian skids to a halt next to us. "Are you hurt?" Christian asks his friend. "Did he hurt you?"

"No," Noel breathes. A little more light appears, and I realize someone turned on their phone's flashlight. "He just...he just grabbed me and dragged me outside. I...I didn't even realize what was happening. Holy fuck, what just happened?"

Alex rubs Noel's arm as Christian glances toward the mouth of the alleyway. "He's gone," Christian says, sounding as if he's reassuring both himself and Noel.

"Police are on their way," Finn says.

"Fuck," Noel mutters again.

Alex wraps his arm around Noel's shoulders, giving him a squeeze. "Come on, sweets. Let's go wait where there's more light."

Noel nods, and we all start making our way toward the sidewalk.

"Sure wasn't expecting us, was he?" Alex says, his voice light. "You should never fuck with porn stars."

Noel huffs a laugh, and Alex gives him a grin.

When we reach the sidewalk in front of the club, I pull Christian off to the side. "You okay?" I ask, running my fingers over his face, checking for damage I pray isn't there. My heart is still pounding.

Christian catches my wrists, his hold gentle. "I'm fine. He just shoved me."

My breath shudders. "Fuck, Christian. That was..."

"I know," he says softly, kissing my palm. He turns enough to face his friend. "Noel, please tell me you're not coming back here."

Noel shakes his head quickly. "No. I'm done. I told our boss I was scared, and he didn't give a shit. He didn't do *anything*. He can find another server."

Christian lets out a breath that sounds like relief. "Okay. Do you want me to..." He cuts off with a soft sound. "Max?"

Noel's head whips around as a man comes jogging swiftly our way from the direction of the parking lot. "Max?" Noel repeats, voice quiet. "What are you doing here?"

The man named Max all but barrels into our group, only slowing once he's in front of Noel. Noel looks shocked as Max sweeps him into his arms. He blinks wide eyes.

"Fuck, are you all right?" Max asks. "I got Christian's text. What's going on? What are you all doing out here?"

As Noel answers a very concerned Max's questions, Christian grabs my hand and gives a little tug. I follow him back inside as Christian grabs Noel's things from the employee room. He tosses a keycard on the small table before we go.

When we get back outside, two police officers are taking Noel's statement. I show them the picture of the guy on my phone, hoping it's enough to identify him. It's late by the time the cops leave, having already gone inside to collect CCTV footage. Everyone looks worn out.

"Um," Noel says, Max's hand in his. "I don't even know what to say. Just...thank you guys. Thank you for coming."

Christian gives his friend's free hand a squeeze. "You don't have to thank us for that, Noel. It's what friends do."

"We've adopted you," Alex says cheerfully. "In case that wasn't obvious."

Noel lets out a wet laugh. "I guess I'll see you guys soon?"

"Count on it," Alex says.

Christian gives Noel a hug before he and Max leave for the parking lot.

Alex hums as he watches them go. "I love love."

Niko snorts. "You don't get matchmaker credit for that one, pint-size."

"What?" Alex squawks. "I was *here*. It counts."

"Anyone want nachos?" Kipp cuts in. He looks around the group, frowning. "No? Just me?"

"It's one in the morning," Dixon says flatly.

Teddy pulls Kipp close, kissing his temple. "I'll get you nachos, doll."

Kipp beams.

"Well, I'd say our work here is done," Alex says primly, dusting his hands. He lets out a happy sigh before shouting, "Porn stars disassemble!"

Several people on the sidewalk startle, turning to look at us.

Dixon groans, covering his face with his hand. "Jesus, small fry. A little tact?"

"Not what I'm known for," Alex retorts, giving Finn's shoulder a tug. "Come on, Ginger Pony, let me ride you so we can get home...and I can ride you. And Grizzly Bear."

Rowan flushes, and Finn shakes his head, but both are smiling as we make our way toward the parking lot, Alex on Finn's back. Alex makes hoof-clomping sounds until Finn pinches his leg. Christian snags my hand, giving me a tired smile.

After saying our goodbyes, we break up to get into our respective vehicles. I'm quiet as I buckle myself in and start the car, and Christian turns to look at me.

"You okay?" he asks.

I nod, getting us out on the road. "Yeah, just... That was scary."

He gives my thigh a squeeze. "I know. And I hate that our boss doesn't care. He doesn't *care*. If he had any measure of security for his staff, stuff like that wouldn't happen in the first place."

"*Our* boss?" I ask, glancing at Christian, whose features are lit by the streetlights. "Noel said the same thing earlier. Is this where you used to work?"

"Yeah," he says. "I got fired for fending off handsy customers."

"That's..." My mouth opens and closes. "That's *bullshit.*"

He huffs a humorless laugh. "Yeah. It is."

I blow out a breath, my pulse racing as I picture what would have happened tonight if we weren't here. Would that guy have been successful in cornering Noel? What if it had been Christian in his place instead? What if this had happened before we'd met? Who would Christian have called for help? His grandma is in an assisted living facility. He's estranged from his mother. The only person I've heard him mention as a friend is Noel.

I grab Christian's hand, holding tight.

"You sure you're okay, Specs?" he asks softly.

I nod, but it feels jerky. "You have me. You have *us,*" I say, hoping he understands. "Even if... Just always, okay? You can always call."

Christian pulls our joined hands to his mouth. He gives my knuckles a kiss, a soft thing, as if he's reassuring me. "I know."

I focus on getting the two of us home safely, but as soon as we're back at Christian's, I pull him into bed, and I don't let go. He doesn't complain, not once. And with my arms wrapped around him tight, I swear to myself I won't let anything hurt this man.

Not ever.

"Ow," Christian says quietly.

"Sorry," I say, immediately loosening my grip.

He rubs my arm with his free hand, giving me a small smile. The two of us are sitting in front of the terrarium, Christian's hand in mine for support.

It's time.

"I like his new shell," he says conversationally. "He picked a good one after his molt."

I nod, but my attention is on the tank in front of us. The new crab is in with Arthur, and although neither has made a single move toward one another, I'm watching like a hawk.

The new crab wriggles a little, and I gasp.

Christian chuckles. "Jesus, you're cute."

"I'm not cute," I shoot back. "I'm freaking out."

He kisses my cheek. "You're cute when you're freaking out."

"That bodes well for you," I mutter. "I freak out a lot."

He hums. "I don't think that's true."

I raise a brow, eyeing him. "I'm kind of particular."

"So?" he says, leaning against my shoulder. "Nothing wrong with that."

"I'm not a go-with-the-flow type of person," I continue. "I live in a constant state of low anxiety and question most everything in my life."

He huffs. "I think you're organized, smart, *kind*, and attentive to detail."

"I color code my notes," I point out.

"Like I said... Cute."

A scoff catches in my throat. "I'm anal-retentive, spend most of my free time studying because I like it, I have *crabs*, and I get off on people watching me have sex."

Christian's eyes dance with humor and something I'm not sure how to name. "Are you trying to convince me of something here, Specs? Because all I'm hearing are positives."

I nearly growl, refocusing on the terrarium. I jolt in surprise. "Where the fuck did Arthur go?"

"He's right there," Christian says calmly, pointing to the corner.

I breathe a sigh of relief. "What if they hate each other?"

"Give them a chance."

"What if—"

"What if," Christian cuts in, "they become the best of friends? What if Arthur, your prickly and guarded hermit crab, finds out he really likes having someone around? Maybe this is the best thing for him."

I look over at my boyfriend, who thinks he's being sneaky.

"Oh, look," he says casually. "Are they fighting?"

My head whips around. "Don't even joke, Christian. I swear to God—"

He shuts me up with his lips. I moan before pulling back, pretty sure I'm supposed to be angry. He follows me, lips capturing mine again, hand anchoring in my hair.

"Not funny," I say, but it only sounds like a groan.

"Kinda funny."

"No," I moan. "We're fighting."

"Are we?" he says, tongue flicking my lip. "We should fight more often."

"Christian," I groan, nearly losing myself as he kisses down my neck. "My *crabs*."

His breath huffs across my skin. "You should really reconsider how you phrase that."

I laugh, a pained sound, as Christian pulls back. He kisses me once, a peck.

"I have an idea," he says before standing up. "Can I grab your laptop?"

"Sure?"

He nods and walks off, grabbing my computer before swinging through the kitchen for a chair. He sets it beside the terrarium and places the laptop on top, and then he's off again. I watch, perplexed, as he gathers pillows and a blanket, dropping them nearby before going back into the kitchen. He sticks a bag of popcorn in the microwave.

My throat feels tight as he returns, stopping to turn off one of the lights so it's a little dimmer. He cues up *Life* on my laptop.

"You're pretty great, you know that?" I say.

He gives me a soft smile as he fluffs his pillow. We lay the blanket over our laps, the bowl of popcorn between us, and watch the show.

After a minute, Christian says, "I feel like I'm kinda starting out in life, you know? Like I'm just now at this point where I'm thinking about my future and what I want that to be. I don't... I don't have a lot, Emil. There's not a lot I can give you. But you said once that we should make the best out of what we have, and that's something I can promise to do. I promise I'll do my best to make you happy every day because I'm pretty sure, if we let it, *this* could be our future."

"Christian," I say, nearly at a loss for words.

He swallows, gaze on the popcorn between us. He looks self-conscious, not something I'm used to seeing. I give his chin a nudge so he looks at me.

"You have *so much* to give," I tell him seriously. "I don't need fancy dates or expensive gifts. I like walking with you in a stone-paved garden. I like writing my papers while you sew. I like... I like *this*. I like all of it. So whatever ideal you're comparing us to, don't bother, okay? You've made me happier than any other person has in a very long time. I don't need *things*. I just want you."

His lip wobbles, and I brush his hair back. It's so soft when he wears it down, and not for the first time, I marvel at the beauty of it. Of *him*.

I've always thought of Christian as strong. It shines out of him in the way he stands and walks and carries himself. He's proud of who he is, and he lends that strength to those around him. He makes me feel safe and secure when we're together. And he looks out for those who've proven themselves trustworthy.

It's easy to forget that Christian is young. That he has insecurities like the rest of us. That, for all the ways in which he's world-wise, this is new to him, and he may need an occasional reminder that he's on the right track.

"We're not ever going to be like anybody else, you and me," I say, tracing his eyes and the gentle slope of his nose with my gaze. "A closet exhibitionist-slash-psych geek and a gorgeous, skirt-wearing seamster who happens to enjoy fucking said exhibitionist in front of others?"

He huffs a small laugh.

"But it doesn't matter," I say truthfully. "The pieces of us are suited to one another, as impossible as that seems. I mean, seriously, how did I even find you?"

"I think it was asbestos," he says softly.

I bark a laugh, and he smiles.

"My point is I can see a future with you, too, Christian. And if you're planning on making me happy every single day, well, get ready. Because I'll be doing my best to make you happy, too."

"Well, shit," he says, sighing dramatically. "However will I manage to cope?"

I bump his shoulder. "Stop being cute."

"Can't," he says simply. "I'm always cute."

I catch his lips with my own, biting gently. Releasing. "This...the two of us? It's perfect, okay? Now restart the episode because *someone* made me miss David Attenborough's voice."

Christian shakes against me as he laughs. Finally, he breathes in, smacks a kiss against my lips, and reaches for the laptop. I spare a glance at the crabs, but neither has moved. Utterly content, I lean against my boyfriend's side, knowing there's nowhere else I'd rather be.

Chapter 24
CHRISTIAN

Emil fidgets with his collar, straightening the already straight material.

"Nervous?" I ask him.

He glances at me in the mirror over his desk. "A little. I haven't talked to my parents since I yelled."

I hum. "Do you think they'll be upset?"

"No," he says quickly. "I think they were surprised more than anything. Henry said they've been more...attentive, though. He said it's horrible, even though he sounded happy about it. So I'm glad they listened. That they seem to be making an effort with him."

But not with you?

I don't voice the question aloud, but it surprises me that his parents haven't mentioned Emil's uncharacteristic outburst to him. If he ever yelled in front of me or, Christ, *at* me, I'd be worried. I'd know something was wrong.

I'm trying to keep an open mind, but what I've learned about Emil's parents so far hasn't endeared them to me. Same with his older siblings, who seem just as aloof when it comes to their middle brother. The only one I'm excited to meet is Rebecca. Emil talks about her with warmth, same as Henry.

Pushing off the bed, I walk over to Emil and wrap my arms around his middle. He sighs as I settle my chin on his shoulder.

"You're tall in those heels," he says softly.

"Mm." I kiss his cheek.

"You look great," he adds.

"So do you. Ready to go celebrate Thanksgiving?"

He heaves out a sigh. "Yeah. Let's go."

Emil drives us to his parents' house across town. The bottles of red wine and the rolls we're bringing sit in the backseat. I didn't wear a skirt today, not because I was worried about anyone's reaction—at least his family is open-minded in that regard—but because I wanted to dress up, and I had the perfect outfit to do so.

My slacks are a twist on a tuxedo pant. They fit my waist snugly, with just enough looseness through the hips to be respectable, but they're slim and tapered down to my ankles. The fabric is matte black, but a small stripe along each side of my leg is shiny satin. My accompanying shirt is a white button-down, similar to Emil's blue one, but the material is silkier and the sleeves have the slightest billow to give them shape. My boots, as Emil mentioned, have a tall heel but are otherwise simple black.

Emil gave me his fervent stamp of approval and even picked out my little white pearl belly button jewelry that no one but him will see.

Emil himself looks handsome, but he always does. His button-down is understated, his pants are simple black but fit him well, and his hair is brushed back neatly, glasses perched on his nose. I find myself smiling as I watch him drive, and he seems to sense it.

"What?" he asks, glancing over at me.

"Nothing," I say quietly. "I just... Sometimes I look at you, and I never want to stop."

Emil blinks, staring out the front windshield. "Shit, Christian."

"I know," I sigh. "It's creepy."

He huffs a laugh. "It's not. It's... I think it's the nicest thing anyone has ever said to me."

"My little exhibitionist," I mumble fondly.

He gives my thigh a half-hearted smack. "It's not that," he says, laughter in his tone. "It has nothing to do with being turned on. Although, yes, that does kind of turn me on."

I snort.

"It's just that no one else cares enough to look," he says, nearly breaking my heart. "But, somehow, you really like what you see, don't you?"

"I kind of hate that you even have to ask that," I admit. "But yes, I really, really do."

He nods, his lips forming a partial smile. *Emotional* happy, that's what it is. I brush the corner of his mouth with my fingertip, laughing when Emil snaps at me playfully.

When we get to his parents', a few other vehicles are already in the drive. Emil parks along the edge of the street and turns off his car with a steadying breath. I reach for our items in the backseat.

"Bread or wine?" I ask, hoping to distract him from his nerves.

"Bread," he says, taking the rolls from my hand. He opens his door, and I do the same.

Emil doesn't knock; he simply walks inside the house. Immediately, a few people look over from the living room adjacent to the entryway, and there are a couple *Emils* thrown out in greeting. Emil smiles as he takes off his shoes. I follow suit, leaving my boots by the door as an older woman walks over to us.

"Hi, dear," she says, tugging Emil in for a hug.

"Aunt Lilah," he answers, hugging her back with one arm. "It's good to see you. This is Christian, my boyfriend."

"Well aren't you just gorgeous," she says to me, holding out her hands. "Want me to take those bottles?"

I hand the wine over. "Sure, thanks."

She hums. "Emil, I haven't seen you since last Thanksgiving. What've you been up to?"

"Lilah?" someone calls. "Does this casserole need to go in the oven?"

"Oh, excuse me," Emil's aunt says, walking off with the wine.

Emil holds up the rolls. "Let's drop these off in the kitchen."

I nod, following Emil further into his parents' house. Several people are in the large yet simplistically designed kitchen, some putting final touches on dishes, a few others standing around with drinks in their hands. Emil sets the rolls on a white marble countertop.

"Want something to drink?" he asks me. "Wine, water, hard alcohol?"

I huff a laugh. "Not right now. But thanks."

He nods just as his name is called. With a little head cant, he leads me over to a small group of people standing beside the kitchen table. Just like before, Emil introduces me as his boyfriend, and then he goes around the circle, pointing out his brother Julian, his sister Eloise, and their respective wives.

"It's nice to meet you, Christian," Eloise says. Like Emil, she has brown hair and glasses, although her frames look more like a fashion statement than a necessity. "Did you two meet at school?"

"Emil graduated last year, remember?" Julian puts in before taking a small sip of his wine.

"Actually, I'm working on my master's," Emil corrects.

Julian looks surprised by that, but Eloise nods. "That's right," she says. "Are you still on track for clinical psychology?"

"Oh, um," Emil says, poking up his glasses. "I wasn't, uh... I was never actually..."

He peters out, and I slip my hand into his. "He's getting his master's in experimental psychology," I say proudly. "And then he'll go on for his doctorate."

Emil gives my hand a hard squeeze.

"What do you do with experimental psych?" Allie, Julian's wife, asks. "I've never heard of that."

Emil opens his mouth to answer when another woman swoops in. "Hey, hon."

"Mom," Emil says, returning her one-armed hug. "Um, this is Christian, my boyfriend."

"Nice to meet you," she says, looking at me with the same eyes as Emil. "Would you like anything to drink?"

"Oh, no, thank you."

She nods, focus shifting back to Emil. "I need to get the soup ready, but I'll catch up with you later?"

"Yeah, sure," he says.

His mom hustles off, and I watch Emil's face go through a myriad of complicated emotions.

"You would not *believe* the surgery I scrubbed in on this morning," Julian is saying. The conversation veers to Julian's job, and Emil stands beside me, nodding in all the right places, clearly listening. His eyes, though, are someplace else.

I give Emil a little tug when it's polite to do so, the others talking about Eloise's recent trip to Africa now.

"Do you think Rebecca is here?" I ask.

His face brightens at that. "Probably. Come on."

I follow Emil into the living room, where more of his family are gathered. He does another round of introductions. There's Uncle Bart. Aunt Sylvia. Cousins Mark and Calvin and Jessa. Emil asks Mark about his budding agricultural business. He knows about Bart's hospital visit for his knee. He remembers Calvin's girlfriend Gloria, who couldn't make it today.

No one seems to know a damn thing about Emil.

I field a couple questions, staying away from the topic of porn, since Emil told me no one in his family knows about that. But we talk about how Emil and I met—the PG version of us being neighbors. And I admit I made my clothes when Jessa asks. She seems surprised by that, but not in a bad way.

After talking for a few minutes, Emil moves us along with a polite, "Excuse us." I follow him up the stairs, my chest tight and lungs aching, as if they don't have enough room to expand. It takes me a second to realize what it is I'm feeling. *Indignation.*

We find Henry and Rebecca in one of the bedrooms upstairs. Rebecca flies right off the bed, knocking into Emil. For the first time since we arrived, Emil's shoulders lose their tension. He lets go of my hand to hug Rebecca back.

"Hey, Bec," he says gently. When they disentangle, he gives his siblings a reproachful look. "What are you two doing up here?"

"Hiding, obviously," Rebecca says, plopping back onto the mattress. Henry is sitting on the floor, and Emil walks over, bumping his brother's foot.

"Hey," Henry says, his focus on the same handheld video game he was playing the last time we met. His eyes flick up briefly, first to Emil and then to me. "Hey, Christian."

"Hey, Henry. Nice to see you again," I say.

Rebecca clears her throat loudly. "*Emil*. Are you going to introduce me?"

Emil snorts. "Bec, this is Christian, my boyfriend. Although you already know that."

Rebecca gives me a big smile. "You're really pretty."

I let out a laugh. "Thanks. So are you."

She beams wider.

"Why are you two hiding?" Emil asks, taking a seat on the floor next to Henry.

Rebecca gives him a look he can't see from over his shoulder. "Uh, why are you?"

"Touché," Emil mutters.

I sit down next to Rebecca, my leg against Emil's shoulder. "Will we miss dinner if we're up here?"

Everyone shakes their heads in unison, and I stifle a laugh.

"They'll call us," Emil says.

"Can't miss it," Henry answers.

"Okay, then," I say, lips twitching.

"Is your grandma here?" Rebecca asks. Emil presses his shoulder into my leg, which I take as his way of letting me know he and his sister talked about her.

"No, she wasn't feeling up to the trip," I tell Rebecca.

Truthfully, I think part of it was not wanting to burden me, Emil, and the Reeds. I assured her she was welcome, but my grandma has always been fiercely independent in her own way. She had to be after losing both her husband and her son. Her decision to move into the assisted living facility was a way to ensure I wasn't shouldering the responsibility of looking after her. I couldn't change her mind back then, and neither could I convince her to come today.

Emil and I will go see her tomorrow.

Rebecca makes a sad sound. "That's too bad. Well, at least take some pecan pie home for her. Mom makes great pecan pie."

"That she does," Emil says, giving me a little smile over his shoulder.

I push his glasses up his nose.

When Emil's phone chimes, he whips his head back around and swears. I bite my tongue as he opens up the app he installed on his phone just the other day.

"What's that?" Rebecca asks, leaning over to get a better view of the screen.

"It's a pet cam," Emil murmurs, practically holding his breath as the video loads. One of the crabs is moving, which is why it sent an alert. He has it set to chime at any detectable motion.

We all watch as the new crab makes its way across one end of the terrarium. He and Arthur haven't had a single altercation, but Emil has been doting over them like the mothering crab daddy he is. It's beyond adorable, but I don't dare repeat that sentiment now.

Emil relaxes as the new crab climbs into the submersible water dish.

"Aw," Rebecca says. "He's swimming. Is that the new one? You never told me his name."

"That's because I haven't named him yet," Emil says.

"Emil," his sister says sternly. "You've had him for over a month. He needs a name."

"Yeah," Henry puts in.

Emil huffs a laugh. "I don't know what to choose. Nothing matches Sir Arthurpod, His Royal Cuteness, Burrower of Sand and Creator of Dreams."

Rebecca clicks her tongue. "It doesn't have to match, you doof. He's his own crab. It just has to be right for him."

"Well, shit," I mutter before clamping a hand over my mouth. "*Fuck*, I can't stop swearing around your siblings."

Emil snorts as Rebecca titters a laugh.

We all jolt when someone yells, "Dinner!"

"See?" Henry says, pocketing his video game as he stands. "Can't miss it."

Emil shoots me a grin as the four of us make our way downstairs. Emil's family is so big, there's a table set up in the kitchen and another in the more formal dining room. I follow my boyfriend, plating up at the counter where a selection of classic American Thanksgiving dishes are spread. There's turkey, mashed potatoes, green bean casserole, and cranberry sauce, to name a few. But there's also French onion soup Emil's mom made and a fig spread most of the family slathers on their rolls. I assume those particular dishes are part of their tradition.

Thanksgiving for me growing up was a mishmash of the American holiday and the Korean one my grandma celebrated before she and my grandpa moved to the states. Instead of turkey, my grandma prepared traditional Korean food, and we gathered at her apartment, just me, her, and my mom. It was the one time a year I swear my mother softened, just a little.

My mom stopped coming to Thanksgiving when I turned eighteen, as if her obligation to me was complete. After that, it was just me and my grandma, celebrating Chuseok in November instead of during the eighth lunar month. But it was *our* tradition, and we kept it going.

This was the first year my grandma wasn't able to cook.

"You okay?" Emil asks softly.

I give him a quick nod. "Yeah, of course. Ready to eat?"

He watches me for a moment longer before nodding. We take our seats in the dining room, and I finally meet Emil's dad, who we missed during our earlier rounds. He looks like a gruffer version of Emil, a little harder around the edges and worn by time.

"Emil, how's your semester going?" the older man asks, cutting into his turkey.

Emil finishes his sip of water before answering. "Good. I'm taking this class on cognitive biases that's fascinating. Like the frequency illusion? How, once you actively take note of something, you're more likely to notice it again and again?"

"What do you mean?" I ask.

He turns to me. "Say someone tells you about this all-natural brand of soap they've started buying. All of a sudden, you start noticing it at the store and seeing advertisements for it on TV, leading you to believe you're encountering that soap more frequently. In actuality, it's been there all along, but you simply weren't perceiving it because your brain was filtering out the information, not deeming it noteworthy or important enough to catalogue."

"Like selective vision?" I ask.

"Exactly," he replies, eyes bright behind his glasses. "The truth is we do this all the time. We can't ever trust our own brains to be unbiased because literally everything we see, hear, smell, think is based on our own perceptions of the world and the way we filter data. Two people can look at the same exact painting and see entirely different things. Someone might see beauty. Someone might see pain. Neither are wrong. But no two people will ever look at the world the same way because our worldview is crafted entirely inside our own heads, not outside of it. Imagine what we could learn if we simply asked each other questions instead of assuming our reality was the only one?"

Ho-ly shit.

My heart hammers as I look at my boyfriend. At his soft smile and brightly lit eyes. He's stunning.

"That's a beautiful way to look at the world, Specs."

He grins at me, cheeks flushed, before turning back to his dad. The man is now in a conversation with Eloise, no longer paying attention to Emil. It's small, the flicker in Emil's smile as he faces his plate again, but it's there. A crack. The tiniest break in his armor.

It feels like my own chest is splitting in two.

I grab Emil's hand, tugging it close and kissing the smooth skin. "Would you tell me more about that later?" I ask.

He nods, and, after a moment, I let his hand go.

We finish our meal with his family and stay for a while after that. Without being asked, his mom packs us a to-go bag to take to my grandma, including a piece of pecan pie. I thank her, touched by the gesture.

Rebecca hugs Emil fiercely before we go, and Henry gives him an up-nod that Emil chuckles at. He ruffles Henry's hair, deftly avoiding the swipe Henry takes at him. Rebecca gives me a hug, too, and tells me to watch out for her brother. I decide I like her and Henry the best.

When we get to the car, Emil turns the ignition without a word. I sense his need for silence, so I stay quiet, my hand resting on his thigh during the drive. Once Emil parks behind his building, he doesn't make a single move to get out of the vehicle. His hands grip the steering wheel tightly, knuckles white.

"I didn't need to go into psychology to understand why I am the way I am," he says. "Why I crave attention."

I swear that crack in my chest splits wider, a fissure of aching pain. It's confusion as to why his family seems so easily capable of ignoring Emil. Anger that they're not there for him the way they should be. Family isn't always perfect; I know that. But I wish, for Emil's sake, his were better.

I lift my hand to his face, tracing first the eyebrow nearest me and then cupping the back of his head. "Emil," I say gently, waiting for him to meet my eye. "I see you."

There's an intake of breath, a shuddering exhalation. And then there, in his car, Emil cries.

Fuck, does he cry.

Chapter 25
EMIL

I'm groggy as consciousness greets me, everything muted and blurry around the edges. My eyes feel dry, and I have no doubt they're still red from the crying I did last night.

Slowly, I turn my head, unable to see Christian clearly without my glasses but picking up on the slow rise and fall of his chest in the morning light. I ease away, my need to use the bathroom overriding my desire to stay in bed with my boyfriend. I make sure to grab my glasses before walking out the door.

After relieving myself, I wash my hands, clean my face, and then stare into the mirror for a good minute. I've always considered my looks to be average. And that's never bothered me. I'm fine being average. It's made it easier to blend in.

But now, I'm starting to wonder if I'd only convinced myself I was happy disappearing into a crowd. Expecting otherwise—expecting to be seen—would have meant setting myself up for failure.

My parents don't listen to me. They ask questions. They say we'll catch up. But they don't hear me. They don't try. Julian and Eloise aren't much better.

It's easy to say it's my own fault. I don't speak up enough. I don't tell them it hurts. But for the longest time, I was just a child. I was a child who fell through the cracks, who learned how to shift sideways so it chafed less. They should have noticed. Why don't they notice?

Christian sees me. Would it be so hard for them to try to see me, too?

I brush my teeth angrily, my motions stiff and jerky. I spit angrily, too. I wish I had an appointment with my therapist today because *fuck* do I want to rant and rave. But maybe I have something better.

Christian is still sleeping when I get back to the bedroom. I climb onto the mattress slowly, not sure whether or not I intend to wake him. But he stirs, deciding the matter for me. His eyes blink open, and a slow smile spreads across his face as I crawl over top of him, settling my weight on his body like a blanket. His arms come around me.

"Hey," he says quietly.

"Hi," I answer, brushing his hair back. The strands fall like silk between my fingers, and I repeat the motion, letting his hair cascade to the side again and again. "When do you want to go see your grandma?"

"I told her we'd be there around lunchtime. What time is it now?"

I check the analog clock on my nightstand. "Ten."

He makes a rumbly sound, stretching slightly, even though he never lets me go. "Would you help me make songpyeon before we leave?"

"Um," I say slowly. "Make what now?"

Christian chuckles, looking so damn beautiful I have trouble not kissing him. "It's a Korean rice cake. They're my grandma's favorite and about the only thing I know how to cook."

"Oh. Yeah. I'd love to help."

Christian's smile is like the sun, and I give in, leaning down to catch his lips. They're soft, and he's warm, and when his cock presses up against me, I shift quickly downwards.

His chuckle is raspy. "You're in a mood, Specs."

"I'm always in a mood around you," I admit, tugging his sleep shorts past his hips.

Christian doesn't complain. His cock stands proud, and I take it in my mouth, humming around him as he hardens fully.

"Fuck, Specs," he says hoarsely, hand sifting through my hair. "Jerk yourself off. Let me see you."

I shiver, pushing my pants down and getting a hand around my cock.

"Later," he says breathily, "when we get home, you're going to show yourself off for me. You're going to fuck yourself with your fingers or one of your toys, and I'm going to watch."

Yes.

I suck harder, stroke myself faster.

"And then, before you come, you're going to take what you need from my cock, and you're going to show me how beautiful you look with my name spilling off your tongue."

I come across Christian's leg before I can utter a word, my moan reverberating around his dick. He swears, pumping his hips up, fucking my mouth. I'm still shaking when his release coats the back of my throat.

"Jesus, Specs," he mutters. "Get up here."

I do, climbing up Christian's body and fitting my mouth to his. It takes a while before we make it over to his place, but neither of us seems to mind.

"So explain to me what these are?" I request as Christian leads me into his kitchen. "What'd you call them again?"

"Songpyeon," he answers, pulling a few items out of his pantry. The sun filters in through the small kitchen window, lighting Christian as he stands in front of the counter. "They're a traditional Korean food made during the autumn harvest festival. Think sweet, chewy...basically a dessert dumpling." He grabs a bowl next, setting it down on the countertop. "I already bought the rice flour and sesame seeds, but I don't have pine needles, unfortunately."

"Pine needles?" I ask in surprise.

"You don't eat them," he says, chuckling. "They get steamed with the rice cakes. It makes them smell nice."

"Ah."

"My grandma would make these in different colors. Pink and green and yellow. She made her own rice flour, too, but I don't have the patience for that."

I chuckle as Christian opens the bag of flour.

"Ready?" he asks.

I give him a firm nod. "Show me how it's done."

Christian mixes up the dough for the rice cakes with quick efficiency, and we let it rest while making the filling. Roasted sesame seeds, sugar, honey, a pinch of salt. When the dough is ready, he breaks off sections, showing me how to roll them into balls and then press a well into the center. Once the filling is inside, the dough gets crimped to look like a half moon. Christian's look much neater than mine.

We steam the songpyeon in his grandmother's bamboo steamer. After they're done, Christian drops them in a cold water bath. He gives me one to try, and I moan around the honeyed seeds and soft, chewy dough.

"Fuck," I manage. "We should make these every year."

It takes me a moment to realize why Christian's face has gone all soft. The implication of my words.

"Yeah, Specs," he says, his smile almost bashful. "I'd really like that."

My chest nearly bursts.

Christian loads up the songpyeon, along with the food from yesterday, and we head out the door. I'm used to the route to the assisted living facility, having made the journey several times for my research aide position, but this is the first time I'm arriving with Christian. He leads the way to his grandma's room, knocking on the open door.

"Christian," Mrs. Park says warmly. Christian doesn't hesitate to walk her way, bending down to give his grandmother a hug. "And Mr. Reed. It's so good to see you again."

"Hi, Mrs. Park," I respond.

"Are you hungry?" Christian asks. "We brought lunch."

"Just in time," Mrs. Park says, getting out of her chair. "I was starting to feel a bit peckish."

Christian walks beside his grandma as we make our way down the hall to the communal dining area. Other residents are eating, too, most of them with the same prepared lunch from the facility. We sit at a table of our own, and as soon as Christian pulls out the container with the songpyeon, Mrs. Park's eyes light up.

"Oh, sweetheart," she says, giving his arm a squeeze. She sighs as she picks up one of the rice cakes, popping the entire thing in her mouth.

"They're not as good as yours," Christian says.

His grandmother shakes her head. "They're perfect. Now tell me what's new."

Christian tells his grandma about making the rice cakes with me in her old kitchen. About Thanksgiving yesterday with my family, although he paints the evening in a delicate light. He shows her a picture of the floral skirt he's working on, which she gushes over, complimenting the fabric choice and his impeccable design. She asks about my classes, too, and the research project. I had to give Mrs. Park's sessions over to Lucy, seeing as my relationship with Christian could have made me biased, but she assures me Lucy is doing a fine job. "Although not as good as you," she says with a wink.

Mrs. Park also regales me with a few stories from Christian's youth. He doesn't seem to mind, although he does blush when she tells me about his attempt to dye his own fabric. It didn't go well, but he was only thirteen.

We sit together and talk for nearly two hours, and the entire time, Christian's grandmother is present. It's in the way she listens and encourages us to go on. It's how she never once seems impatient or loses focus when I accidentally ramble a little too long about the philosophical concept of One Mind, in which all beings share a collective consciousness, our individual experiences like an endless spectrum of light cast from the same prism. She's there, in body and in mind, and it's such a stark difference from how I felt last night that I ache with it, both good and bad.

When Christian and I go, it's with a promise to visit again soon.

We're nearly to the door when I say, "Do I accept it?"

It's clear I startled him, but Christian doesn't falter as we walk toward the car. "Accept what, Specs?"

"Feeling small around them," I answer, knowing he'll understand what I mean. "Feeling like I don't matter."

He's quiet for a beat. "You talked to them when Henry was feeling that way."

"It's different."

"Is it?"

I swallow, and we come to a stop in front of the car. "How do I tell the people who raised me that I want them to *care* more? How do I say that, Christian?"

"Just like that," he says gently. "You be honest. Tell them how you feel."

"I'm scared to."

"Why? I know you have an answer, Mr. Psych Major, even if it's not one you like."

I huff a small, pained laugh. "What if I find out they truly don't care?" I ask, my voice breaking. "What if I say something, and it doesn't get better?"

Christian takes my hand in his, playing with the tips of my fingers. His are slightly callused from sewing. "If you never say anything, you're going to hurt. You already are. Isn't it worth the chance that it might get better?"

I let out a breath. "Will you be there?"

He draws me in, arms wrapping around me tight. "Of course, Specs."

"Fuck," I mutter. "Yeah, okay. Soon."

"Soon," he agrees, letting me go.

We get into the car, and for the second time in so many days, we head back home together. Desperate for a way to keep my mind occupied while we drive, I throw out the first topic that comes to mind.

"Christian? Do you ever want to bottom? Not that I need you to," I'm quick to add. "But I know you're an exclusive top for the studio, and I just realized I never asked if you have a different preference for your personal life."

Christian hums, the sound low. "It's not something I've ever enjoyed. Would that be a problem? If I never bottomed?"

"No," I answer immediately, glancing his way. "If you ever want to try, just let me know. But... No, Christian. I like what we have. I don't need that from you."

He offers me a grateful smile.

"Besides," I say, clearing my throat, "it's probably for the best. I can be a little greedy when it comes to your cock."

"Is that so?" he says, smirking now. "I had no idea."

"Shut up," I grumble.

He snorts a laugh, and I can't help but smile to myself.

After we park, Christian heads over to his place to grab a change of clothes. I check on the crabs, putting some fresh grapes and broccoli in their terrarium because, "It's good for you, Arthur and friend. Don't argue." They don't, but Arthur steers clear of the green stuff.

With that done, I take a shower, making sure to wash myself *thoroughly*. Christian still hasn't arrived by the time I'm done, so I flop onto my bed to wait.

My phone pings with a text.

Christian: Looking good, Specs.

I bolt upright, my pulse firing as I look out the window. Christian is in his bedroom next door. Another text comes through.

Christian: Take off your pants for me?

Holy fuck.

The request, near-demand, Christian made earlier comes racing back to me. He wanted me to show off for him. He wanted to watch.

I had no clue he meant like *this*.

How is this man so perfect for me?

Hands shaking, I fumble with my fly. It seems to take forever, but finally, I get my pants down and kick them off the end of the bed. My socks follow.

Christian: You're gorgeous, Specs. Every inch of you. Touch yourself for me. Show me how much your cock is aching for it.

"Fucking hell," I mutter, setting down my phone and lying back. I slip my shirt partway up my stomach and let my hand trail down my abdomen. It feels as if Christian is right in the room with me, gaze hot and assessing. But he's not. He's across the alleyway, just like he was when we first met—when I fucked myself for him after getting that letter, not knowing who my mystery voyeur was, not even caring.

I care now. Because knowing it's Christian watching me, *wanting* me for exactly who I am? It's better than any thrill of the unknown.

I let out a breath as I slide my fingers underneath the band of my briefs, brushing the tip of my cock. He said to go slow, so *slowly*, I maneuver the fabric down below my cockhead, giving him only a peek. The band keeps my dick in place, and I stretch a hand over my head as my other rests on my lower abdomen, thumb running a slow circuit over my slit.

My phone pings.

Christian: Sexy fucking tease. Could you come like that, rubbing just the tip of your cock and your nipples?

Fucking hell. Probably, yes. But there's something else I want.

I reply with one hand, my other still toying with my dick.

Me: You said you'd fuck me.

Christian: Mm. After you give me a show.

Instead of reaching for my nipples, I turn onto my stomach and lower my briefs, giving Christian a view of my ass. I spread my cheek to the side and pointedly make a middle finger, rubbing it over my rim.

Christian: You cheeky shit.

"You like it," I mumble, pressing the tip of my finger inside my ass. I groan, rocking back on the digit.

Another ping comes from my phone, and I curse, fumbling to grab it.

Christian: Get the lube, Specs. Open yourself up. Pretend it's my tongue.

"Fucking..." I hastily type out a one-handed response.

Me: Need 2 hear u.

The call comes through a moment later, and I accept it, tossing my phone on my pillow right after.

"Well hello, stranger," Christian says.

"You're an ass," I mutter, reaching into my nightstand.

He laughs. "Because I like watching my boyfriend pleasure himself?"

My body rolls in a shiver, and I'm not sure if it's because Christian is so good at pushing my buttons or because of the simple word that thrills me every time I hear it. *Boyfriend.*

"You're an ass because it's my finger and not your tongue," I inform him, popping the cap on the lube. I wet my finger and bring it back to my hole, slipping it all the way inside with a sigh.

"You like it, Specs," he says, voice hoarse. "You like fucking yourself for me. You like showing me how much your body begs for it. And I like watching you."

"Why?" I nearly whisper, pumping two fingers in and out now.

Christian hums as my pulse hammers. "Because you're beautiful like this," he says seriously. "You're real. You light up the same way you do when you talk about brains and biases and things I don't entirely understand but want to learn more about. You let go of all the responsibilities weighing you down, and you show me living proof of what it means to be in the moment. To be transparent and wholly yourself, and I admire that. It's how I want to live. I think you're brave, Specs. And I thought I was brave, too. But you make me feel invincible."

My breath puffs out of me, my fingers stilling in my ass. I turn my head, seeking Christian out, finding him watching me. He's too far away.

"Get over here," I rasp.

"Are you sure? I'd be happy to play voyeur a little longer, my kinky exhibitionist."

"Christian. Get over here now."

"All right, Specs," he says softly, walking away from the window. "I hope your door is unlocked."

"It is. Hurry. *Fuck.*"

"On my way."

Christian clicks off the call, and I blow out a breath, every nerve ending in my body alive and sparking. I have no doubt the pleasure centers in my brain are lit like a supernova right now. But there's more, too. There's warmth in my chest. A lightness in my lungs.

There are certain things necessary to our survival as human beings. Eating. Drinking. Breathing. But, sometimes, our brains deem love to be just as essential. It's not a tangible resource. It's not something we can hold or measure in our palms. But we can trace its path throughout our neural networks. We can see the very proof of love's existence in our body.

I have no doubt that by coming into my life, Christian has altered my brain chemistry.

And in doing so, he's changed my world.

Chapter 26

CHRISTIAN

Emil's apartment is quiet when I enter. I lock the door behind me, heading straight for his room. I falter at the doorway.

Emil is on his hands and knees. Or, rather, *hand* and knees. His chest is bowed toward the bed, cheek against the mattress, one hand in the sheets as his other holds on to the dildo in his ass. He's moving it almost leisurely, in and out at a slow pace as if savoring the glide. His ass is aimed my way, giving me a perfect view of every stroke and the way his body yields to the toy, welcoming it in.

"Are you going...to just stand there?" he asks around panting breaths. "Or are you going...to touch me?"

"Fuck, Specs," I mutter, my gaze roaming over every inch of him. He got rid of his shirt, leaving him entirely bare, and I don't think I've ever seen a more enticing sight than this man waiting for me on his bed in nothing but glasses with a fake dick up his ass. "Thank God for asbestos."

"What?" he asks, trying to look back at me.

I shake my head quickly, shucking my clothes. "Nothing."

When I ease onto the mattress, Emil groans. "Thank fuck," he says, making a tortured sound as he pushes the toy in from tip to base. "Need your hands, Christian. Need them...like air."

"Jesus, you get mouthy when you're turned on," I say, appreciative of that fact.

He lets the dildo go the moment my hand touches his, and I grip the base, pumping it in and out. His moan has my gut clenching.

"Look at you," I nearly whisper.

"In me," he rasps, widening his stance, both hands near his head now. "Get in me, Christian."

"You say my name a lot when you're turned on, too," I tell him. "Even in our videos. You beg for Vixen."

"If you think..." He huffs out a breath as I grind the dildo shallowly. "If you think...I'm going to be ashamed...of asking for what I want, you're wrong."

"Never," I assure him, taking his cock in hand. I give him a slow stroke. "It's beautiful. Every goddamn thing about you, Specs. Tell me what you want. Ask for it. *Beg* for it. I want to give it to you."

"Your dick," he huffs out indignantly, making me laugh. "Gimme your fucking dick."

"All yours."

I pull out the lubed toy and drop it on the bed. I'm up on my knees, the tip of my cock slotting against Emil, when I pause.

"Shit, condom?" I ask.

We've never gone without. But neither of us has partners outside of the studio, so if he wants to...

"No," Emil answers, pushing back against me and enveloping the tip of my cock. "Just you. C'mon."

Biting my lip—*hard*—I ease inside Emil's body. He's already loose from the dildo, but he still clasps me like a fist, his internal rings gripping as I press forward, those same muscles trying to hold me tight as I ease back out. Emil groans impatiently, but I take my time, in and out, in and out, until, *finally*, my hips meet his ass.

"Fuck," I mutter, my entire body rolling in a shiver. "I feel like I already came."

He huffs out a small laugh, which makes me groan.

"Christ, Specs. The way you feel."

"My ass loves you," he says.

This time, it's me laughing. "Could I stay here forever?"

He wiggles back on me, hips rolling. "Who would get me food while I study?"

"We can move the fridge."

He chuckles into the bedding before easing up onto his hands. "Sit on your heels," he tells me.

Curious, I do as he asks. Emil moves with me, not letting my cock leave his ass. As I sit back, he settles in my lap, his knees braced wide outside of mine.

"Hold on to me," he instructs.

I wrap my arms around his chest, and Emil starts to ride my dick.

I groan, fingers flexing against his skin. "Fuck, Specs."

His movements are shallow, the position not allowing him more leverage, but when I brace my own hand behind me and punch up on his next downward pass, the both of us moan. We get a rhythm going quickly, the sight of Emil's ass working my dick sexy as all get-out. I keep one hand over Emil's heart as he starts babbling, but when he loses purchase, his sounds becoming more frantic, I slide my palm down to his stomach.

"Can I?" I ask.

He nods his head quickly. "Yes, yes, please. Need it."

I ease forward, and Emil moves onto his hands and knees again, the motion separating us. He understands what I want when I give his side a gentle shove. As soon as he rolls onto his back, I press back inside his body. Emil's groan mirrors my own, his legs embracing me like a lover as I start to move.

"So good," Emil mumbles, taking my thrusts with relish, his body shifting with mine as if trying to pull me deeper. "Like air," he practically breathes, not for the first time.

"What?"

He makes a small sound and reaches for me. "Kiss me. Kiss me, kiss me."

I do. Of course I do.

Emil's lips are soft, but he clings to me with urgency, his cock rubbing against my abs, his body warm beneath my own. He feels familiar. Every inch of him feels familiar to me, even though I'm sure I could spend the rest of my life exploring, finding more and more to learn about this man.

When Emil comes, I'm not expecting it. One moment, our lips are fused together, our bodies rolling like two functioning parts of the same whole. And the next, he's inhaling a shaky breath, and his cum is coating my stomach. My grip on him tightens, my mouth breaking from his as the squeeze of his ass pulls me over the edge faster than I thought possible. I cry out as I unload inside his body. For once, there's no barrier between us, and my cum coats the both of us, making the glide silky smooth as I pump another few times.

"Oh, fuck," I stutter out, doing it again, pumping shallow-ly. "Oh God."

Emil's fingers dance through my hair, gently tugging the strands. "You like that," he says, squeezing around me.

I groan, dropping my face to Emil's neck. He laughs, hands drifting down to my ass. He digs in, heels and fingers both, making sure there's no space between us.

"Do it again," he demands.

Helpless to disobey, I fuck my cum into his body, my dick not yet soft. "Okay?" I ask, not wanting to keep going if he's oversensitive.

"Mhm," he says. "Feels good. Again."

I curse against his skin and pull out further. The glide of my cock inside his ass is effortless, and knowing it's my cum making him so wet has me wanting to take up camp.

How many times could I fill him? How much could he take?

"Fuck, Christian," Emil breathes. "Are you getting hard again?"

"Is it too much?" I ask, lifting my head.

"Don't you dare stop," Emil says, his back arching.

I groan, bending down to latch on to his nipple. His cock twitches against my stomach.

"Don't stop," he mutters again, voice nearly lost. "Don't ever stop."

Not ever.

The address Noel texts me to meet him at isn't his own. "I see things are going well," I say when he opens Max's door.

He grins sheepishly. "Guess you could say that. Come on in. Max is at the bar."

I'd heard Max found a new job. Apparently, he ran out of his shift that night I texted about Noel potentially being in trouble. Luckily, his manager was understanding.

"The bar is open this early?" I ask, following Noel into the bright kitchen.

He nods, pulling tea from the cupboard. "It's directly across from a hotel, so they open for the lunch crowd. Get a lot of businessmen and such. Want tea?"

"Sure," I say, sitting at the table as Noel puts a kettle on the stovetop. A smile quirks my lips. "This looks good on you."

"What's that?" he asks.

"Contentment."

He blushes, grabbing a couple mugs from a rack beside the fridge. "It's, uh...been really nice. Max said I can stay here as long as I want. Which I kind of want to, you know? My place sucks, and his is..." He waves a hand around instead of finishing his sentence. It's a nice apartment. Small but cozy.

"And you two?" I prod.

"Yeah," he breathes out. "We, uh... We're good."

I huff a laugh. "Just good?"

"The man is a god, happy?"

"Very," I say, grinning. "I'm happy for *you*, Noel. You're a good person. You deserve another good person who can see and protect that."

"Like Emil does for you?" he asks, shutting off the teakettle as it starts to whistle.

I let out a breath, my thoughts turning to Specs and the soft smile he gave me this morning when he woke. "Yeah. Like that."

Noel's smirk is knowing. It doesn't escape me how far we've both come in a few short months. Our lives have changed drastically. Hopefully, for the better.

"Tell me about your job search?" I ask.

Noel nods, setting a mug of tea in front of me before taking a seat. We chat for almost an hour, catching up about my sewing and his interview at a coffee shop down the road. It's good, and if for nothing else, I can thank Knee Highs for bringing Noel into my life.

It's midafternoon when I leave the apartment, and the sun is shining brightly, warming the otherwise cool air. It doesn't hit me where in town I am until I turn a corner and come face to face with the diner where my mom works. It's such a surprise that, for a moment, my steps falter. I stare at the mint-green awning and faded paint on the window, feeling ten again, a young boy who went with his mom to work for the day, excited to sit at a worn booth and watch the world pass by. The adventure faded the older I got, just like my relationship with my mom.

Part of me desperately wants to keep moving. Just pass on by and pretend I was never here. But I don't. I cross the street and head for the diner's front door.

The bell jingles as I step through, the establishment mostly empty at this time of day, apart from an older gentleman seated by the front window. He gives me a nod from behind his paper, not even looking twice at the skirt I'm wearing.

Again, part of me whispers to just go. To turn around and leave before anyone else can notice me. Before a *particular* person can notice me.

But that voice feels a lot like fear. And I'm tired of listening to it.

I walk up to the U-shaped counter at the center of the diner. There are chrome stools all around it, the style reminiscent of the fifties. Some diners replicate the aesthetic. This one is just that old.

It takes a minute before the door to the kitchen swings open. It's not a shock, exactly, to see my mom walk through, but I still jolt when our eyes connect for the first time in years. She stutters almost to a stop when she sees me but collects herself quickly. She doesn't bother pasting on a smile, but her expression remains politely distant, if not a little weary.

She looks so tired, and I hate it.

"Christian," she says simply, stopping on the other side of the counter. Her outfit is light blue, her apron white.

"Hey, Mom."

She looks me over, this woman with light blonde hair and icy blue eyes that I used to admire. Used to adore. I wonder what she sees. A disappointment? Her son? A man in a skirt she has nothing in common with except a love for eighties music?

She doesn't say anything about the skirt, but I can tell by the pinch in her brow she doesn't like it. I didn't wear it because of her, though, and I think that's something she's never fully understood. I wear it for *me*. No one else. Her opinion never has and never will trump my love for *me*.

"Have you been well?" she finally asks, just as the silence starts to wear thin.

"Yeah," I say a little wearily myself. Being around my mother feels like standing under a rain cloud. I'd almost forgotten how oppressive it could be. "I've been good. Grandma moved into an assisted living facility at the beginning of the year."

She hums, retying the apron around her waist. She doesn't ask for more details, and I let it go.

"Anything new with you?" I ask.

She glances out the window, as if looking for anything that could possibly be new in her life. "I'm fine," she answers.

It's not an answer at all.

"Did you come for a reason?" she asks, straightening a plastic container of napkins.

Suddenly, I can't stand it. This place. The plastic and cracked leather. The remnants of a time long past and the woman standing in it with disinterest in her tone.

"I deserved better," I tell her.

Her eyes meet mine. She doesn't flinch. Doesn't even look surprised. "I did the best I could, Christian. Maybe it wasn't enough, but...it was all I had."

Her words hit me like a ton of bricks. I can't help but think of Specs. Of his demonstration of neural processes on the comforter in his bedroom. Of hope and wanting to change. I think about the brain maps on his living room wall, how different fear is from love. I think about every person seeing the world through their own lens, through their own biases and experiences, and how I'll never truly know how my mom feels. Where I see beauty, she sees pain.

Maybe I did deserve better. But so does she.

"I'm sorry, Mom," I say sincerely. "I'm sorry you're stuck in the past. I truly am. I hope, one day, you can be happy again."

My mom barely blinks, barely acknowledges my words, and with a nod, I turn to go. My heart is heavy as I walk away. As the door jingles overhead. It's an ache for her. For myself. For the relationship we never had and never will.

There's no telling what this world will bring with all its chaos, with all its beauty. And I still don't know whether or not I believe in fate. Destiny. It's a little hard not to when Emil fell into my life not once or even twice, but time and time again, as if for a reason.

But there's one thing I'm sure of. I'm not destined to end up like my mother. I'm in charge of this life I've been given, and I'm going to make the best of it. I have my grandma. I have songpyeon and sewing. I have nature documentaries and Noel and my new coworkers at Elite 8 Studios.

I have Specs.

I have innumerable things in my life that are *good*. Things that make me happy, that spark joy.

I'm living. I'm *loving*. And that, I know with all my heart, is more than enough.

Chapter 27

EMIL

Christian was acting cagey this morning when I asked if he wanted to drive together to Elite 8 Studios. He told me he'd meet me here. That he had something to do first.

But he didn't say what.

I try not to let it worry me, but I've never been very successful at *not* worrying.

"Emil?" a deep voice says, breaking me from my trance.

"Oh. Hey, Trevor."

"Everything all right?" he asks. Trevor has worked here longer than anyone else. His moniker, Bruiser, comes from the fact that the guy is a beast: big and muscled and almost scary-looking if you didn't know better. In truth, he wouldn't hurt a fly.

"I'm fine," I assure him, although me standing in the entryway to the studio not moving a muscle probably doesn't help my case.

I head alongside Trevor into the building.

"Filming today?" I ask him.

He nods. "Breaking in the newest hire, Sean."

I snort. "Go easy on him."

Trevor gives me a grin. He isn't known for going *easy* on set, but that's part of his charm.

"Can I ask you something?" I say abruptly.

Trevor stops with me outside the break room. "Of course."

"You're married."

He nods. "Sixteen years now."

"Do you think... I mean, is it *wrong* to get off on fucking other men?" As soon as the words leave my mouth, I backpedal. "Shit, I didn't mean to imply there's something wrong with *you*, just..."

"Just yourself?" Trevor fills in, apparently seeing right through me. I wince, but he answers me evenly. "I don't think it's wrong unless you or your partner feels bad because of it."

"And...it's never been a problem for your husband?"

"No," he says, a smile lifting the corner of his mouth. "Isaac... He can be such a brat. He'll play at jealousy, don't get me wrong. But then I come home, rail him over the countertop like he was all but begging me to do, and everything is fine."

I choke a little.

"I fully believe you can be in this line of work while committing your heart to one person and one person alone," Trevor says seriously. "Sex and love...they don't have to go hand in hand. They do, for many. And that's fine. But there's nothing wrong with you, Emil, just because you're not in a purely monogamous relationship."

"I get off on people watching me," I admit for the very first time. I've never told any of my coworkers that. "I crave it. I don't want to stop."

Trevor doesn't look particularly surprised by my admission. "Then I guess it's a good thing you found someone who enjoys it with you, huh?"

I let out a breath. "Yeah. I guess you're right."

He clasps my shoulder gently, squeezing once before letting go. "Don't let other people's opinions bother you, Emil. That way lies unhappiness. I'd rather be happy, wouldn't you?"

"Yeah. I would."

Trevor nods. "Anything else?"

"No. Thank you."

Trevor gives me a smile before continuing on into the break room. I walk past to the locker room, setting my bookbag down once inside. It's quiet at the moment, although I know it won't stay that way for long. There's always activity in the studio. People coming and going. Sex happening inside these walls. I suppose, if I cared what people thought, I'd never be in this business in the first place.

"Christian likes you the way you are," I remind myself, trying to soothe the old, flaring insecurities that are trying to tell me something's wrong. That Christian is pulling away or... *No.* I stop that line of thinking. Nothing's wrong. Everything with Christian is fine. *Easy*, even. "Because we fit."

We do.

His exhibitionist, that's what he calls me. And he's my beautiful voyeur.

My lips twist into a smile, but even so, I make a note to check in with my therapist to hash out some of these swirling insecurities before I self-sabotage the best thing to happen to me in...maybe ever.

"Fucking self-awareness," I mutter, plunking down onto the bench seat in front of my locker. The door swings open not a second later.

"There you are," comes a voice I'm intimately familiar with.

I spin in my seat, pulse hitching when I spot Christian. "*Holy.* Um...what, uh..."

Christian lets the door close behind him, a little smirk on his face as he walks forward. There's a trench coat tied loosely around his body, the bottom hem ending near his knees. Nothing innocent is ever hidden away underneath a trench coat.

"Christian?" I ask, my throat suddenly dry.

He stops a dozen feet or so in front of me, his legs bare apart from the cute black shoes on his feet. Ballet flats, I think. "I have a surprise for you," he says.

"Shit," I mutter, feeling my heart thump wildly in my chest. "Arrhythmia."

"What?" he asks, head cocked to the side as his hands toy with the belt near his waist.

"Uh... I had this theory that you were giving me an ar-rhythmia."

"And?" Christian asks, lips quirking. "Any conclusions?"

"Data points to yes."

He huffs a small laugh. "Should I keep the coat on, then?"

"Fuck no."

Christian chuckles, and without hesitation, he lets the trench coat slip off his arms. It pools on the floor behind him as Christian, my gorgeous-as-fuck boyfriend, this man who's sweet and supportive and perfectly filthy, stands in a multicolored tutu and nothing else. Well, nothing except for his shoes and the dainty silver chain around his stom-ach.

"Fuck," I breathe.

He raises his arms above his head, the extension making him look longer and leaner than normal, and then he spins ever so slowly, legs crossing in the process. He bends toward the floor, and I nearly have a heart attack.

"You..." I manage.

"Told you I'd wear a tutu for you, Specs. Made this one the other night. Do you like it?" he asks, standing slowly upright and then dropping his head back and to the side, neck arched as he looks at me over his shoulder.

I suck in a steadying breath, my chest feeling too warm, too tight, my eyes pricking for no discernable reason, and I say the only thing I can.

"I fucking love you."

Christian freezes, his body going rigid as his eyes widen. It takes me a second to realize what fell out of my mouth.

Shit. "I…"

"Specs," Christian says, dropping his arms and spinning toward me.

"I—" *Fuck.* "I needa take a shower."

I hop up, all but sprinting toward the showers as Christian's, "Emil," follows me. I jump into a stall and pull the curtain closed, my heart pounding, my hand shaking as I twist the shower on. Christian comes to a stop on the other side of the curtain, his form a dark shadow. "Do you need your bathroom stuff?"

Crap. "Um, yeah. Please."

Christian disappears, and a minute later, he returns, handing my toiletries bag over through a gap in the curtain.

"When you're done in there," he says evenly, "there's something I want to say. But I'm not going to do it through a shower curtain."

My heart beats fast, and I curse the words I let slip as I tug off my clothes. I dump them over the top of the curtain, and they fall with a thump.

"I know what you're doing," Christian says, sounding serious yet almost amused. "Just so you're aware."

"Um..." I mumble, letting the shower drench me. My glasses fog quickly. "I, uh..."

"And the only reason I'm not following you in there is because we go on set in five minutes. And I don't have time to dry your hair *and* my own."

I mutter another, "Shit," making quick work of shampooing my hair that most definitely didn't need to be washed.

"You okay?" Christian asks.

No.

"Of course," I squeak.

Christian simply hums. "I'll grab you a towel."

He disappears again, and I rinse my hair. I give my body a quick pass before turning off the water.

When I pull the curtain aside, Christian is standing there, still in his tutu, looking like a gorgeous wet dream, whereas I likely look like a drowned rat. I avoid eye contact as I pluck the towel from his hand and dry myself off in record time. Christian gives my arm a tug as soon as I'm done, and I let him pull me over to the mirrors. He plugs in a blow dryer and sets to work on my hair, fingers drifting through the strands as I clear the water off my glasses.

My eyes catch his once in the reflection, but I look quickly away.

As soon as the blow dryer shuts off, I grab my clothes and round the bank of lockers. I redress as Christian follows me.

"Specs."

"We're gonna be late," I say, fixing my glasses as my heart does its best to drown everything else out.

"It'll be fine," he says calmly.

I shake my head, not wanting to get in trouble with Jerome but mostly not wanting to hear whatever it is Christian needs to say. I don't want him to tell me he doesn't feel the same. That it's too much, too fast.

Why did I think it would be a good idea to date a coworker? How am I supposed to work with Christian if we break up? I can't do...*whatever* this is before our scene.

I head for the door, and Christian makes a sound behind me. "*Specs*."

I'm halfway down the hall when he catches up.

"Stop running," he says, grabbing my arm. "Just...*stop* for a second."

"Can't," I say, heading for Studio 3. "We have to get on set."

"Jerome will understand if we're a minute late," he says, walking briskly beside me.

"I can't do this," I get out, my voice nearly breaking. "I just can't, okay? Don't make me do this right now, Christian. *Please*."

He lets go of my arm, and I heave out a breath, opening the studio door. Christian follows me through without a word, and when Jerome catches sight of us, there's relief on his face.

"Cutting it close, gentlemen," our boss says, waving us on set. I hastily scoot onto the bed, my pulse racing, my stomach feeling hollow.

"Sorry," I mutter, running a hand through my hair to straighten the strands.

"Holy shit," I hear Marco say. "That skirt is sick."

Christian huffs a laugh. "Thanks. Made it by special request."

"You made that?" our boom operator says, sounding impressed. "Damn. Think you might be able to make one for my niece? She loves ballet."

"Absolutely," Christian replies, his weight settling beside me on the bed. I keep my head down. "I'd be happy to. Just let me know her size."

"Awesome, thanks," Marco says. "I'll pay you, of course."

"If we could," Jerome says loudly. "We're a minute out. Quiet on the set."

The crew shuffles around us, getting into place. Christian's hand brushes mine, but I keep my gaze resolutely on the bedspread near my knee.

"Emil," he says softly.

I hum.

He puffs out a tiny breath. "Are you okay to do a scene today?"

"Of course," I say quickly.

He makes an unhappy sound. "You don't seem okay."

"It's fine," I murmur, doing my best to keep our conversation private. "I can still do my job."

"Specs, I—"

"Ten seconds," Jerome cuts in, his hands counting us down. Christian quiets, but his fingers curl around my own.

As Jerome's hand falls away, the camera lights up red.

"Hey, everyone," Christian says, his greeting lacking its usual cheer. Out of the corner of my eye, I see the tablet scrolling furiously with text, and it takes me a second to realize why. *Christian's tutu.* He chuckles softly. "Thanks, do you like it? I made it for someone special."

His fingers tighten against mine.

"Unfortunately," Christian says slowly, "that someone can barely look at me right now."

My heart thumps, a big, forceful thing. I meet Christian's gaze slowly, and his eyes, tightened as they were, soften.

"Hi," he says quietly.

"Hi," I manage.

Christian aims a smile at the camera, taking in a deep breath. But then he shakes his head. "I, uh... Shit."

His eyes meet mine again, so very dark, so very troubled, and he says four words you never want to hear during live production.

"I can't do this."

My heart sinks.

Oh no.

Chapter 28

CHRISTIAN

"W-what?" Emil says, gaze pinging from me to the camera and back.

"I can't do this," I repeat, not giving a shit about the cameras or the people watching or anyone but Specs, who dropped a big fat *I love you* and then proceeded to run away from me as quickly as humanly possible, as if expecting me to break his beautiful heart.

As if I would ever.

"Ch—Vixen," he says, saving his slip at the last moment.

I shake my head, swinging myself toward Emil as he blinks big eyes my way. "No. I'm not okay to do a scene right now, Specs, because I can't handle my boyfriend thinking he's the only one."

His mouth pops open, and I lean closer, threading my fingers through his hair and holding tight so he can't keep running away.

"You're going to listen to me now. Just stop and listen, okay?"

Emil nods in my grip.

"I can't *stand* the thought of my boyfriend believing I don't love him, too," I say clearly, making sure he hears every word.

"Not for one more minute. Not for five. And certainly not for sixty while we put on a show. Of *course* I love you, Specs. And I thought that would be scary, but it's not."

"No?" he asks quietly, his voice barely there.

"No," I say, my lips curving into a smile. "It's wonderful and fucking *good,* and you make everything better. My goddamn midbrain lights up when I'm around you. So stop assuming the worst and just...just *kiss* me, okay? Because I love you—I *love you*—and the whole world can know for all I care."

"You...you love me?"

My laugh is pained. "Yeah, I love you. Were you lying when you said you love me, too? Because, if not, I think I deserve a ki—"

Emil's lips cut off my remark, and I let out a whimper, tugging him in tight, trying my very best to fuse our lips together. The pain that was twisting tight in my chest ever since Emil fled into the shower stall finally unfurls, bringing with it that same swoop of joy I felt when Emil first uttered those words, "*I fucking love you.*" My gorgeous kinky neighbor. My shy exhibitionist. My remarkable boyfriend with the big brain and the even bigger heart.

"Fuck, I love you," I mumble against his mouth.

His sound is equal parts happiness and aching relief. "You do."

Another laugh. "Yes, I do."

"I do, too," he says, his hands shaking against the sides of my neck.

"Yeah, I kinda got that," I mutter affectionately.

He huffs a laugh between kisses. "God, Christian, the tutu is hot."

"There he is," I say, kissing one corner of his mouth and then the other. "You back with me, Specs?"

"Sorry I jumped into the shower with all my clothes on," he mutters against my lips.

I nearly snort. "Uh-huh."

"I was scared."

I let out a breath, tucking my face against his neck and hugging him tight. "I know. You don't have to be."

"I know that. I do," he says just as quietly. "It's just... I'm still a work in progress, okay? I might fuck up sometimes."

I lean back enough to catch his eye. "I think you're lovely."

Emil's gaze pings between my eyes, so very soft, a little trepidatious in a way I think comes from years of falling by the wayside. Of feeling unseen and, by extension, unloved. "Don't give up on me," he says, almost too quietly for me to hear.

"Never," I promise.

He lets out a breath, eyes closing. But then his entire body stiffens. "Oh my God," he mumbles. "Oh...my God. Are we... Are we still filming?"

A throat clears nearby, and Emil's eyes pinch further shut.

I bite my lip before looking to the side. The entire crew is standing silent, watching us. The light on the camera is off, but I'm guessing at least part of that was caught before they shut it down. Maybe I should feel a little more apologetic, but I can't quite find it in me to care.

"No," I say gently, giving the side of Emil's neck a squeeze. "We're not filming."

He winces, looking pained.

"Gentlemen," Jerome drawls. Emil finally opens his eyes, although it looks as if it takes considerable effort to do so. "If I didn't have a chat room full of viewers practically creaming themselves for the chance to watch two boyfriends in love getting it on in my studio, we'd be having words right about now."

"Sorry, Jerome," Emil mutters, his voice quiet but carrying in the otherwise silent room.

Jerome raises a brow, arms crossed, but I swear he doesn't actually look upset. "I'll send you the clip for your wedding. That's twice now. Videographer fees can be forwarded to Nathaniel." I'm fairly certain he's joking, but he goes on quickly. "We're done for today. Can I tell your avid fans you'll be back next week?"

I glance at Emil, who blushes but nods.

Grabbing his hand, I say, "Yeah. We're on for next week."

"Beautiful," Jerome says dryly. As he turns to walk away, he mutters, "First Dix and Adonis, and now this. Nate," he practically barks. Nathaniel heads his way. "Tell me why we spent so much effort on producing fake boyfriend videos last year? Maybe we should get some real couples in here. People eat this shit up."

Jerome's voice fades as he and Nathaniel head out of the studio. Once the door closes behind them, the rest of the crew snaps to, conversation starting up again as our coworkers begin disassembling the set.

Marco gives us a grin, his boom resting against the floor. "Super cute, you two. Congrats."

I huff a laugh as Emil nudges his glasses up his nose. "Thanks," he mumbles.

Marco heads off, joining the others, and I give Emil's shoulder a bump with my own. "Wanna get out of here?"

"Please," he whispers, practically falling against my chest. He tucks his face away, voice muffled. "Let's go home and just hide away for a couple years, okay? If Alex calls, don't answer. He'll never let us live this down."

I snort. "I dunno. I kind of liked it, Specs. Telling everyone I love my cute-as-heck boyfriend on a live stream? I'd do it again in a heartbeat."

"Yeah?" he asks, lifting his head.

"Mhm. Maybe next time, I can fuck him, too."

Emil's breath catches.

"Because I know how much he loves being railed while everyone watches," I say quietly, brushing his hair off his forehead. "Loves being on display, dick hard and chest flushed with arousal. Loves squirming and begging and showing off how gorgeous he is. How honest. How real and utterly captivating. And I love it, too."

"Shit, Christian," he mutters, shaking his head. But his eyes are soft, like maybe those words were exactly what he needed to hear. "Take me home."

"Yeah, Specs. Let's go."

"Do you think they're talking to one another?" I ask Emil as we lie on my bed, the pet cam open on his phone.

We started out at his apartment after coming home from the studio, but after Emil shoved his pants down, presented his ass, told me to *fucking wreck him already*—and, of course, I did—we migrated over here. I wanted to get a little work done on my skirt for the awards ceremony. It's nearly ready.

Now, we're lying on my mattress, legs tangled, Emil snacking on chips while we keep an eye on his crabs. They're close to each other, not touching but moving around.

"That's how they talk, right?" I ask. "By rubbing their legs together?"

Emil hums, finishing his chip before answering. "They do. It doesn't look aggressive, does it?"

I huff a laugh. "No. That'd be more..." I brandish my fist in the air. "Right?"

This time, it's Emil chuckling. "I wonder what they're saying."

"*I like your shell*," I say with a high voice that's meant to imitate a crab. "*Thanks, I like your claw. So big.*"

Emil snorts. "You're such a dork."

"I think that's you."

"Then we're both dorks," he counters.

"Fine by me."

Emil looks at me a little sheepishly. "I, uh... I named him."

I jolt, and he startles in turn. "You did? You named the new crab?"

He nods, a blush rising on his cheeks.

"Well, shit, Specs. I'm waiting on pins and needles over here. What'd you name Arthur's new buddy?"

His lips twist a little, and he fidgets with his glasses. "Hermin."

It takes me a second. "Hermin the hermit crab?"

"Mhm."

Jesus Christ, this man *will* be the death of me. "That's the fucking cutest, Specs. Okay, what's the rest of it? I know you have more."

He presses his lips together before saying, "Do I have to?"

"Uh-huh. Spill."

Emil lets out a sigh, but the corners of his mouth are upturned when he mumbles, "His Highness, Hermin Park the Gentle, Swimmer of Seas and Friend to All."

My heart starts to pound as Emil returns his gaze to the pet cam. My voice barely cooperates enough to say, "You named him after my grandma?"

Emil's gaze flits to mine, and he shuts off his phone before straddling my lap. He tucks his head under my chin, hiding his face away. "I named him after her *and* you. You're a Park, too. And one of the best people I know. It only seemed fitting to give him your name. He's just like you, after all."

"He is?" I ask, running my palms over Emil's back. My chest feels tight beneath his cheek.

He nods against me. "Mhm. He won over the prickly, guarded Arthur. Just like…"

He trails off, but I know what he was going to say.

"You're not that prickly," I point out.

Emil huffs.

"Specs," I say around a laugh. "You're draped over me like a sweater right now. How would you call that prickly?"

He pokes the side of my stomach, and I laugh.

"Shut up and cuddle me," he mutters.

I squeeze him tighter and kiss the top of his head. "My prickly, guarded nerd. Thank you for trusting me."

His back lifts and then lowers beneath my palms, his breath leaving him gently. "You made it easy."

"That so? Was it because you thought I was an eighty-year-old grandma?"

He groans. "You're still on that?"

"I'll never forget. The *things* you showed me, Specs."

He buries his face against my chest, upsetting his glasses. "*Stop.*"

"I mean, one time you suctioned a dildo to your headboard and rode it so hard you came hands free, remember?"

"I remember," he mumbles.

"Fuck, that was hot. Would you do that again for me some-time?"

"Only if you wear that tutu the next time we…"

He cuts off, and I crane my neck, looking down at the top of his head. "The next time we what?"

He groans a little before turning his face to the side and saying, "I want you to fuck me in the tutu, okay?"

My grin is swift. "Anytime you want, Specs."

"Thank you," he mutters. "Now shush so I can fall asleep on your chest. I have class in the morning."

"I have to pee first."

He groans, an exaggerated sound, but then he gets up and follows me into the bathroom so he can brush his teeth. Back in bed, he all but manhandles me into the same position I was in. Then he sets his glasses on the nightstand and crawls over me.

"You're addicted to cuddles now, aren't you?" I tease, enjoying the weight and warmth of him.

"You've changed me," he says, voice soft. In the dark, I can't see his expression, but it doesn't sound like a bad thing.

I remember Emil telling me once how it was easier not to expect good things than to come to rely on them only to be disappointed. The absence hurts worse. Convincing ourselves we don't *need* affection and love is easier. Or, at the very least, it numbs the pain.

I understand that. Emil and I had different upbringings, but in some ways, they were the same. We both did our best to accept the small space we occupied amidst our loved ones. We tried not to let it hurt.

The fact that Specs isn't afraid of me hurting him is nothing short of miraculous. It's as big and bright as that confession he let slip in the locker room. It's love, and it's trust, and it makes me want to hold on so tight Emil will always know what it feels like to be loved in return. He won't ever have to guess. He won't ever feel unseen or unheard or unloved.

I used to be scared of this. Terrified. But even if, someday, I lose this man with his cheek pressed to my heart, I won't ever regret loving him. I couldn't.

And I think that's maybe most miraculous of all.

"You've changed me, too, Specs," I say into the quiet stillness of the night. Emil doesn't respond, but his chest rises and falls steadily against me. "And I'm so grateful that you did."

Chapter 29

EMIL

I blow out a breath, my nerves frayed. Not because of *this*, exactly. But, well, I'm not sure how he's going to react.

Only one way to find out. Biting the bullet, I send Christian a text.

Me: Which one?

It only takes a moment before Christian appears at his window. My heart beats erratically as he stands there, not moving a muscle. His mouth forms a shape—my name, maybe?—and then he grabs his phone. My own rings a second later.

"What do you think?" I say, my words coming out fast. "Blue or red?"

"Specs," he breathes. "Is that for me?"

My smile is a little shaky. "Merry Christmas."

He lets out a puff of air. "Don't move."

Christian clicks off the call, and I look over at the dress form positioned in front of my bed. The neck is adorned with one blue tie and one red. "I think that went well, don't you?" I ask the inanimate object. Thankfully, it doesn't respond. "He was excited...right?"

Groaning, I tell the butterflies flapping around inside my stomach to chill. When my front door opens and shuts, I bite my fingernail, waiting. Christian appears in my doorway a second later, eyes wide. He's already dressed for Christmas with my family.

I wish I could say I'm more excited, but there's a knot in my stomach that's been there all morning. Today is the day I confront my parents.

I'm not sure I'm ready.

"So?" I say, focusing on Christian.

He doesn't answer, just walks over, takes my face in his hands, and kisses me. I fall back against the bed in my surprise, and Christian follows me down, body blanketing mine as he slowly steals my breath. *Definitely excited.*

"It's too much," he finally says, pulling back.

"It's not," I answer, smoothing my hands over his sides. "You deserve it, Christian."

"Specs," he says, dropping his face next to mine.

"Don't make me return it," I all but plead. "That thing took forever to assemble, and neither Arthur nor Hermin were *any* help."

Christian chuckles against me, lifting enough to see my face. "God, Specs. Thank you. Your gift isn't nearly as good."

I shake my head. "Not a competition."

"It's just a bunch of highlighters and tabs and stuff for your note—"

"Where?" I say, pushing upright and looking around as Christian laughs beside me.

"They're already wrapped and ready to go, Specs. You'll have to wait to open them with the rest of the presents." He pauses for a moment before asking, "Are *you* ready?"

That knot in my gut tightens again, but I drop my feet to the floor and straighten my shirt with more determination than I feel. "Yeah," I say firmly. "Let's go."

Less than half an hour later, my confidence has all but dissolved.

"This is such a bad idea," I moan. "Why did I wait until now?"

Christian gives my hand a squeeze from the passenger seat of my car. The engine is off, my parents' house *right there* in front of us, waiting.

"This is the worst time for this," I go on. "What was I thinking?"

"Breathe, Specs," Christian says gently, his very presence soothing me. "It'll be fine."

"You don't know that."

He hums. "I guess I don't, but I believe it. And I know you can do this. You stood up for Henry. It's time to stand up for yourself."

"It's so much harder."

"Earlier this week, you got spit-roasted by me and Niko while giving new-guy Sean a handjob. Is it really harder than that?"

"Oh Jesus," I wheeze. "Why'd you have to bring that up?"

"Because I knew it'd relax you," he says, the cheeky bastard.

"Relax isn't the right word," I huff out. Although I *do* feel marginally better. "For the record, bringing up our sexual escapades, romantic or otherwise, is far from relaxing."

"Mm. You looked pretty relaxed at the time."

"Fuck-drunk," I correct, letting Christian's hand go so we can get out of the vehicle. "There's a difference."

"Noted," he says, chuckling.

"I don't know why I love you," I mumble, trying to hide my smile.

He snorts. "It's the skirts."

"It's *not* the skirts," I say, grabbing his hand again as we walk up the steps toward the front door. "They're just a bonus."

His smile is warm. "You say the sweetest things, Specs."

"I do not, and we both know it. Most of the shit that comes out of my mouth is a disaster. But you're nice enough not to point it out. *Fuck*. This is going to be a disaster, too. It's not too late to just...leave. We could just leave and try again another time."

"But it's Christmas," Christian says lightly, facing me as we come to a stop at the front door. "Henry and Rebecca are here, and I know you want to see them. Plus, you brought presents."

I grip the bag tighter.

"It'll be *fine*, Specs. You can do this. You're brave and smart and good, and your parents love you. I don't think they want to hurt you."

"I don't either," I admit softly.

He squeezes my hand. "So just be honest with them. I think you'll be surprised. I think they'll turn it around, the same as they have for Henry."

I nod, knowing he's likely right. It's what I've been telling myself over and over since Thanksgiving, after all.

"My therapist says I'm catastrophizing the outcome in my head," I say. "Because then, no matter what happens, it'll be better than I anticipated."

Christian hums. "And you? What do you think?"

"I think I've spent a long time not saying anything, and I'm afraid it's my own fault. That all of this is entirely my fault."

Christian lets out a small breath and steps in close. His wintergreen scent hits me, a gentle cocoon, and then the man himself is wrapping his arms around my shoulders and pressing his cheek to the side of my head. "It's not your fault, Specs.

What did you say to me when I asked you about destiny? You told me we can never truly control others."

"No, we can't," I agree.

"Your parents' actions are not on you," he says. "But now's your chance to speak up. You can stay in the past where nothing is capable of changing. Or you can leap and know that, no matter what happens here today, I'll be there to catch you on the other side, okay?"

"Yeah," I breathe out, my tension dropping. "Fuck, why are you so great?"

"Well, see, I've been dating this really smart doctorate-of-psychology-in-training. And I think he might be rubbing off on me."

I snort a laugh. "I do rub off on you a lot."

"Yes, you do, and I love it," he says, squeezing me before easing back. "Ready to walk in there?"

I brush a kiss against Christian's cheek. "Ready."

I can hear Rebecca and Henry as soon as I open the door. The smell of pine hits me, too, likely from the candles inside the foyer, seeing as my parents' tree is artificial. I let go of Christian's hand to take off my shoes, and it's not long before my siblings cue in to the fact that we're here.

"Hey," Rebecca says, bounding over. She tugs the bag of presents out of my grip. "Thanks."

"Those are for everyone," I call after her, shaking my head as she disappears around the corner. Seeing my brother, I add, "Hey, Henry."

He deigns to grace us with a nod.

"Where are Mom and Dad?" I ask.

"Kitchen," Henry answers.

Turning to Christian, I speak quietly. "Give me some time alone with them?"

"You sure?" he asks, talking just as low.

I nod. "Yeah. I need to do this part on my own. You can keep the youngins busy."

Christian gives my glasses a small nudge. "You got this, Specs."

As my boyfriend heads into the living room, I make my way down the hall. My mom is standing in front of the fridge, putting what I assume are leftovers from breakfast inside as my dad washes dishes at the sink. I stop for a moment, steeling myself.

"Hey."

Mom turns her head. "Hey, hon. Is Christian with you?"

"Yeah, uh, he's in the living room. Could we talk for a second?"

My mom frowns slightly as she shuts the fridge door. "Of course. What's up?"

Feeling like I might fidget out of my skin, I head to the table and take a seat. My mom follows, shooting Dad a glance. He dries his hands before joining us.

"So, uh, I don't really know how to say this," I start, staring at the wooden table. I trace a groove with my fingertip, pulse hammering. "So I'm just going to do it. Sometimes...I feel invisible inside this house. I feel like you guys don't even know what's going on in my life, and that you don't care. And I try to talk to you, but there's always more important things. And...and it makes me feel shitty to even say it, but I want you to *see* me. Sometimes I just...I want to know that you see me."

Silence falls, and I focus on the table, on the tiny divot in the wood, instead of the way my throat is burning. My mom is the first to speak.

"Emil, hon. I had no clue you felt that way. I... I'm sorry for making you feel less important than the other things going on in my life. That was never my intention. I..." She lets out a small breath, but I can't quite bring myself to raise my eyes. "You've always been so fiercely independent, and I didn't realize you needed more from me. From us."

"Your mother's right," my dad cuts in. "It's no excuse. But, son... You were so well-behaved as a child. You never got into trouble. Never needed us to come to your aid. You're smart, and you've been successful at forging your own path in this world. And I guess, like your mother, I thought that meant you didn't need us in your pocket. I'm sorry if we've let you down."

Shit.

My lip wobbles, and I nod a little weakly, my fingernail adding a new scratch into the wood.

"We shouldn't have assumed," Mom says. "Hon, would you please look at me?"

I do, raising my head slowly. I'm unsuccessful in stopping the tear that slips down my cheek, and my mother's face falls. She scoots closer, squeezing my arm.

"Emil, I'm so proud of the man you are. And if I haven't said it enough, that's on me. I think, as parents, it's hard to know where the line is. Julian and Eloise...they hated when I hovered, and I learned to back off. All I've wanted for my children is for them to be happy. To be able to spread their wings and follow their own dreams. But it seems I've made mistakes, and for that, I am sorry. I love you, and I'm proud of you, and nothing could ever change that."

I nod tightly, not knowing what to say.

"Oh, hon," my mom says, standing. She steps forward, wrapping me in her arms, and I hug her back, my cheek on her stomach and my eyes stinging. The next moment, my dad is there, too, his hand on my shoulder, his other smoothing over my hair.

"Emil," my dad says, voice uncharacteristically gruff. "We're not perfect, but we love you unconditionally, and it's been a true honor to see the man you've grown into. One who's inquisitive and kind. One who possesses a great deal of strength to come to us like this. I'm sorry we've ever made you doubt how much we care. If you give us the chance, we'll do better. I swear it."

I nod again, not sure I can manage anything more than that, and for long minutes, that's how we stay. My parents, holding me in the kitchen, carefully bandaging old wounds I thought long since scabbed over.

When I lean back, they let me go. I swipe at my eyes as my mom retakes her seat next to me.

"Would you help me with dinner before Julian and Eloise arrive?" she asks. "We can catch up, and you can tell me about how your research project is going."

"Yeah," I croak out. "I'd like that."

"Christian, too," she says softly. "I'd love to know more about that man of yours and how you two met."

I nearly choke on my spit, but it turns into a short laugh instead. "Yeah. Sounds great."

When I finally leave the kitchen, my eyes are puffy but my chest feels light. Lighter than it's been in some time. I stop at the edge of the living room, spotting Christian sitting on the couch next to Henry. Rebecca is across from them in a chair, her legs folded up as she gestures animatedly.

I catch Christian's eye. He shifts in his seat like he's about to stand, but I shake my head and point toward the stairs. He nods, and I head that way, needing a moment to breathe.

After washing my face in the upstairs bathroom, I meander down the hall, stopping outside my old room. It's a guest room now, the decor more sophisticated than it was during my teenage years. I step inside, sitting on the bench seat in the window that overlooks the backyard.

"Hey," Christian says softly, appearing in the doorway.

"Hi."

He meets me at the window, taking a seat beside me. "All right?"

"Yeah," I say, even though I feel wrung out, numb almost. "It was... It was actually really good. They were really great about it. I wish... I wish I'd said something sooner, you know?"

He squeezes my knee, letting his hand rest there. "You said something now. That's what's important."

"Yeah. *Fuck*, my therapist would be so proud," I say, huffing a laugh and removing my glasses so I can rub my eyes.

"I'm proud of you, too, Specs. Is that weird to say? I never had siblings or a boyfriend to be proud of before. But it's like... Sometimes I look at you, and I get this pressure in my chest and this feeling of *that one's mine, just look at him.* Is that weird?"

"No," I rasp, replacing my glasses. "I feel that way about you, too. You're beautiful, Christian. Inside and out."

His expression softens, dark brown eyes so very warm. "I guess love is turning us into saps, huh? Who knew?"

I huff a laugh. "Literally everyone. Everyone knows that."

Christian snorts. "Well, I like being a sap for you."

"Jesus, that was terrible," I grumble, lips twitching. "So cheesy. I'm not sure I can be seen with you anymore."

He makes a sound of protest before grabbing me around the middle and tugging me onto his lap. I scramble, arms wrapping around his shoulders as Christian buries his face in my neck and nips my skin.

"Take it back," he says, soothing the bite with his tongue.

"Fuck," I breathe, my cock taking interest as Christian's hands smooth down my back and land on my ass. "You can't..." I huff out a breath as his lips brush underneath my jaw. "Can't give me a boner at my parents'. It's not allowed."

"It could be my Christmas present," he says, although his hands travel upwards, back into neutral territory.

"You already got your present, and *ah God*, do that again."

Christian chuckles before obliging, sucking on my neck. Not long enough to leave a hickey, but enough to feel his desire to do so thrumming underneath the surface.

"I take it back," I say on a moan. "You're wonderful and not too cheesy, and later, you can bite my neck for real so everyone knows how proud I am of my perfectly sappy, filthy boyfriend. Okay?"

"So okay," he says.

"Uh, Emil?"

I freeze before scrambling off Christian's lap. Rebecca stands in the doorway, not looking remotely freaked out by what she walked in on, but I feel bad all the same.

"Hey, Bec," I say as casually as I can. Christian adjusts his floor-length skirt next to me. "Need something?"

"Um, could we come in?" she asks, sparing a glance to her side, where I assume Henry is standing.

"Of course."

Rebecca nods before coming into the room, Henry following after her with his video game in hand. "Move over," my sister tells me, shoving me none too gently so she can join us on the window seat. I huff a laugh as Henry settles on the floor, his shoulder bumping my leg.

"What's going on?" I ask.

"I overheard part of your conversation with Mom and Dad," Rebecca says, making my gut swoop. "So I asked Christian what it was about, and he explained."

Christian gives me an apologetic wince, but I shake my head, letting him know it's fine.

Rebecca heaves out a breath. "Can I tell you a story?"

Confused, I nod. "Okay?"

My sister settles her legs under her before she starts to speak. "Once, there was this prince named Emilio."

I huff a laugh, but my sister shushes me, swatting my leg before going on.

"*Emilio*," she stresses, "had the weight of the world on his shoulders. For, you see, he was an older brother, and his siblings looked up to him. When they were scared, Emilio calmed them. When they had nightmares, he snuck into their rooms and told them tales of ogres and giants and princesses in castles. And he never once asked for anything in return."

My throat closes up as Rebecca tells her story, her gaze on her hands in her lap.

"Emilio was so brave, but he didn't seem to realize it. He was brave because he fought battles all on his own. He was brave because he scared away the monsters under the bed. He was brave because he taught two little kids what it means to love from a place that's pure and selfless and kind. He was my hero, you see."

Fuck. Christian grabs my hand when I reach for him, and he squeezes tight.

"But sometimes, heroes go unseen," Rebecca says solemnly. "They never ask for accolades or parades in their honor. So that's why Emilio's little sister wants him to know that she appreciates him. More than she's ever found the words to say. And she loves him. And some day, if she becomes a mom, she'll tell her kids all about their uncle, the prince, the bravest man she knows. The best storyteller. And hopefully, Emilio will know that there are people out there who are better because of him."

My sister doesn't protest in the least when I pull her into my arms. She hugs me back, sniffling quietly as I lose the battle against my own tears. Henry is still holding his game, but he stopped playing the moment Rebecca started talking, and his hand is curled around my leg, a hug in its own right.

"Thank you," I manage to tell them.

Sometimes people are capable of surprising you. They show up when you need them the most. My parents, my siblings, Christian... They showed up for me today.

I've never been very good at change. New shells. New homes. Speaking up simply because it's time.

But change can be good. Great, even.

And the important people... Well, I think they change right along with you.

Chapter 30

CHRISTIAN

I smooth my shirt as I stand at Emil's door, glancing down to make sure my outfit is in pristine condition. It was a short walk over here, but I still want to look perfect for my boyfriend. The one who gave me the courage to make this outfit in the first place.

When he opens the door, I think I might have just accomplished it.

Emil's eyes flare wide, and he doesn't speak for the longest moment, his gaze raking up and down my body.

"Holy shit," he finally breathes. "Christian... You look...*stunning.*"

"You like it?" I ask, lips curling into a smile.

"I want to crawl under that skirt and show you how much."

I bark a laugh. "I don't think there's room for you beside all the tulle."

Emil shakes his head, eyes roving over the floor-length skirt. It's made from the embroidered fabric I picked up not long ago when Emil and I went shopping. The base is a gentle snow white, but starting at the waistband and cascading downward in increasing volume are flowers in a variety of colors. They lift from the fabric, the petals fluttering gently each time they pick up a breeze. At the bottom hem, the flowers are heaviest, so dense the white is no longer visible. My top is simple: a sleeveless, white crop top that ends a couple inches above the skirt's waistband, a snowy canvas by which to draw the eye downward.

Judging by Emil's expression, the effect is exactly what I was going for.

"Gorgeous," he says simply, finally stepping back to let me in. "Anything you need to do before we go?"

"I'm all set," I tell him, walking inside. My subtle makeup is on, and my hair is pulled half-up, a few strands falling loose in front to frame my face.

Maybe this is just an awards ceremony for a rather niche porn market, but I'll be proud to walk into that ballroom with Emil on my arm.

"You look handsome," I tell him, following Emil into the living room as he checks on Arthur and Hermin. He's wearing dark gray slacks with a matching vest, the simple white shirt and bright blue bowtie he paired it with a nice complement to the textured gray.

"Thanks," he says, glancing over his shoulder, a shy smile on his face. "I just need to feed these two, and then we can go."

"What are they having today?"

"Cantaloupe and kale," he answers.

I huff a small laugh. "Bet Arthur will love the kale."

"He won't, the diva," Emil says, putting it in the terrarium regardless. "But Hermin seems to like it."

"Has anyone ever told you you're a wonderful crab daddy?" I ask, stepping close and wrapping my arms around his waist. He inhales a breath, stomach moving under my palms.

"Alex, actually. But it sounds less weird coming from you."

I hum, kissing his cheek, just as Emil's phone pings. He pulls it from his pocket.

"Your mom again?" I ask, looking down at the screen.

He makes a small hum of acknowledgement. "Yeah. She's been smothering me lately." The uptick in the corner of Emil's mouth lets me know exactly what he thinks about that.

"Good," I say, glad his parents are staying true to their word and giving Emil the attention he deserves.

He sends a reply before turning in my arms. "Ready to go?"

"Let's do it."

The awards ceremony is being held at a hotel downtown. Emil and I get a ride so he doesn't have to worry about driving us home afterwards. Much to my surprise, there's a red carpet set up outside of the hotel entrance, and a small group of reporters are standing by, throwing questions at the people heading inside.

"Holy shit," I mutter. "Is it always like this?"

"People love their porn," Emil answers, lips twitching.

It's not mayhem as we step out of the vehicle, but a few cameras spin our way. I notice Trevor up ahead, a slim redhead on his arm as they walk through the doors.

"Felix, Vixen," one reporter calls. Honestly, I'm surprised they even know my name. "Is it true the two of you are a couple?"

Emil bumps up his glasses. "It's true."

"Vixen, who made your outfit?" the same reporter asks.

"Oh. I made it myself."

"He's an incredibly talented seamster," Emil adds.

I give his arm a little pinch, but he looks unrepentant as he leads me past the flashing cameras. Someone asks if our relationship is open outside of the studio, but Emil tugs me forward, so I follow his cue, heading with him into the hotel lobby.

"It's mostly gossip columns," Emil tells me once we're inside. "Hardly anyone reads it."

"Still, I kinda feel like a star."

He gives me a smile before his gaze catches across the room. "Oh, there's Alex. C'mon."

Our blonde coworker squeals when he sees us coming, disentangling from his boyfriends to meet us halfway. "You guys look *amazing*. Christian, that skirt!"

"Thanks," I say, giving it a swoosh. "Is everybody here already?"

Alex nods, inserting himself between Emil and I and leading us forward like a gentlemanly guide. "They're inside at our tables. I was waiting for you two. Mal is here tonight. And Cas."

I know from what Emil's told me that Mal was a performer before my time. Cas, of course, I've met. With Jason and Jason's...Brad.

Alex's boyfriends follow us hand in hand as we make our way into the ballroom, Alex keeping up commentary the whole time about who's here from competing studios and those who are slated to win awards tonight. Apparently Alex is in the running for a scene he did involving fisting, and Dixon and Niko are up for an innovation award for a video in which they fucked inside a zero gravity booth. I'll have to check that one out later.

Our coworkers are split amongst three large tables inside the ballroom, and we get a cheer as we join. Emil introduces me to Mal and Henrik. I notice a cane beside Henrik's chair, as well as the fact that his bright green eyes wander in a way that suggests he might be blind. Mal, who looks like a surfer if I ever saw one, has a smile on his face as Alex regales us with a detailed explanation of how Henrik and Mal met while Mal was escorting.

"It was love at first sight," Henrik adds when Alex finishes his story, to which Mal snorts.

"And you two?" Mal asks, his hand laced with Henrik's on the table. "Did you meet at the studio?"

"Oh, no," I answer, giving my boyfriend a smirk. "We met before that when Emil gave me a pornographic peep show."

Emil groans, dropping his head into his hands.

"Most days for three months, actually," I go on with a grin. "We're neighbors, so I watched him through the window. He didn't even know who I was until I started at Elite 8 Studios."

"Wait, what?" Alex squawks, eyes bouncing wide. To Emil, he says, "You didn't tell me it was more than once!"

"How freakin' sweet," Niko interjects. "I don't think fate could have handed you a better meet-cute, Emil."

Alex cocks his head. "And why's that?"

Niko takes a sip of his drink before answering. "Because he's an exhibitionist."

A beat of silence passes—a *long* beat—and then Alex goes, "*What?*"

Niko looks around the table. "We didn't all know that?"

Alex's wide eyes swing Emil's way. I muffle a laugh against my palm as Emil's cheeks redden.

"Excuse me," a worker says, stopping at the table beside ours where Trevor is seated. "We need a word with the owners real quick."

"Of course," Trevor says, standing. He gives his husband—Isaac, as I learned—a quick kiss before walking off with the employee.

"Owners?" Alex asks, popping up in his seat. "What's that mean?"

Isaac stops staring after Trevor long enough to say, "Because he started Elite 8 Studios."

Silence falls again, and then Alex screeches, "*What? What is even happening right now? Trevor owns the studio? Did you know this?*" he asks Niko, who shakes his head. "Who knew this?"

"Shit," new-guy Sean mutters. "Really makes you wonder what his story is, huh?"

Several heads nod as Alex continues interrogating the group, determined to find out who knew Trevor owned the studio. Jerome and Nathaniel, I note, are conveniently absent, getting drink refills at the bar.

It isn't long before the lights flicker, and the adult entertainers and crew members present quiet, finding their seats. It's my first time at such an event, so I'm not sure what to expect. But, as it turns out, it's like any other awards ceremony, just with more dicks.

Alex wins an award for taking half a forearm up his ass, and although Dixon and Niko don't win theirs, they were runners up. Our studio also receives a commendation for excellence, a fact that makes Jerome flush with happiness, although I'm sure he'd deny it with every ounce of his being.

By the time the awards ceremony wraps up, my cheeks hurt from smiling, and Emil is hanging off my arm, buzzed and, if I had to guess, a little horny. I give his cheek a kiss as we stand to grab waters from the bar.

"It's weird," Emil says.

"What is?"

"This," he answers, sweeping a hand toward the tables where our coworkers, new and old, are congregated. Some of the attendees have started filtering out, but I'm guessing with this many porn stars inside a hotel, the night is far from over. I know, assuming all goes well, ours is just beginning.

Most of our group is still inside the ballroom. Alex is sitting on Rowan's lap, his arm around Finn's shoulders. Cas and Jason are huddled close, looking at something on one of their phones. Mal is whispering into Henrik's ear, the older man smiling coyly. Marco is hanging off his chair, talking with a few individuals from another studio I don't know. Jerome and Nathaniel are standing near the stage, chatting with Trevor and Isaac. Dixon is entertaining a very rowdy Niko, the latter practically giving Dixon a lap dance the bigger man is doing his best to look grumpy about. Teddy and Kipp were making out in the corner a minute ago but have since disappeared. And some of the newer talent and other crew are mingling, Noel's cousin Tanner included.

"So many of the people I started with are gone or are going, like Dixon," Emil says. "And now, there are all these new faces, you know? Feels like the turn of an era."

I hum.

"I'll miss them, but...I like where we're headed," he says, looking at me. "I like that I'll be there with you."

My chest squeezes tight, and I bring Emil's hand up to my mouth, kissing the back of it. "I'm glad I get to spend my days with you, too, Specs. I'll forever be grateful I lost my job at the club and all but fell into your lap."

He huffs a short breath.

"And whether it was asbestos or fate or pure luck," I say, "I wouldn't pick a different path than the one that led me to you."

"Christian," he says quietly, his fingers tightening around mine. "Thank you for leaving that letter on my door. For showing me you were someone I could trust. I'm so very glad you're not an eighty-year-old grandma."

I shake my head, a grin on my face. "Such a shit."

"But I'm yours."

"That you are," I agree, twisting his hand in mine. "I have a surprise for you. Are you ready to go, or do you want to stick around a bit longer?"

Emil glances back at our tables. There's a small smile on his face as he sets down his empty water glass. "I'm ready. What's this surprise?"

"Telling you would ruin it," I point out, giving Emil a tug. I catch Tanner's eye, nodding before Emil and I turn the corner out of the ballroom. We stop at the elevators, and Emil raises an eyebrow.

"We're going up?" he asks.

"Yep."

Emil tucks his lip between his teeth, a hint of mischievousness in his expression. "You know, I never did like surprises before you."

"And now?"

"And now..." he says. "Now, I hope you never stop surprising me."

The elevator pings, doors opening, and I can't help but grin. "Hang on to that thought, Specs."

Chapter 31
CHRISTIAN

When Emil and I reach the tenth floor, I find our room and pull out my keycard. The door unlocks with a subtle click, and I drag my boyfriend inside, letting him go to flick on the lights. Rounding the bed, I grab the bag I stashed here earlier in the day.

"Give me just a minute," I tell Emil, sauntering into the bathroom. He looks perplexed, but he sits down and removes his shoes as I shut the bathroom door behind me.

As I'm changing, my phone pings with a text. I'm relieved to see my plan is falling into place exactly like I'd hoped. Quickly, I get into my rather simple outfit, and then I hang my floral skirt on the shower rod and check myself over in the mirror. *Perfect.*

Emil's eyes bounce wide when I step out of the bathroom wearing nothing but my tutu. His throat bobs, and he tracks me with his gaze.

"Remember what you asked me to do in this skirt?" I say, heading for the door that leads to the adjoining room.

"I wanted you to fuck me in it," he says thickly.

I hum, flipping the lock on the door. When I ease it open, the lights in the other room are off, not letting me see much, but a quiet throat clear confirms our guest is waiting.

"What are you doing?" Emil asks.

"You told me once that you trusted me to keep you in check if we were in public," I say. "You made me promise I wouldn't let you do anything you shouldn't."

He nods, brow scrunched.

"But I know how much it turns you on to have someone watching," I go on, heading his way. Emil lets me tug him to his feet, and I walk backwards, bringing him over to the dresser stationed beside the door. Circling behind him, I set one hand on his stomach, the other at his chin. I aim his gaze through the darkened doorway. "There's someone in that room who's going to watch."

Emil's breathing hitches, his stomach dipping and swelling beneath my palm.

I lean in close, my lips at his ear. "They're going to watch me undress you and bend you over this dresser. They're going to watch as I tongue your ass open. And they're going to watch while I fuck you delirious. If you don't want that, tell me now."

"I want it," he says, voice a whisper.

"Mm. Thought so, my little exhibitionist. Hold on."

Emil's hands scramble for the dresser, and he braces himself as I unbutton his slacks and tug them down to his ankles. He looks back at me, his face flushed, his eyes half-lidded already. I give him a wink before pulling his briefs down to his feet. His cock is fully hard, the tip already glistening with precum.

I run a hand up the length of it as I stand, my finger passing over his slit before I lift it away. Emil lets out a strangled sound, his arms shaking as I set to work on his bowtie. I pull it free and then tackle his vest. Last is his shirt.

As soon as Emil is naked, clothes discarded on the floor, I kick his legs wide. He groans, dropping down to his forearms.

"The person in that room will see everything I do to you," I tell him, dropping to the floor and palming his ass. "They'll see the way your dick begs. Hear every sound from your mouth, every moan as you ask for more."

I lean in, licking over Emil's asshole, and he curses.

"Can you imagine what you look like right now?" I ask, rolling my thumb along his rim. "How perfectly needy. How gorgeously flushed."

A moan leaves his lips as I tongue him again. "Christian," he groans.

"I'm right here, Specs. Do you think they can see how wet your dick is already?" I roll my palm over the head of his cock in demonstration, and he lets out a garbled moan, his knee buckling before he rights himself. "Do you think they're imagining what they'd do to you given the chance?"

"Get something inside me," he says hoarsely. "Now, Christian."

"Mm. Love that mouth," I say before licking him broadly. The moment I press my tongue inside his body, he keens.

"Yes, yes, God, *fuck*," he starts to ramble. "More. Don't stop. Fucking—*ah*. Get me ready for your cock, Christian. Need it."

"I know, beautiful. Hold on."

Emil groans as I press a finger inside him, wet with lube from the bottle I left for this purpose. I work him open quickly, adding a second finger as my boyfriend squirms back against me and begs me to hurry. To *hurry up, already, come on.*

"So gorgeous, Specs. Look at you."

"You'll be looking at...my cum on this dresser if—*God*. If you don't get in me soon," he huffs out.

I nip his ass cheek, loving this man more than I can possibly say. As soon as he's loose enough to take three fingers, I pull out and stand up. Emil widens his stance, hair falling messily over his forehead as he looks back at me, elbows planted on the dresser.

"C'mon, Christian," he begs, eyes skipping down to my skirt as my hand disappears to wet my cock. "Do it. Do it, c'mon."

"Fuck, I love you," I say aloud, flipping the tulle of my tutu out of the way so I can press the head of my cock to Emil's hole.

"I love you, too, but if you don't get in me, I'm gonna—" Emil's words cut out as my crown pops inside his ass.

"You were saying?" I ask, grabbing ahold of his hips as I work myself in.

He hangs his head. "Fuck, I'm gonna come."

I huff a laugh. "Not yet. Up on your hands."

Emil pushes up onto his palms, grunting when I snap my hips the rest of the way forward. I give him a few hard thrusts, waiting until his sounds turn frantic before I still. Flush against his back, I latch on to his neck, sucking and soothing with my tongue as Emil groans.

"What do you think they see right now, Specs?" I ask, redirecting Emil's attention to our voyeur.

He whimpers.

I give his cock a slow stroke, and Emil starts to tremble. "You like having their eyes on you, don't you? You like showing off."

"Christian," he whispers.

"I like showing you off, too, Specs. I want the world to see how gorgeous you are. I want them to see how beautifully you take my dick, like you were made for it. I want them to see how much you goddamn love this. And I want them to see you come on my cock without you so much as laying a hand on yourself. Can you do that for me?"

"*Fuck.*"

"That's the idea," I say, punching my hips. Emil cries out, and I move my hand to his shoulder blades, pressing down. "Back on your elbows, Specs. Hang on."

Emil drops down instantly, bent over at the perfect angle. The sound he makes when I pull all the way out and slam back in again is one I know I won't ever forget. It sounds like joy. Like abandon. It sounds like someone who knows exactly what they want and have succeeded in getting it. It's smug. It's gorgeous. It's the man I love shouting his desire for anyone to hear.

"Is this...what you wanted, Specs?" I ask between breaths, fucking Emil hard enough to rattle the dresser. "You wanted...to be owned...by a man in a skirt?"

"You," he huffs out, his ass clenching around me. "Wanted *you.*"

Fuck.

"You have me," I tell him seriously, wetting my fingers before bringing my hand around to Emil's chest. I tug on his nipple, and he gasps out a breath, his ass spasming around me again.

"Christian," he breathes.

"What do you need?"

"You," he says, his ass cheeks jiggling with every slam of my cock in his body. "T-talk to me."

"You want me to tell you how hot you look right now? How good your ass feels clenched around my dick?"

He groans.

"Want me to tell you what I think our voyeur is seeing? Your cock, hard and bobbing in the air. Your muscles straining and your cheeks flushed red. Your ass swallowing me again and again and *again*."

"God," he moans.

"You look like a wet dream, Specs," I say, flicking his nipple with my thumb, fucking him hard enough that he loses his grip. "But you're mine, isn't that right?"

He nods quickly.

"That's right. So c'mon, my little exhibitionist. Squeeze me. Strangle me. Show our guest who you respond to and paint this goddamn dresser."

Emil comes with a hoarse cry, his entire body shuddering, his ass clenching around me so tight I curse. I grind into him shallowly, the heat and pressure making it impossible not to follow him into orgasm. It's like a kick to my gut as my cock jerks inside his body, emptying, flooding his ass as I grapple to keep myself upright. Emil groans, his body milking me in little bursts, the both of us shaking as we try to catch our breaths.

"Holy fuck," Emil finally says, rolling in a shiver.

"Okay?" I ask, stepping back enough to slip from his ass. The evidence of his orgasm is splashed across the dresser.

He nods, but he's shaky when he reaches for me, so I wrap an arm around his waist, helping him over to the bed. He flops onto it unceremoniously, not objecting when I encourage him to roll to the side so I can get the sheets out from under him.

"You fucked me to death," he mumbles, a sleepy smile on his face.

"What a way to go," I retort, running my fingers through his hair before plucking off his glasses and setting them on the nightstand. "Be right back, okay?"

He hums, his eyes already closing. Not bothering to cover myself any more than what the tutu conceals, I head to the adjoining room, shutting the door to a crack behind me. Tanner flips on the light near the couch.

"Hey," I say. "Thanks again, Tanner. I appreciate you helping us out."

He stands up with a chuckle. "Uh, yeah, man. Anytime. That was seriously hot."

I grin. "Glad you enjoyed it. See you at work?"

"You bet," he says, giving me a two-finger salute as he heads for the door. He pauses with his hand on the doorknob. "Hey, Christian? I'm really glad Emil has you. I've worked with him for years, but... I've never seen him as happy as he's been these past few months. You're good for him."

My throat feels tight as I nod. "Thanks, Tanner. That means a lot."

His lips quirk into a smile, and he heads out the door. I shut off the light before rejoining Emil in our room. He's still sprawled out in bed, and I drop my rather soiled tutu on the floor before sliding in next to him.

He rolls to me instantly, his head finding a home on my shoulder. "Was there really someone watching?" he asks, voice drowsy.

"There was."

After a moment, he says, "Thank you for doing that, Christian. I just... Thank you."

"Yeah, Specs," I answer, wrapping my arms around him tight. "Boyfriends who play together stay together, isn't that right?"

He huffs a small laugh. "It sure won't be boring, that's for certain."

"What's that?"

"Our future," he answers, a gentle smile on his face. "Our life together. It's gonna be unpredictable, and I can't wait."

My chest squeezes, heart aching in the best possible way. "Yeah, Specs," I say softly. "It's gonna be great."

Epilogue
EMIL

Three-and-a-Half Years Later

"So, tell me. Have you had any recent concerns over your urge to be watched?"

I smile at the tactful way in which my therapist worded that. She could have said my *kinky exhibitionist lifestyle*, and I wouldn't have batted an eye.

"No," I tell her honestly. "My job at the studio is keeping my impulses in check, and Christian..." I blow out a breath. "He's great. He helps reinforce my boundaries."

She gives me a warm smile. "That's wonderful, Emil. I'm going to be honest with you. We've been seeing each other less frequently these past couple years, and I think you're at a point where you might not need these sessions anymore."

I nod because I know she's right.

"I'll always be here if you want to check in," she goes on, "but you're immensely self-aware when it comes to your own psyche, and with your insecurities about your exhibitionism and the tension with your family having all but resolved, I'm not sure I'm offering anything more than a listening ear at this point."

"Yeah, I get it," I tell her.

She leans forward slightly. "This is a good thing, Emil. It's always a good day when I can tell my patients goodbye and know it might be for the last time. But again, my door will remain open, okay?"

"Yeah. Thank you, Rose. I appreciate everything you've done for me."

She gives me a gentle nod. "Take care, Emil. And congratulations. Are you excited to start your doctorate next semester?"

My grin is swift. "Can't wait."

Rose sees me out the door, and I let loose a breath. It feels like relief, almost, to know how far I've come in the past several years. I'll miss Rose's gentle encouragement, but she's right; I'm in a good place. Christian and I are solid. My relationship with my family is better than it's ever been. And my studies are progressing exactly as I'd hoped.

There's not a single thing I have to complain about, really.

When I get home, Christian isn't inside the apartment, but Arthur and Hermin greet me from their terrarium below the sprawling cherry blossom tree on the wall. The three of us moved into Christian's place not long after we celebrated our first New Year together. I haven't regretted the change once.

"Arthur. Hermin," I greet, dropping down to a crouch. Arthur is barely in sight, just the tip of his shell exposed. But Hermin is in the water dish, his little orange legs propelling him around. "Glad to see we're behaving. I have something special for you guys tonight. They had watermelon at the store. Are you excited?"

Neither crab answers.

"Yeah, yeah, keep it contained, fellas."

As I stand, I notice a flash of blue in my periphery. I follow it into the bedroom, where a gorgeous velvet jacket is hanging from the dress form I gifted Christian for our first Christmas together. His craft has expanded in the three years since. Not only is he officially a business owner now, but he's had a steady stream of commissions ever since his picture was taken at the awards ceremony. When people found out he made that skirt himself, it was game over. He picks and chooses his clients now, and he's been thinking of expanding and hiring an employee or two.

Christian still works at the studio, but he's cut down his hours to part-time. I don't mind. We get plenty of chances to enjoy one another on video, the live streams still being our favorite. Our fans haven't gotten sick of watching two guys in love get it on for their viewing entertainment. And my boyfriend knows exactly how to push my exhibitionist buttons, ensuring the both of us love it, too.

"Specs?"

I smile, heading back out into the living room. Christian is standing just inside the door, his hair a little windswept, pieces falling from his bun.

"Hey," he says warmly. "Wanna take a walk?"

I cock my head. He's up to something. "Sure. Where are we going?" When Christian opens his mouth to answer, I cut in. "Let me guess. It's a surprise?"

His smile turns into a grin. "Bingo."

Shaking my head, I shove my feet into shoes, and the two of us head out the door. It's warm and sunny out, the summer season having kicked off a couple weeks ago. We walk hand in hand down the sidewalk, Christian updating me about his grandma. I was bummed to miss out on today's visit, but I know I'll see her soon.

When we reach the entrance to the meditation garden, Christian tugs me to a stop. "Feel like enjoying a little inner peace?" he asks.

"With you? Always."

Christian unlatches the gate, and we walk through. A few birds chirp amongst the gentle noise of traffic as we wind down the narrow path toward the center of the garden. The grass is lush and green underfoot, and when we reach the manicured lawn, I follow after my boyfriend, stepping stone to stone.

He's the first to take a seat at the bench in front of the pond, and I lower myself down beside him, our legs pressed together. Christian sets his palm on my thigh.

"No ducks today," he notes.

"They'll be back."

He hums. There's a slight breeze, and it makes it feel as if the mural on the wall across the water is alive. I could almost imagine the flowers blowing in the wind, the smell of pollen carrying over the air.

"I saw Noel earlier," Christian says.

"Yeah? He and Max doing okay?"

He nods. "Yeah. They sent in their application for adoption."

"That's great. They'll be awesome dads."

"Yeah," Christian says, a faraway look in his eyes. His lips twitch into a smile. "I never thought much about kids, you know?"

I do know. We've talked about it before.

"I never thought I'd have someone of my own," he goes on. "So imagining anything beyond that was a moot point. I feel like...like my world opened up when I met you, Specs. Like I started living."

"Christian," I say softly.

He slips off the bench, going down on one knee. I let out a gasp.

"Emil," Christian says, his voice whisper-soft over the wind. "There was a lot I never knew was possible before I met you. I didn't know how it could feel to love someone so fully that you wanted to spend all your time with them. I didn't know a single person could be capable of inspiring hope, that they could make you into a better person and help you to grow. I didn't know I wasn't dreaming until I met you, and suddenly, every day was a dream come true. And no, you're not allowed to tell me that was cheesy."

I huff a laugh, and Christian pulls something from his pocket. I swear I stop breathing. For a moment, there's nothing but him and me and the space between us, wide open with possibilities.

"If this world really is chaos," he says, opening his hand to reveal a ring, "then you're the most fortunate improbability I've ever encountered. I don't want to spend a single one of my remaining days without you, Specs. You and David Attenborough."

I laugh and swipe at my cheek.

"Plus Arthur and Hermin, of course," he adds, lips twisting. "The four of you... You're it for me. Would you be mine, Specs? For the rest of our lives?"

"What's that saying?" I ask, my voice sounding wet. "The husbands who play together stay together?"

Christian's grin is blinding. "Is that a yes? Are you saying yes?"

"Yeah, Christian," I huff out, dropping to the ground in front of him. "I'm saying yes. I'll be your husband." I pick up the ring, slipping it onto my finger. The silver gleams in the light, a promise, a beautiful declaration. "For as long as my brain is capable of electrical impulse, you'll be on my mind, in my heart, weaving through my body. I'll be yours, and I'll be proud to call you mine. My beautiful voyeur. My fellow crab dad. My fiancé. Soon, my husband."

"Shit, Specs," he rasps, fingers drifting over the metal on my finger.

"I think I was yours from the beginning," I tell him truthfully. He always made me feel good, *safe*, even before I knew his name. Even before I saw his face or felt his lips against my own. "Thank you for choosing to be mine."

"I didn't really have a choice when it came to you," he says, scooting closer in the grass, his hands coming up to frame my face. "I fell in love with you, piece by piece. This brain. This heart. Even these glasses."

I laugh, and Christian strokes his thumbs over my cheekbones.

"I love you, Specs. And I'll keep on loving you for as long as I draw breath."

Never in doubt, I press my lips to his. It's wintergreen and warmth and trust. It's a fluttering in my stomach and resolution in my chest. It's the feeling of the man I fell in love with loving me right back.

And, in the end, isn't that what we're all searching for? Our great big love? The real-life story we'll tell those who come after us?

I know I found my happily-ever-after.

And like hell will I ever let go.

The End

About the Author

Information about Emmy Sanders and her complete list of works can be found on her website. Subscribe to her newsletter, join her Facebook reader group, Emmy's Enclave, and connect via email or social media:

www.emmysanders.com

Find online:
www.facebook.com/emmysandersmm
www.instagram.com/emmysandersmm